"THOSE WHO LIKE STEPHEN KING . . . WILL THRIVE ON MICHAEL SLADE." —*Macon Beacon*

"The king of psychothrillers. Readers who relish monsters wearing a human face must read a Michael Slade novel." —*Midwest Book Review*

"Will raise hackles, eyebrows, and blood pressure everywhere. . . . Gives you real shock value for the money . . . the most gruesome I have ever read." —Robert Bloch, author of *Psycho*

"Would make de Sade wince." —*Kirkus Reviews*

"Slade knows psychos inside out." —*The Toronto Star*

"Allow yourself to be seduced . . . and you will encounter the most violent, most complex monsters to stalk innocent and otherwise since *Psycho*'s Norman Bates." —*Ottawa Citizen*

"The kind of roller-coaster fright fans can't wait to ride." —*West Coast Review of Books*

"Well written, very well researched. A gripper." —*London Daily Mail*

"One of the hallmarks of a Slade novel is the extensive research behind each story. Readers come away from Slade books not only entertained—and terrified—but also enlightened. Slade villains are among the most twisted, evil creations to adorn the printed page. The nervous tension of Slade novels is enhanced by the realization that no one is safe—any character could be killed or maimed at any time." —*Cemetery Dance*

"Compulsively terrifying . . . an advanced course in psycho horror . . . convulsively terrifying." —Alice Cooper

continued . . .

ALSO BY MICHAEL SLADE

Special X Thrillers

MICHAEL SLADE

KAMIKAZE

A SIGNET BOOK

SIGNET
Published by New American Library, a division of
Penguin Group (USA) Inc., 375 Hudson Street,
New York, New York 10014, USA
Penguin Group (Canada), 90 Eglinton Avenue East, Suite 700, Toronto,
Ontario M4P 2Y3, Canada (a division of Pearson Penguin Canada Inc.)
Penguin Books Ltd., 80 Strand, London WC2R 0RL, England
Penguin Ireland, 25 St. Stephen's Green, Dublin 2,
Ireland (a division of Penguin Books Ltd.)
Penguin Group (Australia), 250 Camberwell Road, Camberwell, Victoria 3124,
Australia (a division of Pearson Australia Group Pty. Ltd.)
Penguin Books India Pvt. Ltd., 11 Community Centre, Panchsheel Park,
New Delhi - 110 017, India
Penguin Group (NZ), cnr Airborne and Rosedale Roads, Albany,
Auckland 1310, New Zealand (a division of Pearson New Zealand Ltd.)
Penguin Books (South Africa) (Pty.) Ltd., 24 Sturdee Avenue,
Rosebank, Johannesburg 2196, South Africa

Penguin Books Ltd., Registered Offices:
80 Strand, London WC2R 0RL, England

Published by Signet, an imprint of New American Library, a division of
Penguin Group (USA) Inc. Previously published in a Penguin Group (Canada) edition.

First Signet Printing, November 2006
10 9 8 7 6 5 4 3 2 1

Copyright © Headhunter Holdings Ltd., 2006
All rights reserved

 REGISTERED TRADEMARK—MARCA REGISTRADA

Printed in the United States of America

For Bev Vincent and Steve Kimos

Everyone talks about fighting to the last man,
but only the Japanese actually do it.
—Field Marshal William Slim

We're going to bomb them back into the Stone Age.
—General Curtis E. LeMay

Zero Hour

Pearl Harbor, Hawaii
December 7, 1941

Like a swarm of hornets buzzing in from the north, the Japanese planes dove out of a Sunday morning sky to bomb and then strafe the hangars and aircraft that lined the bottom edge of the A-shaped runways at Hickam Field. *"Tora! Tora! Tora!"* While Commander Mitsuo Fuchida repeatedly signaled the code word "tiger," meaning "total surprise," back to Admiral Chuichi Nagumo on the *Akagi*, flagship for the strike force, Corporal Joe "Red" Hett was shaving in his digs on the Hawaiian air force base. Having spent Saturday night at liberty in the bars, brothels, dance halls, and clubs of Pearl City, the airman was nursing a hangover from consuming too much booze at a late-night poker party in the new enlisted men's beer hall, dubbed the Snake Ranch.

"Damn Marines!" Hett muttered on hearing the first boom. "Some trigger-happy jarhead must've let one go."

Boom! Boom! Boom!

As the coral foundation beneath the barracks shuddered, Hett cut his cheek.

The flyboy glanced at his watch beside the sink. 7:56.

Then the concussion from a closer blast crashed the ceiling fixture to the floor.

The "Red" in Red Hett was a reference to the fiery hue of his hair, which was almost as crimson as the blood that now streaked his shaving cream. At this moment, Joe wore khaki trousers and loafers, and had U.S. Army Air Force dog tags strung around his neck. Bare-chested, he sported the deep tan he'd earned from goofing away his days off on the sands of Waikiki. That's where he was destined now—to doze in the sun and wake up to an eyeful of wicked wahines in skimpy beachwear. What better peacetime posting was there than this?

BOOM!

KAMIKAZE

The Hale Makai Barracks, Hickam Field's newest structure, was a huge, octopus-like complex with wings jutting in all directions. It served as quarters for more than three thousand enlisted men. So violent was the explosion caused by the direct hit on the mess hall at its center that it blew soldiers out the windows of the upper floors. On the ground floor, the bomb scattered diners, tables, chairs, and trays of grub, and shrapnel killed thirty-five men as they gulped down their bacon and eggs. Machine-gun bullets rat-a-tat-tatting through shattered windows ricocheted off metal footlockers to perforate bunks. By the time Red Hett, razor still in hand, got down the stairs and out the door, blood-spattered survivors in tattered clothes were already crawling amid the rubble or staggering around in a daze.

Chaos!

As his eyes adjusted to the glare, Joe caught sight of a young GI, a Colt .45 flapping in a holster on his hip, dashing hell bent for leather along the road between the barracks and the hangars that bordered the airfield. He was obviously on guard duty.

"The Japs are here! It's war!" he shouted as he ran past, a modern-day Paul Revere raising the alarm.

As Joe turned to watch the guard sprint down the street, the roar of an airborne engine zoomed in from his other side. With tracer streaks leading the way, bullets stitched across the ground, throwing up puffs of asphalt dust in their wake. They drilled through the guard as red mist and continued on ahead. A Zero fighter shot by Joe and soared over its kill before the GI crumpled down dead. So close to the road was the plane that it almost seemed to be landing, and through the open cockpit, Hett got a glimpse of the pilot. With his helmeted head and square goggles, he resembled a creature from outer space. Wrapped around his brow and rippling in the breeze was a white scarf, the *hachimaki*, a traditional symbol of courage. Hell, Joe could even see the gold in his teeth!

"Meatballs," Hett cursed as the plane began to climb. The word was slang for the Rising Sun painted on the underside of both wings.

Clang! Clang! Clang!

Shiny shell casings ejected by the Zero's guns showered the street and bounced around until motionless.

Casting aside the razor, Joe ran to the cut-down guard. The corpse lay sprawled beside a patch of green grass littered with petunia blossoms and red hibiscus. Crouching, the flyboy relieved the holster of its .45 and craned his neck around.

Sandwiched between Diamond Head to the east and Pearl Harbor to the west, Honolulu's Hickam Field was home base for the U.S. Army Air Force's bombers on Oahu. From the plumes of thick, oily smoke mushrooming ominously into the sky above the anchorage, Joe knew the ships of the Pacific Fleet were sunk or damaged. Ahead of him, at the end of the barracks, the Stars and Stripes hung limply at the top of its flagpole. Nearby, a sergeant was struggling to mount a machine gun in a bomb crater. The attack had blown open the guardhouse, releasing its prisoners, and the escapees rushed to help the sarge set up the .50-caliber weapon.

Save the planes, thought Hett.

A row of double hangars lined the curb to his right. Between the tent-roofed buildings fronting the flight line, Joe saw the Zeros flash by with their wing cannons blazing and heard the shriek of dive bombers jazzing the base. Hickam had no anti-aircraft guns, no air-raid shelters, no slit trenches. The guard force was armed solely with pistols. As a defense against sabotage—the only threat contemplated by those in command—

Hickam's twenty B-17 Flying Fortresses, thirty-two almost obsolete B-18s, and twelve A-20s were dovetailed wingtip to wingtip out on the concrete mat. Sparkling in the sunlight and easy prey, they'd be smashed to smithereens by this sneak attack if something wasn't done.

The boom-booming and bang-banging was loud enough to rupture eardrums in the iron alleyway between the hangars. With one fist gripping the .45, Joe covered his ears as he darted for the runways. He burst out onto Mat A to find it hell in the Pacific.

Bombs fell like black rain from a cloud of high-altitude Japanese planes. Looking up, Hett had the sensation that every bomb was heading straight for him. Dive bombers off the *Shokaku* had launched the initial assault on Hickam Field while twenty-four men labored in Hangar 11 to roll out B-18s for an eight o'clock training flight. A bang-on strike through the roof had killed twenty-two outright and cut the legs off the other two. Now, as the hangar's twisted framework licked the sun with tongues of flame and ongoing explosions blew out skylights, windows, and doors, officers and enlisted men in a hodgepodge of Sunday attire—uniforms, skivvies, aloha shirts, and pajamas—fought the fire, salvaged equipment, or tended to the wounded.

His bathrobe gaping to expose his nudity, a captain came reeling out of the smoke with blood streaming down his face, shaking his fist at the planes and bellowing, "I *knew* the little sons of bitches would do it on a Sunday! I *knew* it!"

Bwam! He got mangled by a fragmentation bomb.

From Joe's standpoint, the base was a sea of fire. Every swoop by a Val dive bomber took out something else: a supply building exploded in a hail of nuts and bolts and wheels; the chapel succumbed, even with the supposed protection of God; the Snake Ranch beer hall had served its last drink; the firehouse and its engines were made permanently unavailable to fight this inferno, while broken water mains uselessly spurted geysers into the air. Down, up, and away screamed the bombers, dipping so low that some struck telephone lines, then tore off with wires tangled around their wheels.

Until now, the Yanks had scoffed at the skill of Jap pilots, and blood was the price of that arrogance. After each Val dropped its load on a target, it veered into a figure eight to strafe the field repeatedly, winging back and forth, its guns chattering, along one cross-leg and then the other. The gunners, riding backward in the rear seats, glowered at Joe with each pass and tried to pick him off with bullets that zinged from the concrete just as they do in the movies. Meanwhile, the Zeros flashed around like silver mirrors, their aerial ballet tightly choreographed as they fanned over the bomb-cratered moonscape to rip the flight line to pieces.

Zoom, circle, *fire* . . .

For a moment, Joe thought one Zero was sprinkling toothpicks on the roof of Hangar 9, but then he grasped that it was sending the structure up in splinters.

One tin hangar still under construction rattled hollowly, as if stones were hitting metal, then suddenly bullets were ricocheting around inside like the balls in a pinball machine.

A blinding explosion of gasoline *foomed* up from the flight line as ground crews dodging bullets tried to haul machine guns and ammunition out of the disabled Flying Fortresses. *Foom! Foom! Foom!* Off went a chain reaction as bomber after bomber was consumed by the ravenous fire. Flaming, gibbering men were hurled away from the wrecks, flailing their arms like phoenixes desperate to rise from red hot ashes.

Acrid smoke choked Joe's lungs.

Blasts were coming at him from both above and below ground, quaking the concrete under his shoes as the terrible concussion and the deafening pressure wave of each massive explosion blew his breath away. Through gaps in the white pall that roiled across the mat, Joe watched an improvised crew scramble into an undamaged B-17. As guns poked out of the turrets, the pilot got three engines going and taxied off across the pitted battlefield, but he was unable to coax the recalcitrant engine to kick in. Splats of lead from vulturous Zeros soon tattooed the plane's wings.

Into the thick of this flew a dozen more planes.

The Japs are really coming now, thought Hett.

Then he wondered, Where did they get four-engine bombers?

When he recognized the new arrivals as B-17s, Joe grasped that they were twelve Flying Fortresses the base had expected from the mainland.

The crew members probably thought the approaching planes were a meet-and-greet from the U.S. Army Air Force, until the Japanese Zeros opened up with their wing cannons.

Low on fuel and with their turret guns packed away, the B-17s had no choice but to go for emergency landings. Zeros strafed one as it ran the gauntlet down to the field, setting off magnesium flares in the radio compartment. A fire broke out in the midsection of the lumbering bomber, and as the burning plane thumped down heavily onto the runway, the tail section snapped off. As it skidded to a halt, what was left of the forward fuselage stood up like a penguin, forcing the battered airmen out to run for their lives. As they scampered across the Tarmac, a fighter pounced down and took out the flight surgeon in a withering hail of bullets.

Another Flying Fortress was also in deep trouble. Three Zeros were clinging to it like vampire bats, slamming slugs from their nose guns into its engines. Flames erupted from one cowling, then a second. Joe saw the white star on the blue circle as the crippled U.S. bomber passed directly overhead, and that galvanized him into action.

By chance, a freelance photographer was at Hickam Field to shoot a pictorial spread on Pearl Harbor for *Life* magazine. Cowering in one of the hangars, the cameraman spied the shot of a lifetime passing right before his eyes, so he bolted from his bomb shelter to follow the bare-chested airman out onto Mat A.

As he snapped his first picture, a discus of spinning shrapnel came whirling toward him from the fiery flight line. Dropping his camera, the photographer stretched out on the concrete as if sunning himself on a quiet Sunday morning. Though his severed head and hands plopped down next to his body, no blood appeared. So hot was the shrapnel that when it decapitated him and sliced off his hands, it cauterized his neck and wrists. The blood coagulated before it could spurt.

The sole image captured in the now broken camera was of Joe "Red" Hett standing defiantly in the open, the blasted bombers of Hickam Field ablaze beyond him. Legs astride and back arched, he was emptying the Colt .45 as fast as he could pull the trigger into the belly of a Japanese Zero above his head. Ejected shell casings spat from the pistol. His dog tags bounced off the muscles of his chest as he swiveled to give the muzzle enough lead on the plane. His half-shaven face was a symbol of the sneak attack. Outrage flashed in his eyes, and his lips snarled back from his teeth. Whatever Joe was yelling at the pilot whose head stuck out of the cockpit, those words would never see print.

The photo, however, made the next issue of *Life*.

By capturing America's reaction to the Day of Infamy, that image became an icon of the war.

Divine Wind

Tokyo, Japan
October 27, Now

Now in his eighties, Genjo Tokuda often thought back to the years when his father had taught him how to follow the Way of the Warrior.

He pictured the two of them in the Zen garden, a realm for deep contemplation amid serenity. The pond was streaked with lolling carp and edged with mossy rocks. Wisteria draped the vermilion bridge that spanned from earth to paradise. The path through the stone lanterns promised a mystic journey.

"Imagine a time," his father said, "more than six hundred years ago, when the samurai were the knights of Japan, the shogun was their leader, and the emperor—as now—was divine."

The boy pictured feudal Japan in his mind.

"Genghis Khan," his father continued, "had conquered more land than any warrior before him. Mongolian horsemen thundered west from the Pacific Ocean to the far edge of Russia. Kublai Khan, his grandson, wished to conquer more, so he sent an emissary here to demand that we bow to his rule."

Father and son sat together in the teahouse by the pond.

"Did we?" Genjo asked.

"We refused to answer. So Kublai Khan dispatched forty thousand barbarians on hundreds of ships to enslave us. When the weather turned, a typhoon struck. Two hundred sinking ships drowned thirteen thousand men. The surviving Mongol invaders had little choice but to retreat back to China."

"We won."

"But not for long. Kublai Khan was not a man to stomach defeat. Seven years later, one hundred and fifty thousand warriors boarded a thousand ships, then sailed here to crush us. They landed on our beaches. We fought back. For fifty days, the battle raged. Gunpowder explosions blackened the sky. Arrows from their bows rained down on us. But we had *bushido*—the Way of the Warrior—the code by which a samurai transcends his fear of death. It gives him the peace and power to serve the emperor faithfully. And to die well, if need be."

Genjo could see them in his mind's eye.

Those samurai of the shogun, the "barbarian-subduing general."

Way back when, in 1281, they stood in their helmets, breastplates, shoulder guards, and belly wraps on the sacred shores of Nippon, slicing and dicing the foreign invaders to pieces with the blades of their flashing swords.

Banzai!

"The emperor is divine. Heaven favors us. So as the battle onshore reached a climax, a wind howled out of heaven and attacked the Mongol ships. For two days, enormous waves pounded our coast. Ships rammed together or slammed against the cliffs. Swamped ships foundered on the rocks. Ships by the hundreds sank into the sea, drowning Mongols by the tens of thousands. Those who clung to splintered wrecks were picked off by our archers. Those trapped ashore were slaughtered or surrendered to become our slaves. A fifth of the vast fleet retreated home to

China in defeat, and the myth of the invincible Khan was shattered throughout the Mongol Empire."

"We won," Genjo repeated.

"Yes," replied his father. "We never lose a war. The Divine Wind. That's what we called it. That storm of heavenly favor sent by the gods to save us."

Kamikaze.

That was the name of the sword.

Kami for Divine.

Kaze for Wind.

Kamikaze. The Divine Wind.

His next lesson in *bushido* took place inside the Shinto shrine that bordered the garden. Father and son entered through the *torii* gate, a pair of upright wooden poles topped with two crossbeams. As he passed from the outside world to the divine realm, Genjo eyed the lion-like stone dogs on either side of him. One with mouth open, the other closed, the *komainu* guarded the sacred shrine. Pausing at the water trough, father and son purified themselves by rinsing out their mouths and washing their hands to show respect to the gods. In the worship hall, they tugged a rope attached to an overhead bell to let the *kami* know they were present. To show gratitude, each threw a coin into the offering box. After bowing deeply, they clapped their hands twice, also to ask the gods for attention.

Before them stood the *honden*, the main hall, where the gods were in attendance.

Genjo couldn't see them, but he knew they were there.

His ancestors.

Samurai.

Warriors turned into gods.

On this side of the threshold, the *daisho* was mounted on a wooden rack. The big sword—*daito*—and the small sword—*shoto*—fused together as *daisho*, the sign of a samurai. Others were allowed to carry one sword or the other, but only samurai carried both.

Reverently, with both hands, Genjo's father raised the big sword off the rack. In the stillness of the shrine, amid the serenity of the garden, the boy heard the glistening steel sing as the blade slipped free of its curved scabbard.

"Kamikaze," his father said, invoking the name of the sword. "We make the best swords in the world. This sword began as iron mixed with carbon. Then fire, water, anvil, and hammer forged it into this. See how it curves? That's for strength and sharpness. See how it shines? Polishing adds perfection. Etched into the blade are the words 'Four Body Sword.' Do you know what that means?"

"No," said Genjo.

"It means that the sword tester stacked the corpses of criminals one on top of another and—starting with the small bones, then moving up to the large ones—cut through them with this blade. 'Four Body Sword' means Kamikaze will slice through four men."

"Why does it have a name?"

"The *katana*," his father said, "is the battlefield sword. This sword is a samurai's most treasured weapon. It's part of him. It's the soul of his warriorship. So he gives it a name."

"Kamikaze?" Genjo asked. "Why name it that?"

His father moved several feet away from his son and took up the stance of a samurai poised to strike.

"Close your eyes," he said, "and listen well."

Genjo closed his eyes.

Not a sound.

Then—*shhhhewwww*—he heard the blade whip past his face.

"Did you hear it?"

"Yes, Father."

"That's Divine Wind."

* * *

Years later, just before Genjo went off to war, his father had summoned him to the Shinto shrine. On seeing the younger Tokuda arrive in his uniform, the man who had taught him the Way of the Warrior smiled from ear to ear. In the presence of the *kami,* their ancestral samurai gods, the elder Tokuda raised the *katana* once more from the wooden rack and, with pride in his eyes, passed it to his son.

"Kamikaze," his father invoked. "Strike down the barbarians with your Divine Wind."

Genjo stuck the battle sword through his belt.

Returning to the rack, his mentor lifted the *wakizashi* off the lower hooks. The shorter sword was less than two feet long. It was the sword a warrior used to commit seppuku.

Seppuku.

Hara-kiri, in other words.

His last lesson in *bushido* had taught Genjo how to regain honor if he should lose a battle or shame himself. With his sword in front of him, sitting on a special mat, he would open his white kimono to bare his abdomen. Taking up the *wakizashi,* he would plunge the blade deep into his gut. The initial cut would slice from left to right, then he would yank the steel upward to spill out his intestines. A bow of his head would signal his assistant to decapitate him with a sweeping stroke of the *katana*.

"Come home victorious," Genjo's father said. "Or do what must be done."

He gave his son the short sword to stick through his belt.

Genjo had the *daisho*.

He was samurai.

It used to be that you could spot a yak a mile away. In fact, the name yakuza says it all. *Ya* means 8, *ku* means 9, and *sa* means 3 in Japanese. Those numbers add up to 20, a losing hand in a game of *hana-fuda* (flower cards), so yakuza members enjoy being the "bad hands" of society.

Kazuya had laughed at paintings of the first yaks—the "wave men," the "crazy ones"—of the 1600s. Their flamboyant clothes, hairstyles, and extra long swords were a hoot. Theirs was a time of peace, when samurai were idle, so leaderless *ronin* had wandered Japan, committing thefts and causing mayhem.

The yaks of the 1950s had looked outlandish too. The sunglasses, dark suits, white shirts, dark ties: they dressed like hoods enforcing black-market deals for Al Capone. Tough guys who endured hundreds of hours of pain for full-body tattoos shaped like long underwear. Thugs with less than ten fingers.

The rat pack was in by the 1990s. It was cool for yaks to flaunt punch-perm hair, shiny tight-fitting suits, and pointy-toed shoes, all so long out of style in America. With gang pins on their lapels and logo signs on their social clubs, they wheeled through the streets in big, flashy Lincolns and Cadillacs.

Until they got hammered.

As Japan's national proverb says, "The nail that sticks up must be hammered down."

Kazuya was a yak for the new millennium. That he was born to be yakuza was obvious from his name: in English, it had the same six letters as the Japanese mafia. Ostentation was a luxury of the past. It had died when Japan's economic bubble burst—thanks to the yakuza's undermining the banking system through loans that swiftly turned into bad debts. Pissed-off politicians had passed a 1992 act aimed at dismantling groups with a certain percentage of members with criminal records. No longer could the yakuza depend on their open alliance with right-wingers in the political and corporate arenas. Japan's National Police Agency had the teeth to go after them, so twenty-first-century yaks would have to blend in.

Yaks like Kazuya.

The new ninjas of Japan.

There wasn't a tattoo on his body, and he had all his fingers. A lot of toned-down yaks dressed according to a code: *Shiro nara shiro. Kuro nara kuro.* If you wear white, wear all white, from your hat to your shoes. If you wear black, wear all black. Kazuya, however, was into deep, deep cover. So in a country where conformity was highly valued and outward signs of individuality raised suspicion, he dressed like a well-paid *salariman*, the sort of corporate high-roller who paid Kazuya handsomely for "comfort women."

Kazuya was a business-suit yak.

His business was to cater to the kinky side of Japan's overstressed, buttoned-down "salary men." The hard-core pornography: he imported it. The sex tours to Bangkok, Manila, Taipei, Seoul: he ran them. When it came to "selling spring"—a Japanese euphemism for pimping young girls—he was without equal. Some were unwanted children from China, where boys were preferred in the one-child system. Others came from the Philippines, where girls lured out of poor villages with the offer of good jobs ended up stripping and hooking in the bars and clubs of the *mizu shobai*, Kazuya's "water business." But what raked in the biggest bucks were his "date clubs," places where, for a hefty membership fee, doctors, lawyers, and corporate execs could select and fuck a North American blonde.

Blondes are big in Japan.

Hollywood South and Hollywood North are magnets for buxom young actresses desperate to break into films. Fluent in English, Kazuya knew L.A. and Vancouver as well as he did the head of his cock. A couple of times a year, he flew to both to scout for undiscovered talent willing to perform "comfort work" on the casting couch between screen tests for Asian films.

He figured that's why they'd assigned him this job.

Because he spoke English.

And because he knew Vancouver.

The yak who met him at Tokyo's airport was his uncle. He could tell from the squint of the old guy's eyes that he was none too pleased. His uncle was one of the old-school yaks with the full-body tattoos; he'd been recruited by the *gurentai* hoods who had sprung up after the war, back in the days when Genjo Tokuda ruled the Ginza district.

Originally, yaks had inked tattoos to boast about their crimes: a black ring was added to the arm for every offense committed. Later, tats became both a test of enduring pain and the mark of the misfit who refused to adapt. His uncle Makoto's inking—a mural of dragons, gang insignias, flowers, and Noh masks—covered his torso, front and back, both arms to below the elbow, and his legs to mid-calf. Also, his pinky was gone.

"What went wrong?" Makoto asked.

"I lost control of the car."

"Were you speeding?"

"So they say."

"Who?"

"Vancouver police."

"Did they charge you?"

"A traffic ticket. I paid the fine."

"How late were you?"

"An hour," Kazuya replied. "There was no one by the figurehead when I arrived."

"Fool," his uncle said, ushering him to the car. "You shamed yourself. And you shamed *me*."

The instructions had been simple. He was to fly to Vancouver, just as he did to scout blondes, and drive around Stanley Park to the *Empress of Japan*'s figurehead, which was mounted on the seawall walk alongside the harbor. There, moments after the boom of the Nine O'Clock Gun, he would be met by a man with the code name Kamikaze. The stranger would hand him a vial of blood to smuggle into Japan.

But with time to kill before the meeting, Kazuya had indulged his passion for blondes and fast cars. He was a good-looking guy, if he said so himself, and he liked to use the bedroom to collect his finder's fee from the blondes he selected for Japan. Blondes like the one he'd met over a drink in a bar that afternoon. Japan was a crowded country—not like Canada—so Kazuya had rented a fast car to enjoy the wide-open spaces with the sexy blonde. Unfortunately, the yak had spun out on his way back into town. And that was why he'd failed to meet Kamikaze.

The Ginza district is the Times Square of Tokyo. Destroyed by bombing during the war—only the Wako Building, with its clock tower, and a few structures in the side streets survived—it was now, by day, the swankiest shopping spot in Japan and, by night, a dazzling, neon-lit fantasy of restaurants, clubs, and bars.

The club where the car stopped occupied the upper floor of a two-story building that fronted a towering skyscraper of sun-splashed glass. The stubby structure had once been the headquarters of Genjo Tokuda, back when he was the most feared hood in Tokyo. It was now a private club for fossils like Makoto, old-time thugs who were quickly giving way to slick yaks like Kazuya.

Clang . . .

Clang . . .

Clang . . .

Relentless clanging filled the pachinko parlor on the floor below the club. Walking through the gambling den, Makoto and Kazuya passed by rows upon rows of people whose eyes were locked on the tiny chrome balls of the pachinko machines. An elevator at the back wall ascended to the top floor, but the doors wouldn't slide open until Makoto fed an electronic card into a slot.

Smoke swirled through the air of the private upstairs club. Here, the game was *cho ka han ka*, "odds or evens." The player shook a pair of dice in a black bamboo cup, then set the cup down on a mat. Compared with the pachinko parlor, the private club was deathly quiet. The gamblers surrounding the table, their drinks held by comfort women, slapped cash onto the mat and bet "odds" or "evens." Since all the men were yakuza, ten thousand dollars was bet on a single play.

"That's all," said the dice man.

The thugs withdrew their hands from the cash mat.

"Play," said the dice man.

Opening the cup, he looked inside and declared, "Evens."

In the far corner of the club, a sumo-sized man was being fawned over by bowing underlings who reacted to every order he gave with *"Hai! Hai!"* "Yes! Yes!" The comfort women massaging his shoulders were young enough to be his granddaughters. Both wore unbuttoned white blouses over short, pleated schoolgirls' skirts and knee socks. The girls covered their mouths and giggled at something the old yakuza said, and feigned surprise when he ran his fat hands up their thighs. On spying Makoto and Kazuya, he dispersed his hangers-on with a brusque wave of his hand.

The door beside the fat yak's chair opened into a backroom. Not a word was uttered as the three men crossed the threshold and the door closed behind them. Two knives and two lengths of string lay on a table scarred by hundreds of gouges. Without hesitation, Makoto went straight to the chopping block, picked up one string and clenched it between his teeth, then wound a tourniquet around the pinky of his good hand to cut off circulation. Having numbed the finger and reduced its flow of blood, he grabbed the nearer knife and whacked it down like a headsman's ax. *Yubi o tobasu.* He "made his finger fly."

Yubitsume, "finger cutting," went back to the days of the samurai. It's how a warrior made amends for misdeeds to his boss. When a samurai sword is held properly, most of the strength in the grip is applied by the pinky finger. Without that finger, a samurai was weaker in battle and more dependent on his master for protection. Since old yaks thought they were modern samurai, they stuck to that tradition.

But not Kazuya.

There'd be none of that shit for him.

The pain must have been excruciating, yet no sign of it showed on Makoto's face. The fat yak passed him a towel to bandage his hand and a sheet of paper in which to wrap the severed finger. An old fridge stood against one wall. Back when Genjo Tokuda had ruled with an iron grip, that was where he was rumored to store the fingers his men had chopped off to quell his wrath.

Crazy fuckers, Kazuya thought.

Come into the modern age.

The modern trend was to do away with *yubitsume*. When yaks went under cover, missing pinkies stood out. The funniest story Kazuya had ever heard was about a yakuza boss who wanted to stop finger cutting among his thugs. He gave the order to his middle men to eliminate the practice. When one of those underlings made a wayward thug mutilate himself for some infraction, the boss was furious. So what did the middle man do to atone for infringing the no *yubitsume* order? He performed *yubitsume* on himself!

Crazy fuckers.

Putting a pearl in your penis: *that* Kazuya could understand. When his uncle Makoto had gone to prison—that record was why he couldn't make the trip to Vancouver—he'd cut into the skin at the tip of his cock and inserted a pearl to create a bulge in his manhood. A pearl for every year he was in jail. That, they say, gives women pleasure when you fuck them, so it makes up for the time a yak has spent away from his sexual partner.

A ladies' man like Kazuya could see the logic in that. But when it came to fingers, *that* seemed stupid. He required all the fingers he had to keep the ladies happy.

Because Makoto wasn't directly responsible for the mishap in Vancouver, the finger on the table was an *iki yubi*. A "living finger."

What these old-school yaks really wanted was

a *shinu yubi*. A "dead finger" from the one who was directly responsible—namely, Kazuya.

"No," Kazuya said.

"Fool," his uncle snapped.

The door at the rear of the room accessed an elevator that took them up the face of the sky-scraper backing the two-story building. The city of Tokyo bowed down at their feet while they were carried all the way up to the top floor. There, the doors were opened by someone who controlled a ring fence of security devices—metal detectors, bomb-sniffing sensors, hidden cameras, Taser darts, knockout gas jets.

The doors slid open.

The three stepped out.

And Kazuya got the shock of his yakuza life.

So sunlit was the penthouse that he might have been in heaven. In front of them, a man was seated on an ornate chair. He appeared to have samurai warriors guarding him. The suits of ancient armor were genuine and belonged in a museum, as did the thirteenth-century Mongol War antiques that were on display for this modern shogun's exclusive pleasure. Traditional Japanese instruments—a banjo-like *koto* and a wood flute—played soft music. Two samurai swords hung in a rack on a foot table set before this octogenarian.

Adorned with the crest of his family, a *tanto* knife slung through its belt, his kimono was gray, in keeping with his dignified age.

Tokuda! thought Kazuya.

The *kumicho*—the supreme boss of the post-war yakuza—had lived in seclusion for so long that he'd taken on a mythic status. But here he was in the flesh, the burned half of his face an ugly scar. The old yaks on either side of Kazuya were moving toward their master, heads bowed and thumbs tucked under their palms as a sign of respect, so the young yak approached too. The thumb was the most important finger, the last to be cut off by a disgraced underling.

Suddenly, Kazuya found himself sweating.

"A vial of blood?" he'd said to his uncle back in the car. "How important can that be?"

More important, it now appeared, than he could have imagined.

Important to Tokuda!

The floorboards were thick wooden planks that had been laid down to squeak as they were trod upon. A nightingale floor like the singing of birds. A shogun was always in peril because the man who assassinated the shogun could become shogun himself. The same was true for the *kumicho*. A nightingale floor was constructed so no one could sneak up on the shogun, and that's what gave rise to the legend that ninja assassins were able to walk on the walls and the ceiling. To get close enough to kill the shogun, an assassin would have to find a way to bypass the boards.

The three men ceased treading when they reached a white sheet that had been spread on the floor. From dips in the cloth, Kazuya knew it covered some kind of grate. Skirting around his side of the white mat, the fat yak placed the paper containing Makoto's bloody finger on the table at Tokuda's feet.

The *kumicho* said nothing.

He stared at the offering, then stared at Makoto's bandaged hand, then nodded his head.

Never had Kazuya seen a glare as menacing as the one that fell on him. Tokuda's eyes locked onto the slick yak's hands. His lips moved as if he was counting fingers.

"You dare to dishonor me?" he snarled.

"I—" began Kazuya.

"Shut up!" Makoto whispered.

Tokuda beckoned his injured henchman to approach, then reached down and lifted the battle sword off the rack in front of him.

Makoto took it.

"You dishonor yourself," Tokuda said, sneering at Kazuya.

Grabbing the short sword from the rack, the *kumicho* passed it to the sumo-sized yak.

Both men bowed away from their master, careful not to turn their backs on him, and returned to their original positions flanking Kazuya.

"Sit," Makoto said, indicating the white sheet on top of the grate.

When Kazuya hesitated, he was shoved to the floor.

Behind him, the young yak heard the long sword slip free of its sheath. He began to tremble when the fat yak laid the short sword on the mat in front of him, a white cloth wrapped around half of its shining blade.

"Redeem your honor," Tokuda ordered.

Still refusing to believe that his failure in Vancouver had come to this, the dumbstruck yak made his most serious—and final—error by shaking his head at the *kumicho*.

Shhhhewwww!

The last sound Kazuya heard was the Divine Wind.

Yubitsume

Vancouver, British Columbia
October 30, Now

It wasn't hard to spot them. Though a deluge of tourists came surging out of the chute from customs clearance at Vancouver International Airport, the two jumbo jets they'd arrived on had come from Asia. So not only were Joe and Chuck Hett two of few Caucasians in a mass of non-white faces, but father and son were also both a head taller than most of those around them.

"Hi Red. Hi Dad." Jackie greeted the two men from the sidelines.

"How's my favorite granddaughter?" Joe Hett replied, leaning over the waist-high Plexiglas fence that separated those deplaning from those waiting for them and wrapping his arm about her shoulders to cinch her into a hug.

"I'm your *only* granddaughter."

"That's why you're my favorite."

"Good flight?"

"Terrible. I got better service in bombers during the war. Look at these guys," the octogenarian said, sweeping his arm wide to encompass the crowd. "All the way from Japan, I'll bet they got super-service. On a hop, skip, and jump from New Mexico, I got a cup of dishwater and the chance to *buy* a snack."

"How 'bout you, Dad?"

"Terrible," echoed Chuck Hett, joining the three-generation family hug. "I had to listen to Red grouse most of the way."

"Music to your ears, son."

"So you think, old man."

"Hey!" Joe protested as he was shoved from behind. The man who'd pushed him into Jackie was a tough-looking bodyguard clearing a path for his boss, a well-protected Japanese mogul surrounded by a posse of goons. Though now in his eighties, Joe was the sort of Pacific War vet who never backed down from a fight, so he came off the Plexiglas fence like a boxer absorbing a punch.

Grabbing hold of the offending hand and wrenching it aside, he surprised himself, his son, and his granddaughter with the force of his counterattack. The eldest Hett literally tore the pinky finger off the bodyguard's palm.

"I'm *standing* here!" Joe snarled, stabbing his finger at the ground and directing his challenge toward the hub of the entourage. "Tell him to back off!"

"Easy, Red," Chuck said soothingly. "You gotta give a speech. You want to be in a wheelchair with stitches in your face?"

"I'm waiting!" Joe persisted, refusing to give an inch.

From her vantage point on the other side of the barrier, Jackie suddenly saw what was really at the heart of this confrontation. The Japanese mogul was also in his eighties, so these two had faced off—at least figuratively—in the Pacific War. With half his face an ugly scar, the elderly Asian looked even tougher than Joe. If the scar dated back to the war, that was gasoline on this fire. And since he was the boss of the goon who'd given Joe the shove, her granddad was blaming his old enemy for the new insult.

As for the fingerless man, he was ready to let Joe have it. The way his good hand was flattened, it would be a karate chop. So Jackie's hand hovered by her holster, just in case.

For a moment, the standoff was frozen in time.

Jackie eyed the bodyguard.

The bodyguard eyed Joe.

Joe eyed the bodyguard's boss.

And the boss eyed Jackie's uniform.

A command in Japanese. No more than a single word. That's all it took to defuse the powder keg. Reeled in by the mogul, the fingerless thug backed away from Joe. On a cue from their boss, the Japanese gangsters turned their backs dismissively on the American vet and headed for the exit.

"Man," Joe fumed. "I fought a war for *this*?"

Still grasping the prosthetic finger, he pushed it from between the knuckles of his fist, flashing the fuck-you finger at his insulters as they left.

"I think our pit bull's hungry," Chuck said to his daughter. "What shall we eat?"

"Sushi?" Jackie suggested.

From the airport on Sea Island, in the mouth of the Fraser River, the three Hetts drove north across the bridge toward downtown Vancouver, stopping at a White Spot Restaurant for lunch.

"So this is where all the draft dodgers went?" observed Joe as they parked the car and walked from the lot. Typically for late autumn, the sky threatened rain.

"The wet ones," Jackie replied.

The Hetts were one of America's warrior families. Their bellicose bloodline went back to the Revolution, when Jerome Hett had fought the Redcoats at the Battle of New Orleans. Since then, every generation of Hetts had engaged in war—Joe in the Pacific Theater of the Second World War and Chuck in Vietnam. Only with Jackie had the cycle been broken, and the irony was that now she wore red serge.

"I blame you," Joe said as they were ushered to a restaurant booth and handed menus.

"Blame me for what?" Chuck asked.

"Turning my only granddaughter into an expat."

"I'm not an ex-pat, Red," Jackie corrected. "I was born here. I have dual citizenship."

"Maybe," Joe said. "But you're a Yank at heart. If your dad hadn't taken your mom on that tour of NORAD bases, she wouldn't have gone into premature labor in the Arctic, and I wouldn't have a Canuck redcoat as my heir."

"*I'm* your heir," Chuck said.

"You wish," Joe chortled, winking at Jackie.

On her suggestion, all three ordered the same

meal: a hamburger, no fries, with a vanilla milkshake.

"Triple-O?" the waitress asked.

"Yes," said Jackie, answering for the men.

"What does that mean?" Joe asked. "Some sort of Canuck code?"

"You'll see, Red."

"He sees red all the time, our pit bull," Chuck goaded.

Actually, Red was a nickname that could apply to any of the three Hetts seated in the booth. With her flaming red hair and emerald green eyes—not to mention the uniform she donned for special occasions—Jackie was the best candidate for the sobriquet. Today, she sported the working uniform of the Royal Canadian Mounted Police: a blue forage cap with a yellow band and the bison-head crest of the force just above the peak; a blue, waist-length Gortex jacket over a gray shirt and blue tie, with the words "RCMP GRC Police" on both shoulders and zippered slits along both sides to give her easy access to her handcuffs and gun; blue pants with a yellow side-stripe; and black ankle boots.

There was still red in Chuck's hair, though it was overpowered by a lot of gray. Today, he wore a turtleneck with a bomber jacket. Raised in the shadow of a flamboyant father, Chuck had been relegated to the role of straight man. But within their family, he gave as good as he got. Joe had helped set the Rising Sun in the east, but Chuck—in his post-Vietnam years with Strategic Air Command—had been the Hett who'd run the hammer and sickle down the flagpole. Recently, he'd retired to the Hetts' adopted state of New Mexico, where Joe had owned a ranch in his years with the 509th.

Red, however, had been Joe's nickname for so long that neither Chuck nor Jackie had ever called him anything else. He wasn't Dad or Granddad. He was simply Red. Always had been, and always would be. Red's hair might now be white, but his personality still teetered on the edge of conflagration, ready to flare up at any moment. His face was crinkled and leathery from his decades in the Southwest's sun, and probably permanently tanned by the Big Hot One he'd witnessed during the war. Thin-blooded from life in the desert, today Joe was bundled up as if he were flying to Siberia.

The food arrived.

"Now *that's* what I call a burger," Joe announced a few minutes later, Triple-O sauce dribbling down his fingers and his chin.

"Want another?"

"Uh-huh."

"Dad?"

"Deal me in."

Beckoning to the waitress, Jackie placed an order for three more Triple-Os.

"Crack the code," Joe said.

"Triple-O asks for extra relish and mayonnaise. That's why you're so messy."

"He isn't messy," Chuck said. "Red's just old. Back home, he puts on a bib with a drool cup for every meal. After he straps on his geriatric Pampers."

"Okay, that's it. Put up or shut up, son." Joe planted an elbow on the table and held up his hand to arm-wrestle.

"No way." Chuck grimaced. "Look at the gunk on that paw. I'd be wrestling a greased pig."

"Speaking of pigs," Joe said, "what'd you make of that Jap at the airport?"

"Uh . . . Red," Jackie said diplomatically.

"I know, I know. It ain't PC. That's why it's not correct for you to use the word. But I'm too old a dog to learn new tricks. Back in the forties, every newspaper called them Japs. As did the president. So pardon me if that's what I call the banzai brigade I fought. If it's any consolation, the ones born after the war aren't Japs. And you can bet your booty that Jap had a slur for me."

"You're a pig, not a dog," said Chuck.

"And pigs don't have paws," countered Joe. He began to suck the relish off his fingers with gusto. "Damn, that's good. If I'd had some of this Triple-O sauce at the airport, I'd have bitten the remaining digits off that goon, then spat the bones out at the puppet master."

"You'd be dead now, Red," said Jackie.

"I've whupped his kind before."

"I doubt he lost that finger in an industrial accident. I suspect that guy's a yakuza. Offend the boss and that's the price a Japanese gangster pays."

"I saw that movie," Chuck said.

"So did I," said Joe.

"*Black Rain*. With Michael Douglas."

"*The Yakuza*. Robert Mitchum."

"Let's see your war trophy, Red," said Jackie.

Joe withdrew the prosthetic finger from his pocket and set it on the table.

"Looks realistic. May I borrow it for a while?"

"Why?" Joe asked.

"To swab it for DNA. If it turns out that those thugs are up to no good, it might come in handy."

"My granddaughter the cop," Joe said proudly,

speaking to Chuck but nodding at Jackie. "So when do we get a tour of the stables where you work?"

"After lunch."

The next round of burgers arrived just in time for Joe to mess up his sucked-clean fingers. "What do they call this creation?" he asked as he smacked his lips.

"The Legendary."

"Gotta be a legend to go with that?"

"Back in the twenties," Jackie related, "this hustler called Nat started selling hot dogs at Athletic Park, an old baseball stadium. In time, he moved up to selling Triple-O burgers out of his Model T and had carhops running from vehicle to vehicle. They stuck cedar planks across the windows as trays. Nat made a fortune, and over the years his burgers became legendary."

"That's how we'll make our fortune," Joe advised Chuck. "Corner the Triple-O franchise for the States."

"Before long, it'd no longer be Legendary, would it?" Jackie said. "Just super size."

"I blame you," Joe groused.

"Blame me for what?" asked Chuck.

"Turning my only granddaughter into an un-American."

*   *   *

"Your fame precedes you, Red," Jackie said over coffee. Having cleared the dishes, the waitress had wiped their table. Fetching a newspaper from her briefcase, the Mountie folded it back to a full-page feature, then set it down for the men to see.

"Hell in the Pacific," trumpeted a big black headline across the top of the page. That was followed by a photo collage and information on the upcoming Veterans of the Pacific Conference, where Colonel Joe "Red" Hett, who'd flown with the 509th Bomb Group, would be the keynote speaker. Introducing him would be his son, Colonel Chuck Hett, who'd recently retired from Strategic Air Command.

"Heed my advice: don't grow old," said Joe, thumping his thumb down on a photo of himself as a crinkle-faced cowboy. Bookending Joe were picture arrays that captured the start and the finish of America's involvement in the Second World War. In the middle of each was a photo of Joe striking back at the Rising Sun.

"Handsome guy," he said, pointing at the photo of him blasting his pistol at a Zero.

"Is that really how you met Grandma?" Jackie asked.

"Yeah," Joe replied. "She saw that photo of me in *Life* and wrote to me in the Pacific. We corresponded all through the war, and the first thing I did after VJ day was travel to Indiana and look her up. We married a month later."

Jackie sighed. "Love at first sight."

"Yeah. Plus I was horny."

"Which spawned me," said her dad.

Chuck and Joe were the only family Jackie had left. Her mom and her grandma had died together in a car accident, and Jackie was an only child. It occurred to her that "only" was the greater part of "lonely," and she felt content with both men here.

"Striking photo," Jackie said, indicating one of the shots flanking gun-blazing Joe.

"Taken by a Kate. See the fish in the water?"

"A Kate?"

"A Nakajima B5N torpedo bomber. Who could remember a name like that? Or the Aichi D3A dive bomber? Or the Mitsubishi A6M fighter?"

"Obviously *you*!"

"I just wrote a speech." He winked at her. "Anyway, we called the torpedo bombers Kates, the dive bombers Vals, and the fighters Zekes or Zeros. You're looking down on Battleship Row.

By 'fish,' I mean Japanese Long Lance torpedoes that had been adapted for shallow water."

"What am I seeing?"

"Hell in the Pacific, like the headline says. The Japs were out to conquer Asia, and we got in the way. To contain them, we froze their assets in the States, slapped on an oil embargo, and stopped our exports to Japan. But we didn't want to fight 'em, any more than we did the Nazis. Then the Japs turned their eyes on Southeast Asia, with all its oil and natural resources. They knew we'd react militarily to aggression in that region, and they figured if they hit us with a preemptive attack that knocked out the Pacific Fleet, we would sue for peace."

"They figured wrong," Chuck said, "and turned what basically had been a European tussle between the Nazis and the Brits into a world war with us."

"But not before Pearl got hammered. Eighteen ships, including all eight battleships, were sunk or heavily damaged. Three hundred and fifty planes were smashed. More than two thousand servicemen died, and twelve hundred were wounded. Luckily, the *Lex* and the *Enterprise* were out at sea, delivering aircraft to Midway and

Wake islands, or the Japs would have got our carriers too."

Joe turned the paper around so Jackie could follow what he had to say about the photo.

"The Kates came snarling in by twos and threes, past Hickam Field—where I blasted at the Zero—and dropped their fish into the harbor to slam into Battleship Row. As you can see, the boats are tied up nose to tail at moorings on that side of Ford Island. The single battleship in front is the *California*."

Bang! Joe hit it with his fist.

"The *California* sinks. Those next two ships, side by side, are the *Oklahoma* and the *Maryland*. Behind them are the *West Virginia* and the *Tennessee*."

Bang! Bang! Joe pounded the outside ships, prompting looks from quizzical diners.

"See the shockwaves in the water from the previous explosions? See the wakes of more torpedoes speeding in? The enormous spouts of water from where hulls have been hit are soaring higher than the funnels of the ships. The outside two are oozing oil and starting to list. The *Ok* is about to capsize, the *West* is gonna sink. Both ships on the inside are damaged, but they'll stay afloat."

Joe poised his fist above the table.

"The next two are the *Vestal* and the *Arizona*. Both have been hit by—"

Jackie cut in. "*Vestal*'s not a state."

"The *Vestal*'s a repair boat, not a battleship," Joe explained. "Both have been hit by bombs. Bringing up the rear is the *Nevada*, torpedoed and belching smoke. Minutes after this photo was taken, another bomb knifed through four of the *Arizona*'s decks. It detonated deep in the forward magazine. The blast blew a fireball more than a thousand feet into the air. That killed close to a thousand men. The explosion was seen and heard for miles. Jap planes, at ten thousand feet—"

"Don't bang the table," Chuck interjected. "Simulate the blast and you'll have coffee cups flying." Chuck turned to his daughter. "Khrushchev and his shoe," he said.

Too young to catch his meaning, Jackie let the comment pass over her head.

"Jap planes rode out the shockwave at ten thousand feet," said Joe. "There was only one survivor forward of the bridge. Fuel gushing out of the hull ignited, and fire spread along Battleship Row. A seaman named Zwarun was locked in the brig on drunk-and-disorderly charges. Poor guy went down with the ship. Two days later, the fires were finally extinguished. All they found of the skipper was his class ring."

"Is that the explosion?" Jackie asked, diverting Joe's attention to the next photograph.

"Uh-oh," Chuck said. "Don't get him started."

But it was too late.

"*That* photo," Joe growled, "is one of the most memorable images of the Pacific War. And it's a fraud. It shows the *Shaw*, not the *Arizona*, blowing up. Because it's the best blast on film from Pearl Harbor, guess what shot gets used?"

"What's wrong with that, Red?"

"Where's the *Nevada*?" Joe asked, tapping the photo beside the iconic image of him shooting at the Zero. "It should be there," he said, fingering the water beneath the raging fireball. "But the heroics of the *Nevada* have been erased."

"Why?" Jackie asked.

"So the devious War Department could dupe the American public. The only battleship to sail during the attack was the *Nevada*. Though it had been hit by a fish and was streaming smoke, it cruised past the death and destruction on Battleship Row. As the *Nevada* slipped between Ford Island and the floating dry dock across the water, in front of Hickam Field—"

"Where you were?" Jackie cut in.

"Right," confirmed Joe. "Anyway, as the *Nevada* sailed by, three bombs that might have struck it hit the *Shaw* instead. The *Shaw* was in the dock for work on its depth-charge gear. Most of the crew were ashore. As it went up in a spectacular explosion, a shutterbug on Ford Island captured the huge fireball you see in this photo. There, in front of the fireworks"—Joe tapped a space that was empty water—"you should be able to see the gun turrets of the battleship."

"I don't get it," Jackie said. "Why erase the *Nevada*?"

"Supposedly, to keep public morale high. From Pearl Harbor on, censorship ruled. You couldn't find a picture of Americans who died for their flag. This image has been cropped from the original to reduce the smoke and eliminate the damaged *Nevada*. The War Department thought such photos would stop parents from enlisting their sons. It was only two years later, when the Marines took heavy casualties while storming Tarawa, that the public got to see multiple dead."

"Same thing in Iraq," Chuck said. "Remember the stink that arose when people saw the photos of all those flag-draped coffins in the belly of a plane?"

"Right," said Jackie.

"If you die for your country, you become an embarrassment," said Joe. "A thousand heroes died on the *Arizona*, but they got censored. The *Shaw* made a good photo, so it came to represent the war. And the *Nevada* got airbrushed out."

"Your blood pressure, Red," warned his son.

Joe's face was turning the color of his nickname.

"I know, I know. Still, it picks my ass. You reach my age, you're *sick* of all the lies. Vietnam was a lie from start to finish, and it could have cost me my son. It did cost all those on that wall in Washington. And for what? There are no WMDs in Iraq, even though we flaunted all those phony photos at the UN. More body bags. And for what? Liars in the war rooms aren't the guys who fight. When push comes to shove, we're the ones who pay for their lies—in *our* blood!"

A haunted look crept into Joe's eyes.

"And not just our blood."

His finger slid across the newspaper from Pearl Harbor to the photo array on the far side of his present-day headshot.

"*That,*" he said, "was the biggest lie of all."

Banzai

Hong Kong
Christmas Day, 1941

She refused to let her fear show as she walked the hospital wards, giving what comfort she could to the shot-up and mangled soldiers. As a girl in small-town Alberta, where her dad ran a grain elevator, Viv Barrow had fantasized that she was Florence Nightingale. She saw herself wandering with her candle among all those British heroes who'd been cut down in their prime—or so she had imagined—in that disastrous Charge of the Light Brigade in the Crimean War. Yearning to play "the lady with the lamp" to modern-day soldiers, Viv had trained as a nurse at Edmonton's

Catholic hospital. On the day she graduated, she had hopped a train for the long, winding trip through the Rocky Mountains to Vancouver. There, Viv had applied to nurse for the military, and after a brief stint on the hospital boat that sailed to and from the West Coast Native villages, she got the chance to ship out to Hong Kong.

So here she was, walking the wards in St. Stephen's College, a two-story boys' school nestled on a rocky slope near Stanley village. Serving as a makeshift hospital for soldiers who'd been wounded defending the British colony against the Japanese army, the school flew a Red Cross flag on its low-pitched roof.

"Nurse?"

"Yes, Corporal?"

"I can still *feel* my leg."

"That's common," Viv assured him, averting her eyes from the stump left when surgeons had amputated the limb just below his pelvis. "We call that phantom pain."

"If the Japs come, I'll protect you."

"Shush," Viv said. "Get some sleep. It's Christmas Day. And I've heard"—she leaned down and whispered in his ear, as if confiding something top secret—"that Dr. Black has a case of whisky in the headmaster's office. He'll break it open at noon for a Christmas party."

"Save me a dance?" the soldier asked.

"I promise," Viv replied.

Tension had grown throughout the Pacific in 1941, and London had asked if Canada could help reinforce Hong Kong, in the hope that would deter Tokyo from taking hostile action. On November 16, two thousand soldiers with the Royal Rifles of Canada and the Winnipeg Grenadiers had arrived, bringing the defenders to fourteen thousand strong. The ill-equipped and half-trained Canadians assumed they were in for a snooze of garrison duty, but less than eight hours after the sneak attack on Pearl Harbor, fifty thousand warriors with the Japanese Imperial Army had swept down from China to invade Hong Kong.

Since then, only fearful news had reached the hospital, and each report was followed by an influx of fresh casualties: shell-shocked men with limbs that had been blown off as the battered battalions fell back to the Gin Drinkers' Line, a ten-mile rampart of trenches and pillboxes stretching across the rugged hill country of the mainland; gruesome head wounds suffered during the retreat across Victoria Harbour for a do-or-die stand on the island. A week ago, the enemy had waded ashore under cover of darkness, and since then they had been grinding down whatever stood in their way, blasting with their guns and gut-stabbing with their swords and bayonets. Now they had punched through the Wong Nei Chong Gap, in the central highlands, and last night, they had rampaged drunkenly around Stanley village and down this peninsula.

If Fort Stanley fell, so would Hong Kong.

Never had Viv been so relieved to see the break of day. Last night, ominous sounds in the black-ness had those trapped in the isolated hospital on edge. They could hear the fighting in Stanley drawing inexorably closer. Now and then, the odd bullet had zipped out of the dark as moaning men, sweating from fever, fidgeted about on their cots. Some cried out from whatever night terrors gripped their minds.

At one point, Viv had teetered on the verge of a primal scream, so wound up from stress that she feared she might snap. For release, she seized a British captain who had given her the eye and led him into a closet to fuck against the wall. With his pants around his ankles and her skirt hiked up to her waist, the two of them had slammed each other as if dawn would bring the gallows.

Even after he exploded in her and Viv bit down on his shoulder to stifle her orgasm, the two had kept on clutching and writhing until both their fear and their passion were exorcised.

Now, as dawn reddened the windows of the packed main hallway and its adjoining classroom wards, the same British captain was trying to convince Dr. George Black to evacuate St. Stephen's wounded to the fort.

"No," said Black, the lieutenant-colonel in charge of the wards. "I think it's safer here."

"Safer!" Viv's lover was incredulous. "How can that be? We're on the road from the village to Fort Stanley. How long will it be until the Japs come banging on our door?"

Black was a white-haired, soft-spoken medical man who had worked in the colony for fifty years. His staff consisted of two medical officers, seven British nurses and Viv, four Chinese nurses, and four British orderlies, all of whom cared for about a hundred patients. This morning, the doctor wore his hospital whites with a Red Cross armband.

"Frankly," said Black, "I'd sooner be here than with the soldiers at Fort Stanley. Guests at the Repulse Bay Hotel weren't harmed because there were no able-bodied soldiers on the premises. I'm sure that's what will happen to us."

"Doctor!" Viv exclaimed, shifting from eavesdropping on the men to interrupting them.

"Yes?" said Black.

"Look!" Viv pointed her finger to hundreds of dark silhouettes backed by the bloodred sky shimmering beyond the nearest window.

"Don't be alarmed," Black said to calm the patients in the central hall. "The Japanese are here. But there's a Red Cross flag on the roof, and I'll tell them to leave us alone."

Viv watched as Black strode into one of the classrooms and tore a white sheet from a bed. Armed with that flag of surrender, he crossed to the front door and swung it wide to confront the enemy. In heroic British tradition, he barred the threshold with his arm and announced boldly to the point man of the Japanese vanguard, "This is a hospital. You mustn't come in."

A moment later, the back of the doctor's head blew out in a spray of blood and bone.

"Banzai!" shouted Genjo Tokuda as he and two hundred Japanese soldiers, bayonets fixed and drunk on liquor looted from a bar, stormed St. Stephen's College. An old man holding a white sheet opened the door, so Corporal Tokuda, leading the charge, shot him between the eyes. As each soldier rushed into the Red Cross infirmary, he trampled the sheet and bayoneted the doctor.

Shriek after shriek filled the hall as steel sank into flesh. Fifty-odd patients were run through in their beds, the invaders tearing off bandages to reopen half-healed wounds. When a Chinese nurse tried to protect an invalid, she got skewered too. Before long, those who had swarmed the hospital in helmets, khaki jackets, breeches, and puttees were soaked head to toe in blood. So slippery was the floor that the soldiers struggled to keep their footing as they fanned out to satellite wards to jab their blades into other casualties.

When a British captain sought to shield a Canadian nurse, Genjo Tokuda gutted him with his bayonet. Eye to eye with the dying man, the Japanese warrior kept him upright on his buckling legs so he could witness the death throes of someone bleeding out like a samurai committing hara-kiri.

The nurse was Viv.

The captain was her lover.

Viv's memory must have shut down, for the next sound that penetrated her consciousness, after all the screams, was a British voice shouting, "They say that anyone who can get to the front door will be spared."

Numb from shock, Viv shuffled toward the rectangle of blinding light. Like animals wading through a flood of blood to Noah's ark, the patients who had not been slaughtered in their beds strained for the door, some trailing blankets behind them. Viv stooped to help the legless soldier with the phantom pain, dragging the amputee with her the rest of the way.

At the door, the colony's conquerors were searching their captives for cash and valuables. Spotting a knife tucked in one man's belt, they bayoneted him. They even took the prayer book from the padre. Having lost all sense of time, Viv felt as if she were wandering through the landscape of a dream. A nurse's watch hung upside down on her chest so she could read the time or take a patient's pulse by looking down at her breast. The soldier who searched her tore it away with such force that he ripped her uniform and exposed her brassiere.

The soldier sniggered.

Then Viv was marched away.

Eight nurses were imprisoned in a stifling room. As morning wore on, the temperature climbed toward 120 degrees. The buzzing of flies was enough to drive the women insane.

"Are they going to kill us?" asked one nurse, her thumbnail bitten to the quick.

"We'll bake to death," another moaned. "God, this heat! The Black Hole of Calcutta must have been like this."

With much of the U.S. Pacific Fleet at the bottom of the sea, Japan had launched a multipronged attack on Southeast Asia, hurling its might against the Philippines, Midway, Thailand, Wake, Guam, Singapore, the Dutch East Indies, Malaya, Burma, and here. The sooner the Rising Sun flapped over Hong Kong, the sooner these soldiers would be off to seize other riches. So the task was to force the last stronghold at the tip of this peninsula—Fort Stanley—to surrender.

The men who had made it to St. Stephen's door were locked away in a windowless storeroom on the second floor. About sixty prisoners of war were packed into a ten-by-twenty-foot space—so many that they had to take turns at sitting and lying down. As the heat of the noontime sun hammered the roof, the Japanese began selecting captives for the torture room.

The gibbering from the first pair to feel the dismembering edge of the sword electrified the air within St. Stephen's. The butcher's bill recorded four chopped-off ears before the men were finally slaughtered. Genjo Tokuda was with the squad that transported the doomed. To push the sweating prisoners back from the door long enough for his cohorts to haul out the next two, he fired a couple of quick shots into the huddle of POWs.

The youngest of the captives was shaking with fear.

The defiant soldier next to him appeared to be a vet from the First World War. Tokuda knew just enough English to catch what the old hand said to the youth: "Look, kid, we're gonna die today. But the one thing we're gonna do is die like Royal Rifles. So don't let these fuckers scare you."

"Him," said Tokuda in Japanese, so his comrades dragged away the old vet as one of the second pair. He too died pleading for mercy after they stabbed out his eyes.

Then it was back to the cell.

"Canada," Tokuda said, pointing at the young soldier who had quaked with such fear.

"Yeah," choked the Rifle, trying his hardest to muster his courage. "To hell with you. Go ahead. Kill me, you bastard!"

Tokuda struck him with the flat of his sword.

"Canada . . . Cowboy!"

The Rifle frowned. "Sure . . ." Hesitation. "Cowboy," he said. His puzzled face seemed to ask, What's going on here?

Tokuda stepped back and twirled his free hand

above his head like a cowboy whirling a lariat. "Yip-yip-yip," he mimicked.

Another slap of the sword, this time to the side of the boy's head.

Tokuda drew an imaginary pistol with his empty hand.

"Cowboy . . . You."

With blood running down his gashed cheek, the Canadian pantomimed a quick-draw back.

The Japanese laughed.

And they left him alive in the room.

Wails and cries filled St. Stephen's as the butchery went on. Worse yet were the interludes of silence, for they meant that Tokuda and his squad were on their way back to the second-floor cell for more POWs to dismember. Every time that door swung open, Tokuda slapped his hip with his hand and then aimed a finger at the Rifle. And every time, the youth drew in return.

Finally, there was enough hacked-apart flesh in the torture room to serve the conquerors' plan. Four more Royal Rifles were led off to what they assumed would be their deaths, but instead they were forced to watch while Japanese swords cut the tongue out of one man from the previous pair and chopped off the other man's ears. After, the commander's interpreter told the four reprieved soldiers, "Go to Fort Stanley and tell your leaders what you have seen. Hong Kong must surrender, or all will be killed like *this*!"

Writhing and crying, with soldiers gripping her arms and legs, one of the Chinese nurses was carried out of the stifling room. Where she went, Viv could only guess, but quickly female screams began to echo through the hospital.

Soon, the Japanese were back for another nurse. From the smell of whisky on their breath and the bottle gripped in one's hand, Viv knew the soldiers had cracked open the case of liquor that Dr. Black had been saving for the Yuletide party. What a savage Christmas! she thought as another Chinese nurse went into hysterics.

The sight of the struggling woman being dragged from the room flooded Viv's brain with images of the Japanese army's 1937 Rape of Nanking. If what they said was true, over three hundred thousand people in China's capital city were beheaded, burned, bayoneted, buried alive, and disemboweled. Eighty thousand women and girls were raped by the invaders. But the one image Viv couldn't shake from her mind, no matter how hard she tried, was that of a pregnant woman who was sliced open after death so her rapists could present the fetus to their commander on the end of a bayonet.

Viv wondered how many soldiers here had also participated in the Rape of Nanking?

Now, all four Chinese nurses were gone from this bake oven. Was it too much to hope that Japanese soldiers might loathe the thought of touching colonial women?

No! They're coming back!

Off went the first Englishwoman, then she too began to shriek. Each time the Japanese returned, their uniforms were stained with more blood. But nothing unnerved Viv as much as how one of the men was ogling her, as if he could burn the clothes off her body with the intensity of his lust.

Two more British nurses.

Then they grabbed Viv.

Whatever she had feared she was going to see, it was nothing compared to the scene that greeted her from the door to the torture room. So many pieces of bodies were piled on the floor that blood had crossed the threshold and pooled by the opposite wall. Naked and pierced with sword wounds, Viv's seven nursing compatriots lay sprawled in postures that meant they'd been pinned down and gang-raped.

On instinct, Viv turned to bolt, but she found

herself facing the corporal who'd ogled her in the holding cell and was now undoing his pants.

"You—" he said as others tore off her clothes.

Viv lashed out.

"—*mine*," Tokuda declared.

Heather Stables

"This is where you work?"

"Uh-huh," Jackie replied. "The Heather Stables."

"Stables?" said Joe incredulously. "When I asked you over lunch if we were going to see the stables where you work, I didn't expect *actual* stables."

A sweeping lawn fronted the beamed facade of the Tudor building at the corner of Heather and 33rd. If you didn't know what city you were in, you might think that you were approaching the front door of Shakespeare's birthplace in Stratford-upon-Avon. The grass on either side of Special X HQ was strewn with autumn leaves.

"You Mounties sure do treat your horses royally," said Joe.

"Actually, it was built as a boys' school back in the twenties," said Jackie. "In 1921, we purchased it as a barracks for two hundred redcoats. We tacked on four stables for 140 horses. The mounts are long gone, but the name stuck.

"Hi Fred," she said to the commissionaire just inside the door. He was a mounted policeman who'd retired but couldn't get the red serge out of his blood, so now he secured the door with the Corps of Commissionaires.

"Good day, Corporal. Who do we have here?"

"These two hoods are fugitives from New Mexico who've come to fleece the vets at the upcoming convention. He's Joe the Fish—my granddad, I regret to say. And he's Cut-'em-up Chuck—my dad—from the most wanted list."

"Tough-looking hombres," Fred said.

"Ha!" barked Joe. "You should see my granddaughter. Evil seed if ever there was one. Beady eyes. Broken nose. Cauliflower ears. And a mouth that knows no respect for its elders."

"Sign in, gentlemen. We've got a cell waiting."

After signing the visitors' record, Joe and Chuck

were issued clip-on passes. They paused for a moment to take in the entrance hall, a vault that soared two stories over their heads. Facing the entrance was the bullpen. It looked more like a museum than it did a squad room. To the left were staircases up and down. Mounted above the descending stairs was a huge bison head, like the one in the crest on Jackie's peaked hat.

"Your mascot?" Chuck asked.

"Yeah. We almost lost him. The trophy was stolen recently, but we got it back. Had him cleaned and remounted, and now he looks like he's right off the plains."

"What's up there?" Joe asked.

"The chief's office. He's got the front corner."

"And down below?"

"The cyber cellar. Our ViCLAS linkage system, which is like VICAP in the States. And psych- and geo-profilers."

"The eggheads, huh?"

"Yeah," said Jackie. "But not him. The guy coming up the stairs is the Mad Dog."

"Mad Dog, huh? Times have changed. I can recall when the Mounties had dogs that were *actually* hounds."

"Sergeant Preston," Chuck said.

"And his mutt, King."

"The Mad Dog's the main man on our SWAT team. Emergency Response Team, in our tongue. If push comes to shove," Jackie said, "we sic him on the bad guys."

"No wonder," Joe replied. "He's got muscles on his muscles. We coulda used him at the airport with those goons."

She ushered them across the hall and into the bullpen. This squad room was like none they had seen before. No cops in shirtsleeves and shoulder holsters, working at desks crammed closer than olives in a jar, surrounded by mug shots from the underworld. This was like a sheriff's office in the Wild West, with frontier firearms decorating the walls and a Maxim machine gun from the gold rush set up on the floor. Mannequins displayed the garb of legendary lawmen. But instead of Wyatt Earp and Bat Masterson, these pith helmets, Stetsons, and scarlet uniforms had once clothed Bub Walsh and Sam Steele.

"Red, Dad, this handsome guy is Sergeant Dane Winter. He and I are a team."

Winter came out from behind a desk next to a Winchester rifle and shook hands with both Hett men. Sandy-haired and athletic, he was in his thirties. The sergeant wore a uniform like Jackie's, but with an extra chevron. Joe wondered if Winter was bedding his granddaughter.

"Dane's granddad flew in the war, Red."

"Oh?" responded the eldest Hett. "When did he enlist?"

"September 1940. During the Battle of Britain."

"I thought of that."

"What?"

"Joining the RAF. *For Whom the Bell Tolls*. Hemingway's Robert Jordan taking a stand. We weren't in the war, and I wanted in. Fighting the Nazis was a good fight."

"Something stop you?"

"My pop," said Joe. "He knew we were heading for a showdown with Tokyo. He told me, 'Let the Brits fight that war. You get ready for what's coming.'"

"A twist of fate," said Dane. He indicated the newspaper on his desk. It had been folded back to the *Life* magazine shot of Joe shooting at the Zero.

"Your grandpa fly Spits?"

"Halifax bombers."

"So he was one of Bomber Harris's boys?"

"From '42 on."

"Where'd he see action?"

"All over the map. In the Battle of the Atlantic,

he took part in the Channel Dash and the destruction of the warship *Gneisenau*. Over the Third Reich, he was in on the Thousand Bomber Raids. Then he was in North Africa in the months leading up to Monty's victory over the Desert Fox at the Battle of El Alamein."

"I'd like to meet him," Joe said.

"He died recently."

"Sorry to hear. We're all dying off, us old vets. That, no doubt, is why they asked me to speak at the con."

"Well, you were in on some pretty big stuff."

"Dresden?" said Joe. "Did your grandpa fly that raid?"

"No," replied Dane. "He missed that. Got shot down in the raid on the V-2 missile factory at Peenemünde in August 1943. He spent the rest of the war in a POW camp."

"He was lucky," Joe said. "That was overkill. No warrior should have to carry Dresden guilt."

They were interrupted by the ringing of the phone on Dane's desk.

"Sergeant Winter," he answered.

The conversation was brief.

When he hung up, Dane turned to Jackie and said, "Sorry to rain on your parade, but the chief wants us in his office."

"Red, Dad," she said, "these are the keys to the car. You're on your own for a while. I'll draw you a map of the scenic route to the convention hotel, and I'll explain how to get around Point Grey to the airport if you want to check out the plane."

"Plane?" said Dane.

"The fireworks. Tomorrow night."

"Right," he said. "I forgot. Tomorrow's Halloween."

Hung along the walls of the wide staircase that angled up to the chief's office were paintings and photographs that depicted the history of the RCMP from its formation in 1873 through to the present day. The Special External Section of Canada's national police—Special X, for short—investigated criminal cases with links to other countries. Cops from forces around the world climbed these steps, and the powers that be wanted to leave each one with the impression that—as the unofficial motto goes—"The Mounties always get their man."

To be successful, you must look successful.

Promotion sells.

"What happened at Dresden?" Jackie asked as she and Dane went up the stairs.

"I caught that too."

"Caught what?"

"Your granddad is haunted."

"He didn't used to be. He was the ultra-patriot. But he's lost moral certainty over the years."

"Since when?"

"Vietnam. That was the start. He bought into the government's lie that we were fighting Communists, and he couldn't understand why we got our asses whipped. At least, not until he learned that Ho Chi Minh had issued his declaration of independence from French colonial rule in 1945. Red saw then that we had stepped into France's shoes. The fact that Ho was a Communist was about as relevant as Jefferson's owning slaves. The crux was that both men were ardent nationalists. So we ended up trying to suppress an independence movement, just as the Brits did in the Revolution. With the same result."

"I think it's more than that."

"It is," said Jackie. "But that's part of it. My dad got shot twice in Vietnam. He almost didn't make it. My granddad's disillusionment stems from having nearly lost his only son for a lie."

"Then Iraq?"

"Don't get him started on that! But what really shook him was the revelation that President Truman had kept a secret journal at the Potsdam Conference in 1945. Seven years after Truman's death, it finally came to light."

Having reached the landing at the top of the stairs, they knocked on the chief's door.

"Enter," called out Robert DeClercq.

The view from the corner office, even on this overcast afternoon, took in the exuberant fall colors of Queen Elizabeth Park. Facing the two window walls was a horseshoe-shaped desk made from three Victorian library tables. In the crook of the U sat an antique chair crowned with the crest of the Mounted Police. The paperwork on the desk was piled around the computer, printer, scanner, fax, and telephone, marching neatly from the In table to the Out. The picture on the wall behind this workstation was Sydney Hall's *Last Great Council of the West*, a sweeping canvas of redcoats, their hands on their swords, meeting feathered Indians at Blackfoot Crossing. Command structure is the key to crisis management, and this felt like the office of both a macro and a micro overseer. When faced with a Gordian knot of red tape, this officer, like Alexander the Great, would simply draw his regimental sword and slash through to a resolution.

This was the office of a man who got things done.

No bullshit.

"Mr. Roger Yamada," DeClercq said, "meet Sergeant Dane Winter and Corporal Jackie Hett."

The diplomat who greeted them was in late middle age. He bowed slightly and shook their hands, blending both Japanese and North American cultures. His dark, graying hair matched the color of his impeccable business suit; both had been cut conservatively to suggest a reserved manner. His face was a mix of Pacific Rim races.

"Mr. Yamada is with the Japanese consulate," said DeClercq. "As you can see, he was just beginning to fill me in on a yakuza link between our countries."

No time wasted.

Straight to the case on the wall.

The Strategy Wall was the command center of DeClercq's office. It stretched from floor to ceiling along the length of the unbroken wall and wrapped around the corner to the edge of the painting. An expanse of corkboard onto which the chief pinned a visual overview of the most important cases being handled by Special X, the Strategy Wall was like the map tables wartime generals used to plot their campaign strategies.

DeClercq—who was about a decade younger than Yamada—had less gray at the temples of his dark hair and even darker, seen-it-all eyes. Lean and wiry in the blue serge uniform of commissioned officers, he wore the crown and two pips of his rank on the epaulets, the badge of the force as collar dogs on the jacket, and his long-service medal—with three stars known as the Milky Way—on the breast pocket.

"The yakuza," Roger Yamada said, "is not what it used to be. Do you know its history?"

"Educate us," said DeClercq.

Jackie wondered where the diplomat had learned to speak English with a North American accent.

Not in Japan.

"Yakuza members of old prided themselves on following the code of *bushido*. Not any more. The gangs are degraded now. This man"—he pointed at a headshot of a young Japanese on the Strategy Wall—"represents the new norm. He reflects the trend toward declining cohesion and obedience among yakuza members. He just sees crime as a way to make himself rich. He controls the odious importation of child prostitutes from China. His name is Kazuya Ochi.

"Kazuya—I'll use his first name—flies to Vancouver a few times a year to recruit blonde prostitutes. He was last here four days ago. The

75

Japanese National Police Agency suspects that this is where he deals with the snakeheads, Chinese triad smugglers who traffic in underage girls. When he returned to Tokyo, he was met at Narita Airport by his uncle, Makoto Ochi.''

From a leather briefcase, Yamada withdrew a second photograph and passed it to DeClercq.

The chief tacked a mug shot of a tough-looking thug to the Strategy Wall. Makoto's face was crisscrossed by scars.

"The national police followed them to a building we know well in the Ginza district. That, I'm sure you know, is the shopping and nightlife mecca of Tokyo. In 1945, Ginza was all but flattened by four firebomb raids. Everything but the outer shells of concrete buildings burned down. Three weeks after the end of the war, the U.S. military arrived to begin the occupation. Soldiers set up headquarters at Hibiya, just northwest of Ginza, in the heart of the city. That's where the shogun had once built Edo Castle. The Imperial Palace of the emperor now stands on the ruins.

"The yakuza, after the war, were all but annihilated. Since the 1700s, they had preyed as two groups. The *tekiya* were peddlers. Snake-oil salesmen who worked fairs and markets. The *bakuto* were gamblers. Dice men and card sharps who worked towns and highways. The wartime military draft had severely reduced their ranks, and the American occupiers proceeded to sweep away the topmost layer of control in government and business. That created a power vacuum in Japan, spawning a new form of yakuza: the *gurentai.*

"The *gurentai*," Yamada said, "grew into our version of the Mob. Imagine *The Godfather* movies cast in Tokyo. Japan's Don Corleone is Genjo Tokuda. He's the gangster who built the building to which the national police followed Kazuya and Makoto Ochi."

"They went in?" Jackie asked.

"Yes. But only Makoto Ochi came out."

"Is Genjo Tokuda alive?"

"Very much so," said Yamada. "In fact, he's in Vancouver. That's why I'm here."

The diplomat fetched another photo from his briefcase.

DeClercq pinned it up beside the previous two.

Jackie found herself staring at an eighty-year-old Japanese face that was half an ugly scar.

"I know this guy!" she said. "My granddad, my dad, and I just had a run-in with him at the airport."

"That's a good one," Yamada said, referring to the prosthetic finger that Jackie withdrew carefully—

so as not to disturb any forensic traces—from a pouch on her gun belt.

"My granddad scored this trophy by tussling with one of Tokuda's bodyguards."

"A yakuza wears a prosthetic finger when he's traveling abroad. Not to is to advertise that he's a thug. Some are of poor quality and wouldn't pass scrutiny. They fall off at inconvenient times, like during a customs check. The best prosthetics are crafted in London, but they cost a lot. Discount shoppers get theirs in Hong Kong."

"Not a booming trade."

"It used to be. By the early sixties, there were 184,000 yakuza in 5,200 gangs. More men than in Japan's army."

"All under Tokuda?"

"No, but he was the most vicious of the lot. Yakuza cut off their fingers to make amends for mistakes, and he held his hoodlums to an impossible standard of *bushido*."

"How'd he get to the top?" asked Dane.

"Ginza had to start from zero after the war. The Americans seized six hundred buildings around Tokyo and established PXs in the Hattori clock tower—now the Wako Building—and the Matsuya store in Ginza. The PXs—"

"I've always wondered what that stands for," said Dane.

"Post exchange," replied Jackie. "A PX is a store within a military post."

"All of Tokyo became a U.S. military post after the war," Yamada explained. "The Americans rationed food and liquor, and that spawned an instant black market. In Ginza, shanties were hastily hammered together from salvaged boards, and tent stalls mushroomed along the dim streets. The smart businessmen hung out shop signs written in Roman letters or adorned with pictograms so the Americans would know what went on inside. Soon bars, cabarets, dance halls, and pool halls were crowded with GIs. That's when Genjo Tokuda—having been freed under an amnesty that released Japanese prisoners of war—muscled in."

"What'd he do in the war?"

"No one knew. His face was scarred beyond recognition. His only ID was the uniform he was captured in."

"Where was that?" Dane asked.

"Okinawa. Tokuda used his wartime connections to put together a gang of unemployed, repatriated soldiers. He commanded like a general, a samurai ruled by *bushido*. In the beginning, he was just one of many engaged in a free-for-all struggle to corner the black market and control the bars and clubs favored by GIs."

"To pimp prostitutes?" Jackie asked.

The diplomat nodded. "The *gurentai* fought among themselves, as hoods do everywhere. Turf wars erupted, with gangsters trying to kill off rival bosses. In the yakuza, your boss is God. So a gang without a boss is weak and crippled in a fight. Whoever kills a rival boss takes over his gang and territory."

"Capone," said Jackie.

"That's who they mimicked. Right down to the clothes they wore. The legend of Genjo Tokuda is this: A yakuza boss from another district aimed to take over the black market in Ginza. He asked Tokuda to meet him to settle the matter honorably and then pulled a gun he'd hidden under the negotiating table. He triggered a shot at Tokuda, but the gun jammed. Tokuda fled with his bodyguard, but they were pursued by men with swords who caught up to them on the street. The bodyguard was killed. Tokuda was injured. Though wounded in the shoulder, he grabbed one of the swords by its blade—"

"Ouch!" Jackie winced.

"And wrenched it from his pursuer's hands. Swinging the sword, Tokuda counterattacked. He hacked the heads off three men, including the rival boss."

"Is that true?" Dane asked.

"The incident wasn't reported. But that was the start of Tokuda's reputation for vengeance."

"The start?" said Jackie. "There's more?"

"Members of the rival gang ate the ashes of their boss and vowed to avenge his beheading. One night, Tokuda was drinking in one of his Ginza clubs when a would-be assassin walked up to his table, pulled out a pistol, and shot him near the heart. When he got out of the hospital, Tokuda had the Claw—his enforcer—hunt down the triggerman and the others who had botched the hit."

"The Claw?" said Dane.

"Tokuda and his closest henchmen snuck the captives out to sea in a boat. Clad in spongy, air-filled life jackets so they could breathe, the doomed hoods were forced into open coffins on the deck. Slats were nailed across the tops to hold them down. Dividers were fitted around their necks to compartmentalize their heads. Then freshly mixed concrete was poured over their bodies. When it hardened, the gangsters' faces stared up from concrete overcoats. With his bare hands, the Claw gouged out their eyes, and one by one, the blind men were dumped into the ocean. They sank—alive—to the bottom of the sea. The following day, the rest of the rival gang members received a jar full of eyes. They quickly swore allegiance to Tokuda.

"After that," Yamada said, "other gangs were loath to challenge him. He let it be known that no quarter would be given. All he claimed to want was a piece of the pie, and he offered blood brotherhood to rival bosses. Those who accepted sealed the deal with a traditional *sakazuki* ceremony at his home. The alliance was sworn over cups of sake, and a go-between declared the union complete. That done, Tokudo slowly seized control. Instead of a piece, he ate the whole pie."

"What about the police?" asked Dane.

"The civil police were unarmed. Tokuda's gang switched samurai swords for automatic firearms, and soon *they* became known as the Ginza police."

"And the Americans?"

"From 1945 on, their obsession was Communism. Tokuda was a tool for their dirty work. The occupiers agreed to leave his gang alone if he would control the labor unions and crush any movement that might be a Communist initiative."

"Lucky Luciano reached a similar deal with the Allied invaders in Sicily during the Second World War," said DeClercq. "The Allies kept their hands off his army of street criminals, and he offered them the services of the Mafia."

"Kickback deals with occupation officials guaranteed Tokuda freedom from prosecution for his black-market crimes and extortions. He got involved in everything: gambling, smuggling, loan-sharking, prostitution, pornography, gun-running, slavery, and drugs."

"Heroin?" said Dane.

"Methamphetamines. As post-war Japan developed its competitive and frenetic pace, speed became the national drug of choice. The yakuza also bartered it for Western arms."

"Tokuda sounds ruthless. A nasty piece of work."

"He's an organizational genius. Because of his wartime connections, he has a long-standing alliance with the right-wing political nationalists. That's how he infiltrated the corporate world. In the bubble economy of the 1980s, he laundered his dirty money through stocks and real estate. Then he got millions more from the banks in bad debts."

"What's his scam?"

"Sokaiya. The word literally means 'shareholders' meetings men.' Tokuda would buy up a small number of shares in a company, earning his *sokaiya* the right to attend shareholders' meetings. They would gather information on, or create, damaging scandals about the company and its executives—secret mistresses, tax evasion, unsafe factory conditions, pollution, and such. They'd threaten to disclose those scandals at the shareholders' meetings unless their demands were met. If the shakedown was rebuffed, the *sokaiya* would attend the meeting and raise hell, shouting down those who tried to speak and broadcasting the scandals for all to hear. In Japan, people fear embarrassment and shame more than physical threats. One or two shareholders' meetings like that had all executives running scared. In the end, Tokuda got majority stock control of thousands of companies."

"And real estate?" said Dane.

"For that, he used *jiageya,* 'land turners.' As land prices rose, these men blackmailed, threatened, or committed arson to force small businesses or residents off prime real estate. Then Tokuda developed his acquisitions with dirty money."

"What happened when the bubble burst?"

"Nothing," said Yamada. "Tokuda caused the

recession, so he knew it was coming. He cashed in at the height of the false economy and bought overseas."

"Here?"

"Everywhere. America, Europe, Asia."

"Then what?"

"He retired and became a recluse. He lives on the top three floors of a skyscraper behind the building to which the national police followed Kazuya and Makoto Ochi."

"Doing what?"

"He collects shogun antiques."

"Why's he in Vancouver?" Jackie asked.

"We don't know. That's why I'm here. Not once since the end of the Pacific War in 1945 has Genjo Tokuda left Japan. He's always had a passport, but he's never used it. So whatever brings him here now, you can be sure that you want to know."

"Sergeant, Corporal," DeClercq said, "locate Tokuda, follow him, and see what he does."

"I can help," Yamada said, "with a phone call. May I summon my sister from the car?"

The woman who entered DeClercq's office five minutes later was also in her sixties, but she was full Caucasian.

"Hello," she said, bowing as her way of introduction. "My name is Lynda West."

"My *half*-sister," Yamada said, as if reading Jackie's mind. "My mother was Japanese, my father an American GI with the occupation forces. He died before I was born. My mother named me after him."

"Don't let Roger fool you. He's reserved on the outside, but he's not above a prank. We joke that we're related, but we're most likely not."

"We might be," Yamada said. "Your dad *was* in Tokyo during the occupation."

"True," said West. "And I'm Tokyo Rose."

"You could be tested," said Jackie, a cop to the core.

"Heavens, no!" exclaimed the woman. "Joshing is one thing. That would be another. I wouldn't want to know if Dad cheated on Mom. And that would spoil the joke."

"*You* spoiled it," Yamada said, "by outing me. That was my test to see how sharp these officers are."

"Sharp enough," DeClercq replied, "to wonder why Ms. West has a GPS gadget in her hand."

"That's for you," the diplomat said as his "sister" handed the chief the global positioning system.

"A gift from Japan?"

"At Narita Airport, the national police fitted Tokuda's luggage with a tracking device. While we've been talking, my personal assistant has followed it with this."

Barbed Wire

To look at the woman sighing out her last shallow breaths in this crib of a deathbed, you'd never guess that she was once the adventurous nursing grad in the photo. The black-and-white headshot from 1941 had yellowed slightly with the passing of time. From back then, Viv Barrow beamed up at her daughter in the here and now, while Lyn Barrow stared down at the wartime nightingale.

"Were you once that happy, Mom?" she asked.

The dying nurse didn't answer.

Lyn returned the photo to its place on the bedside table. Snapped in Edmonton on the day of her graduation, the Viv in the picture wore a white uniform with a nurse's cap pinned into her upswept forties hairstyle and a starched bib tucked into what was most likely an ankle-length skirt. The twenty-two-year-old RN's complexion was as fresh as country cream; her dark eyes were full of the dreams that only people that age can believe in, and her smile was as bright as the sun on the prairies. Her arm was clutched around a bouquet of roses that had to be blood red.

The hallway outside her hospital room was shushing down for the night. Soon it would be time for Lyn to leave, so she sat down beside the palliative-care bed and reached in through the bars to take Viv's arthritic hand in her own.

"Mom, it's Lyn. Can you hear me?"

No response from the bed.

Over the past few months, it had all spilled out. Some of what Viv told Lyn had come in the form of conscious recollections—mostly stories related by the old woman as she flipped through her wartime photograph album—and some had escaped through subconscious babblings under the effect of drugs.

"That's me on the day I arrived in Vancouver," Viv had once explained, a gnarled finger caressing a photo of her leaning against the shortest of the Stanley Park totem poles.

"This too," she added, sliding that finger across to a snapshot of the suspension bridge high over the Capilano River.

"Where's that?" Lyn asked, touching a cheesy photo of an old wishing well.

"Near the suspension bridge. Did I never take you there?"

"Not that I recall. What are you wishing for?"

Viv was standing beside the well with her eyes closed, about to drop a coin from the palm of her hand.

A pregnant pause.

Then Viv answered.

"Canadian troops were being mustered to go to Hong Kong. I wished to follow them as their nurse."

Instead, Viv had landed a job at the local hospital.

"The first thing I did when I stepped off the train—after finding a room, of course—was phone my name into VGH for a fill-in job. I hadn't slept for two days on the rails, but I was far too excited to rest. So off I went on a walking tour of Stanley Park and a swing across the Capilano suspension bridge. By the time I got back to my room, VGH had called me in."

"To work that night?" Lyn asked.

"Uh-huh," said Viv. "And what I hadn't checked out was the local tram route. It was a two-mile walk to the hospital. I didn't have enough money left for a cab. I didn't know a soul in Vancouver. And no tram or bus connected my room to VGH."

"So who drove you?"

Viv shook her jaundiced head. "Believe it or not, there was a time when the Depression, armament production, and gas rationing meant few people drove cars. I had no choice but to walk."

"In the dark?"

"Yes. During the blackout. As yet, we weren't at war with Japan, but there were rumors of Nazi U-boats prowling the West Coast. There was a fear that ships in the harbor would be attacked from the sea and sunk, so streetlamps were doused, windows were curtained, and my route to work was almost as black as ink."

"Scary."

"All I had was moonlight to guide me there, and the moon was but a sliver. Of course, I was dressed in my nurse's whites. I must've looked like a ghost slipping through the night."

"*Real* scary."

"It was," said Viv. "A wartime seaport. Sailors loose on the town. And some of them attacked women."

"Anything happen to you?"

"Luckily, I was armed. My landlady loaned me a baseball bat and told me to follow the white line down the center of the road. If footsteps came toward me, she said, 'Swing the bat like hell and knock his head out of the park.' "

The black leather cover of Viv's photo album was embossed with a golden sailing ship, its sails billowing in the wind. Stuck to the inside of the front cover was a time-worn shot of a little girl sitting in a farmyard of chickens, her mouth smeared with chocolate. On the first several pages were photos of beaux in the varied uniforms of the Second World War. Their eager faces made Lyn wonder how many survived.

There was no picture of Lyn's dad.

The pages that followed the snapshots of Viv's arrival in Vancouver were filled with photos that captured her first adventure on the golden ship of the album's cover.

Alert Bay was a Kwakiutl village on an isle just off the inland shore of Vancouver Island. It was home to a tribe of totem carvers, a place where the aboriginal potlatch once had spiritual grounding.

Here was Viv tugging on a rope that sank into the sea off the deck of a coastal boat, the *Columbia*. Here was Viv among mythological monsters that had been carved up the trunks of towering cedar trees, the wings of thunderbirds spread as if about to embrace her. And here was Viv sitting sideways on a windowsill in St. George's Hospital, sunning herself with her eyes shut as if lost in Shangri-La.

"I got that job," Viv had said dreamily on the day they started her morphine drip, "soon after I arrived in Vancouver. Back then, Alert Bay was the real thing. Just a few generations earlier, the Kwakiutls were still initiating cannibals into their Hamatsa cult."

"Sounds thrilling."

"It was. The chief's son carved me bracelets."

"Why'd you leave, Mom?"

"To transport a patient. This old Indian woman was brought to the hospital with mental problems. She thought Baxbakualanuxsiwae—the cannibal monster on the totem poles—was trying to eat her. The doctor at the hospital asked if I would escort her here, to Essondale, for a psych assessment. So that's how we ended up in bunk beds in a cabin on the police boat."

"Was she dangerous?"

93

"We didn't think so. I thought she was just a lonely widow in dowdy clothes. She wore a great big hat festooned with all sorts of strange plants. She was a patient like any other to me, so I treated her as if we were sailing down the coast for a physical. That was my mistake."

"Why?"

"I was young and inexperienced. So, foolishly, I let her choose the lower bunk."

"That's bad?"

"You can't hear the squeaks. When a patient climbs out of the top bunk, squeaks from the bed springs wake you up. When she crawls out of the lower bunk, she's silently on the floor."

"That presents a danger?"

"It does if she slides an eight-inch hatpin out of her festooned hat, then looms over you with her arm raised, ready to plunge the weapon deep into your heart."

"You woke up!"

"No, I slept right through. But I had left the door ajar for fresh air. One of the cops onboard had come down to use the head. He peeked in, saw that I was about to get stabbed, and dashed in to grab the woman's hand before it plunged."

"Wow! Another second and there'd have been no more you."

"And no *you*," said Viv.

The photos from Alert Bay were the last shots in the book. When she docked in Vancouver, Viv had called the Canadian army to check on her application to serve as a military nurse. A short time later, she had shipped out to Hong Kong. That's why Viv was in St. Stephen's College at four o'clock on Christmas Day, 1941, when the Japanese soldiers who'd run amok in the hospital since dawn heard that the colony had capitulated, and finally stopped raping and killing the nurses.

Nine months later, Lyn was born.

By then, Viv was a prisoner in Stanley Internment Camp.

Lyn had next to no recollection of being an infant POW. She had, in fact, spent almost three years in that camp, until it was liberated by the Royal Navy in August 1945. Only since her mother's illness had Lyn been able to fit together the pieces of the puzzle that had baffled her for so long. There were two reasons why there were no photos in the album after Alert Bay. The first was that Viv had lost everything—her physical possessions and her mental health—in the fall of Hong Kong. The second was that she would slip into a deep depression whenever the topic of war with Japan cropped up. During the worst episodes, Viv

was committed to the psychiatric ward at Essondale for electroshock treatments.

Consequently, the war was off limits.

Sometimes, bolstered by all the research she had
done in a futile attempt to learn more about her
father—beyond the bare-bones description offered
by her mom—Lyn thought she could vaguely recall her childhood behind barbed wire.

When Lieutenant General Takashi Sakai first announced that all residents of British background
were to be interned, Sir Athol MacGregor, Hong
Kong's chief justice, suggested that streets at the
top of the Peak be designated POW camps. The
chief justice, it seemed, had failed to grasp what
Sakai had in mind. The idea wasn't for white colo-
nialists to look down physically and psychologi-
cally on those who had conquered them, but for
Japanese officials to be able to see Lord Such-and-
such scrubbing latrines as his lady scrounged to
survive.

To that end, Sakai selected several drab apartment blocks that huddled together on the rock of
Stanley peninsula at a depth too low to catch the
cool sea breezes. There, in Spartan quarters built
to house three hundred East Indians, the Japanese
crammed almost three thousand prisoners of war.
So tight were the steaming, crowded barracks that

every space got used: holes under staircases, corners in halls, pantries in kitchens. The internees slept on the floor or in beds made out of boxes. There was one toilet for every ninety captives.

Did Lyn actually recall playing in the gutters as a dirty little girl in Stanley Camp? She had certainly read about the urchins who'd frolicked there after the slaughter, back when the stench of decaying corpses, rotting food, and human excrement hung over the camp like a poisonous fog. The Japanese had left the dead wherever they fell. On the far side of the barbed wire that penned in the internees lay the remains of an English soldier whose sister was in the camp. Each day, she got as close as could be to her brother, while slowly his face became unrecognizable under a mask of flies, his khaki uniform turned green from mold, and putrefying flesh oozed off his bones.

Damn the flies, the bedbugs, and the lice!

They could drive you mad!

Did Lyn actually recall choking down the inedible food? The diet consisted of rice, rice, rice. A bowl a day, undulating with worms and weevils. For color, the POWs concocted "green horror soup," a mix of weeds and garbage scraps—potato peelings, carrot tops, buttercups, and the like—foraged from the guards and eaten out of tin cans salvaged from the dump. If a slice of bread was smuggled through the wire by a former servant, the lucky recipient would use a ruler to make sure that everyone in the room got an equal morsel.

"This'd be a good place for some fat dame who wants to get thin. Look at me, Harry."

"Hey, Sid, see that little girl over there?"

"Aye."

"If the Japs stop our rations, we eat her first."

Was that conversation something Lyn had read somewhere or now remembered?

Sunken eyes and a ghastly pallor were the norm as the gaunt, slovenly wretches shrank from within. So inadequate was the food that it spawned medieval diseases, ones that slowly stripped away the lining of the brain. Tapeworms and other intestinal parasites ran rife, but the ugly agonies were beriberi and pellagra.

Beriberi struck in wet and dry versions. Wet beriberi left its mark on bloated bodies. Push a finger into the spongy flesh of the leg, and that dent would still be there the following day. Dry beriberi was known as "electric feet." It felt as if a blowtorch had scorched your knobby legs. The only relief was to sit for hours with both feet submerged in a bucket of water.

"Cemetery."

"What's that, Mom?"

"That's where they make love."

"Who?"

"Behind the headstones. And in freshly dug graves."

"Who?" Lyn repeated.

"Lovers in Stanley Camp. The cemetery's the only place free from prying eyes."

That seminal conversation had taken place just a few months ago, once Viv began a regimen of powerful palliative drugs. It was the first time she had broached the topic of war with Japan on her own, and Lyn had tried to gently lift the veil on her Hong Kong memories.

"Where was I conceived, Mom? Your daughter? Lyn?"

"St. Stephen's," murmured Viv.

"When?"

"Christmas morning. Before the attack."

"Where?"

"In a closet. Away from prying eyes."

"Who's my dad?"

"Captain Richard Walker."

All those years and that was the first time Lyn had heard his name. No doubt Viv's tongue was loosened by the psychotropic drugs, but perhaps she also welcomed the unburdening that often comes at the end of life. For too long, she had suppressed her wartime trauma, dissolving into sobbing fits if Lyn's dad ever got mentioned. But now her secrets spilled out like the evils released from Pandora's box.

"What became of Captain Walker, Mom?"

"He was killed while defending St. Stephen's."

"Who killed him?"

"The Jap who raped me."

So there it was! The origin of all their mental strife. Viv's because she had to live with the aftermath of rape. And Lyn's because she'd had to endure both her mother's depression and physical abuse in the foster home that had taken her in while Viv was getting treatment at Essondale.

"How did Captain Walker die?"

"Your dad was speared in the gut while trying to protect me from rape. He hung on the blade of a bayonet so the Jap could watch him die. Then I was caged in a room and hauled out again and again to get raped. The Jap said he won me in a card game. 'You mine.' 'You mine.' That's what he said. No one else could rape me. Just him. Just him! Just *him*! He refused to kill me like they did the other nurses. I was still alive when Hong Kong surrendered."

Tears streamed down Viv's cheeks as her heart poured out the emotions she'd repressed since the war.

"The Jap?" said Lyn. "Do you know his name?"

"I heard it once."

"Where?"

"In Stanley Camp."

The day began like any other day in Stanley Camp. The breezeless hellhole was hot, muggy, and thick with mosquitoes and flies. Water was in scarce supply, with drought on the horizon. The *Hong Kong News*, the English-language propaganda sheet, informed the prisoners that a tiger had been seen digging in trash near the fence. They got a rare laugh from that bunk, until a shot rang out and a dead tiger was carried off hanging by its paws from a pole. It turned out that the cat had escaped from a circus during the invasion.

"Who knows what to believe?" said the matron who was sewing alongside Viv. The curlers styling her hair were fashioned from odd bits of telephone wire.

The window framing both women looked out on a yard where a pair of scrawny prisoners threw a baseball back and forth. All clothing in the camp was made by hand. Tea towels and rice sacks

MICHAEL SLADE

were turned into shorts and shirts. Buttons were
carved from bamboo, and old rubber tires were
cut into sandals. When someone died, his rags
would be on somebody else the next day.

"Don't believe *that*," Viv scoffed, jabbing her
sewing needle into a *News* story beside the tiger
report.

"Why?" queried the Englishwoman. "Couldn't
Japanese bombers have wiped out the bridge between Vancouver and Vancouver Island?"

"What bridge?" Viv said dryly.

And that's when the two Japanese soldiers had
come around the corner of the housing block. Neither had been to the camp before, and Viv was
suddenly tense. Both were dressed in uniform,
and both carried swords. They strode across the
yard as if it were their private domain, and Viv
knew they were from the Kempeitai.

The Japanese gestapo.

"I throw the ball," said the *gunso*, the Kempeitai sergeant.

The baseball players glanced at each other, and
one began to shake with the DTs. Not for nothing
was the rampart the Japanese had overrun in early
December dubbed the Gin Drinkers' Line. Some
of the Brits were bottle-a-day men, and the fall of
Hong Kong had deprived them of their gin.

"The ball," repeated the *gunso*. "I know how to play."

"Oh God!" said the matron beside Viv. "He must be the Kamloops Kid!"

The women of Stanley Camp lived in fear of the guards. The ugly shadow of the conquest atrocities hung over them, and there was drunkenness among the Japanese guards. Prowling around the camp at night, they would peer into windows. During the day, they would sneak up behind women in their rubber-soled boots and startle them. At bedtime, it was Viv's practice to wedge the door.

But a far worse threat lurked across the harbor in Kowloon, at Shamshuipo Camp, where military prisoners of war were confined. There, the danger took the form of a grinning young man with a clipboard.

"You're Canadians, eh?" he said, greeting one group of new arrivals. "Is anyone here from Kamloops?"

"I am," a POW replied.

As hard as he could, the interpreter punched the POW in the face. As the Canadian crumpled to his knees, he was smashed across the cheek with the clipboard in Slap Happy's hand.

"My name is Sergeant Inouye," the translator

told those lined up at the gate. "I was born and raised in Kamloops, British Columbia, so I hate your goddamn guts. When I was ten years old, I was barred from my friend's birthday party because his mother didn't want 'a Jap face' in her snapshots. I couldn't get into the public swimming pool because the sign on the wall said, 'No Coloreds, Japs, or Chinese.' In Canada, they called me a 'little yellow bastard.' So now I have *you*, and you bastards are going to suffer."

Slap Happy—the Kamloops Kid—made good on his threat.

According to the rumors that reached Stanley Camp, his signature punishment was to have two soldiers hold down a prisoner while he personally punched and kicked him. He locked men away in solitary confinement and starved them past the point of begging for mercy. To squeeze information out of a hard case, Inouye would drive the man through the jostling streets of Kowloon until they reached a military police station. Along the way, he would read from the Kempeitai's training manual: " 'Torture can include kicking, beating, and anything else connected with physical suffering.' We Kempeitai are good torturers, my friend. You'll find we've taken the phrase 'anything else' and made it an art form."

The POW would come back broken.

Or not come back at all.

"They say the Kamloops Kid went to Tokyo in 1938," the matron whispered to Viv. "He enlisted in the army as a translator and is now the official mouthpiece of Commandant Tokunaga. He's the most sadistic of the Japs at Shamshuipo. I hate to think what brings the Kamloops Kid to us."

"The ball," said the Kamloops Kid for the third time, still grinning like the Cheshire cat.

The second of the two prisoners, a toilet-tissue cigarette dangling from his lip, shrugged and tossed him a pitch.

Back came the ball.

Harder.

"Again," said the *gunso*.

The smoker's next pitch had muscle.

It came back even harder.

"Again," ordered the *gunso*.

The prisoner smirked, wound up, and really let fly, putting a curve on the ball.

The ball shot right between the splayed hands of the Kamloops Kid and struck him in the face.

His nose began to bleed.

From the moment the two men had rounded the corner of the building, Viv's eyes had been fixed on the other Japanese soldier. Now she watched in horror as the corporal drew his samurai sword and, with a two-handed sweep worthy of those ancient warriors, sliced the pitcher's head from his bony shoulders.

The Kamloops Kid swaggered over and picked up the head.

Holding it out before him, he slowly turned so all the spectators could see.

"You'll be counted off in groups of ten," said Inouye. "Should one of your ten try to escape over this barbed wire"—he passed the head to the swordsman, the same man who had raped Viv and gutted her lover during the fall of Hong Kong—"Corporal Tokuda will return to Stanley Camp with Kamikaze—that's his sword—and do *this* to the other nine."

So here sat Lyn Barrow, keeping vigil beside her mom's deathbed, holding Viv's arthritic hand in her own, and watching the sheet rise and fall a little less with each labored breath. She thought of all the suffering wrought by that one man—to her mother and herself—and she soon felt overwhelmed by the injustice of it all.

"Mom, it's Lyn. Your daughter."

Viv's death rattle marked the beginning of the end.

"This, I promise you. I'm going to hunt Tokuda. Then I'm going to kill him."

It might have been a spasm, but Lyn thought otherwise.

Viv squeezed her hand.

Then she died.

Nine O'Clock Gun

Vancouver was still laboring under gloomy, low-level clouds, but a gap had opened on the inland horizon, and there a fat, orange harvest moon glared at the Pacific. Like an island in the ocean, Stanley Park formed a barricade between English Bay and the sheltered harbor of Burrard Inlet.

The watch on Kamikaze's wrist ticked toward nine o'clock as his car left behind the canyons of glittering downtown towers for the shadowed darkness of the urban forest. He drove between the moon-dappled waters of Lost Lagoon and Coal Harbour, then began his counter-clockwise prowl around the park's shoreline. Ahead, at Hallelujah Point, was the Nine O'Clock Gun, a century-old cannon encased in a wire-and-granite cupola. Originally, the gun was fired so that seamen in port could synchronize their ship chronometers with the tide. It had been fired every night since 1894, except during the Second World War, when its blast would have been alarming to Vancouverites.

And it would be fired this evening.

Kamikaze had checked.

Instead of continuing around the park on the seawall road, the car turned inland, toward the aquarium. Parking just beyond that watery animal jail, which had once known better days, the would-be yakuza, dressed all in ninja black, headed for the path that would lead him to his fate. He stalked along it until he came to a sandstone column crowned by a marble lantern with what had turned out to be a not-so-eternal flame.

The Japanese-Canadian War Memorial.

No need to read the plaque.

He knew it by heart.

For as long as he could remember, going all the way back—perhaps—to his early life in that internment camp, Kamikaze had no clear grasp of who he was. It was as if his internal self-image was pathologically out of focus—as if the light within his soul had been snuffed. So that's why he felt as if this monument stood for him, too, even though he had no link to its actual history.

Often, he had come here to sit in the dark and brood.

But not tonight.

Tonight, he would find out who he was.

Or he would die.

To be a Japanese *issei*—an immigrant—on the West Coast was to inherit a history of racial hatred. Back in the 1880s, men had sailed from Japan to follow a dream of riches, and here they had fished, farmed, and mined, or worked in lumber camps and on the railroad. But when it came, the backlash was fierce and angry. The *issei* were denied the vote and citizenship. In 1907, white supremacists rampaged toward "Japtown." They were met by a hail of rocks, and that led to limits being set on future immigration.

The only way to prove themselves loyal to Canada was to fight in the First World War, so 195 *issei* and one *nisei*—a Japanese descendant born here—volunteered. Of them, 54 were killed and 92 wounded, so in 1920, on the third anniversary of the Battle of Vimy Ridge, this cenotaph was raised in Stanley Park. To the lasting memory of those who had laid down their lives, the lantern was lit.

Ha! thought Kamikaze.

You proud fools.

The attack on Pearl Harbor had fanned the flames of hate, and less than ten days later, on December 16, 1941, the lantern was extinguished.

Every Japanese person on the West Coast was forced to register as an enemy alien, and all twenty-one thousand, Canadian citizens included, were driven inland to internment camps. Their property was seized and sold off to whites. Suspected spies and protesters were shipped east to prisoner-of-war compounds. No Japanese were allowed within a hundred miles of the Pacific Ocean.

Later, after the war, the mass deportations began. Internees by the thousands were expelled to Japan.

For the next four decades, the lantern atop this cenotaph remained dark. Kamikaze could barely recall the day he was set free from *his* internment camp, but he knew that whatever had happened to him within its barbed-wire fence had left horrific scars on his subconscious. The first time he had glimpsed this snuffed-out lantern, sometime back in his vague childhood, he had understood intuitively that that's what he had suffered in the concentration camp.

Extinction of his "I'm me" light.

Then had come the August 1985 day when, as if to finally mark the integration of the *nikkei*—the new term for Japanese Canadians—into this racist amalgam, the lantern of the Stanley Park memorial was relit. The guest of honor, seated beneath the shirotae and yoshino cherry trees (so colorful in the springtime, but barren of leaves and blossoms tonight), had been Sergeant Masumi Mitsui. Then ninety-eight years old, he had led the charge up Vimy Ridge, only to spend the next war in the Greenwood Internment Camp with his family. Watching from the crowd, Kamikaze had seen the sense of self light up that old man's eyes, and he had hoped—how he had hoped—that a sense of self would also ignite in him.

But that was not to be his fate, it seemed, for he was neither *nikkei* nor Caucasian.

Instead, he was caged physiologically in a no man's land between the trenches of the Pacific War.

A misfit, he belonged to neither side.

Hated by one camp during and after the war.

Shunned by the other for being genetically unclean.

And so he had resigned himself to his ignoble fate, wandering aimlessly through purgatory, denied entrance to both heaven and hell.

But then . . .

Was it possible?

Could it actually be?

Kamikaze had chanced across his blood link to Genjo Tokuda, the wealthiest and deadliest of Tokyo's yakuza.

Kamikaze had taken his code name from Genjo Tokuda's sword.

The old-school yakuza flatly denied that they were descended from the *ronin*, the marauding samurai who had terrorized Japan in the 1600s. Instead, they carried on the traditions of the *machi-yokku*, the "servants of the town," courageous folk heroes who had stood up to the *ronin*. In doing so, the ancients had protected the poor and the defenseless. That's why the yakuza have a romantic stature in Japanese films. And that's why Kamikaze, in a fantasy born from researching Tokuda, likened himself to Robin Hood.

Would that not be a life with meaning?

To *know* who you are?

But even more alluring to him was the structure of the yakuza. It, like the Mafia, was organized into a pyramid, with a hierarchy based not on bloodline but on adoption. At the top was the gang's godfather—the *kumicho*—Genjo Tokuda. Beneath him were descending levels of underlings, and each underling was bound to his immediate boss by a centuries-old code. The *oyabun* played the "father role," and like any good father, he provided protection and advice to his initiated children. In return, the father had a right to expect unquestioning loyalty and obedient service from the *kobun*, playing the "child role." A *kobun* had to be willing to take a bullet for, and *be* a bullet for, his *oyabun*.

He had to be kamikaze.

He had to be ready to die.

For Kamikaze, it would be enough to be accepted for who he was. The yakuza don't care where you come from—your color, your country, your class—because they initiate the misfits of society. All they require is that you pride yourself on the code of *bushido*, the Way of the Warrior. *Giri*—a strong sense of duty and obligation to other members—is also essential. Nothing in life can be more important than your gang. And yakuza must show sympathy for the weak and for people ground down by the powers that be. Violent death in a struggle against the tyranny of oppressors: that is a most poetic, tragic, honorable fate.

Your boss becomes your father.

Your gang members become your bothers.

That alone would be enough for Kamikaze.

But his fate—it seemed to him—was to be more than that. For his *oyabun* was destined to be the *kumicho* himself. If the link Kamikaze had discovered in some old British colonial records was correct, then Genjo Tokuda would be both father figure and actual father to him.

According to his watch, it was time to go. So the would-be yakuza in his ninja black followed the densely shadowed path north from the cenotaph to a vantage point near the dragon-like figurehead of the *Empress of Japan*. Its fanged jaws seemed to snarl fearsomely at the humped mass of mountains beyond the moon-streaked harbor.

At five minutes to nine, a black limousine rounded the lighthouse at Brockton Point and stopped at the curb directly in front of the figurehead, as instructed.

Kamikaze crouched in the dark.

No one got out of the idling limousine.

Boom! The Nine O'Clock Gun, just around the point and out of sight, blasted south toward the towers of the downtown core. Its reverberations echoed back at the park. Before that phantom battery fell silent for another day, the far rear door of the limousine opened. A featureless figure strode quickly to the base of the figurehead, and Kamikaze abandoned his hiding place on the opposite side of the road. Reaching the seawall, he walked east toward the limo and engaged the waiting man.

"I'm Kamikaze."

"Call me the Claw. Get in," the bodyguard ordered, indicating the yawning rear door.

So stocky was the Claw that his body seemed fit for a gorilla. He was balding and had a prominent mole on his cheek. Not a word escaped his lips as they drove through the peninsular park. The fact that Kamikaze wasn't on the floor with a sack pulled over his head meant that this was either the first day of the rest of his yakuza life or the beginning of a one-way ride.

So be it, he thought.

No turning back.

From the dragon figurehead, Stanley Park Drive ran parallel to the seawall, along the south shore of the harbor. On the inland side loomed Lumberman's Arch, a huge, wonky structure that resembled a lopsided *torii* gate to a Shinto shrine. Ahead, the Lions Gate Bridge, with its necklace of lights dipping from the dual supports, spanned First Narrows and landed at the foot of the mountains.

The limo zigzagged to the crest of Prospect Point and drove onto the causeway bisecting the park. As the car bridged the neck of ocean joining the outer bay to the inner harbor, the harvest moon peered into the tinted windows like a pudgy-faced groupie at a rock concert.

The end of the bridge saw Marine Drive branch left and right. The left fork conveyed them into West Vancouver, the richest municipality in Canada. No sooner had they entered than they turned up Taylor Way, the road that climbed Hollyburn Mountain to the British Properties. Up, up, up they snaked to the crown of the city. The irony was not lost on Kamikaze.

During the Depression, the Guinness family of Ireland, brewers of good beer, had purchased this side of the mountain to create an exclusive community. To populate the British Properties, they built the Lions Gate Bridge in 1938. Then, to make sure the properties *stayed* British, they sold the lots with covenants that restricted ethnic Asians.

Times, of course, had changed, and tonight the

limo drove into the multi-car garage of a magnificent mansion that had been bought with money laundered by Genjo Tokuda's yakuza.

The garage closed automatically.

"Get out," said the Claw.

No *bakuto* had ever tried a gamble as daring as this. Those dice men and card sharps who had worked the towns and highways of medieval Japan would have been proud of him. When he found his wartime birth record in colonial government papers, Kamikaze mailed a copy to Genjo Tokuda's headquarters in Tokyo's Ginza district, along with an offer to provide a blood sample for DNA tests. At the firing of the Nine O'Clock Gun on October 25, he wrote, he would be waiting near the figurehead of the *Empress of Japan* in Vancouver's Stanley Park. There, he would introduce himself as Kamikaze to the man Tokuda sent to meet him, and then would hand over the genetic fingerprint that would prove they were father and son.

The no-show five days ago had prompted Kamikaze to courier a follow-up letter to Japan:

Father, you dishonor me. I wish to become a yakuza. What I can offer you for that honor is set out below. The timing is such that we must move

quickly, so again I will be waiting near the fig-
urehead of the Empress of Japan *when the Nine*
O'Clock Gun fires on October 30.

So there he had been tonight, and here he was
now, being ushered into an aerie of glass with a
view all the way south to the U.S. border. He was
about to lay his cards on the table in the hope that
Genjo Tokuda would accept his *ya*, his *ku*, and his
sa as a "bad hand" worthy of respect.

Tokuda was in Vancouver. Kamikaze knew
that.

He had watched the *kumicho* and his gang exit
the customs area at the airport earlier today.

By the glow of the moon, the only illumination
in the eagle's nest, an old man entered and sat
down on an ornate chair. In a wooden rack on
a coffee table in front of him was his *daisho* of
samurai swords.

Smuggled in? Kamikaze wondered.

A rebel spirit and a willingness to commit
crime, that's all it takes to join today's weak yakuza. So low have recruiting standards sunk that
most new members are *bosozoku*, street punks no-
torious for racing motorbikes. Such riffraff are an
insult to how it was in the days when Tokuda's

samurai prided themselves on their ancestral ties to *bushido*.

With that in mind, Kamikaze knew what to do.

With one arm outstretched and his other crooked behind his back, he bowed in deference to the old *kumicho* and introduced himself.

Tokuda had only half a face, thanks to the scar, but he studied his putative son with eyes that seemed to pierce like laser beams to his genetic core.

"Speak," said the Claw. "I'll translate."

So Kamikaze addressed Tokuda from his heart.

An hour later, father and son, in kimonos adorned with the family crest, sat face to face on ceremonial mats. The father's kimono was gray. The son's was white. Custom said that Kamikaze required a guarantor, but the only guarantee Tokuda had needed was the sight of his own features in his son's mixed-race face.

The ceremony that father and son were about to undergo would solidify their blood connection. Tonight, the blood was symbolized by sake, which the Claw mixed with salt and fish scales, then carefully poured into cups. Since Tokuda was both *kumicho* and *oyabun*, his cup was filled to the brim. As *kobun*, Kamikaze got less.

Both men drank a bit, then exchanged cups.

KAMIKAZE

To seal their blood connection, which in their case was real as well as symbolic, each man drank from the other's cup.

Having made his commitment to the yakuza, Kamikaze followed Tokuda and the Claw out to the moonlit deck, where the three gangsters gazed down at Vancouver.

"There," said Kamikaze, pointing to the south shore of the harbor. "That's the target."

The Last Frontier

The Mad Dog's baritone belted out the bottom end of "Happy Birthday" as Brit, his sexy ex-stripper, ex-hooker wife, exited from the kitchen with a candlelit cake in her hands and sang the upper vocals like the heavenly angel she surely wasn't. Had a Peeping Tom been lurking out there tonight, the sight of Brittany Starr, plunging neckline and all, would have lured him over the white picket fence and across to the dining-room window of the sage green bungalow. Inside, he'd see a cheery fire blazing in the hearth and, on the mantel, an eagle feather that had been given to the hostess with the mostest and her testosterone-poisoned husband at their recent wedding. One look at that Neanderthal would probably convince

Tom to beat a fast retreat, rather than chance a beating at the hands of the muscle-bound Mountie.

Too bad.

As an expert in such matters, Tom would have correctly deduced that the happy couple screwed night and day.

"Make a wish," Brit said, setting the lazy-dazy cake down in front of their guest.

Had Ghost Keeper not been an honorable friend, and the Mad Dog his blood brother, he might have wished for Brit. Instead, he wished for a week off to go hunting and sweat-lodging in the Nahanni's Headless Valley.

Pheeew!

The inspector blew out the candles.

"I'll huff, and I'll puff, and I'll blow your house down," Brit said as she scraped up the candlewax from a table setting even Martha Stewart would have admired.

"Sorry."

"Must be all that puffing on your peace pipe, Tonto," said the Mad Dog.

"Eddie? The gift," Brit prompted, while slicing the cake.

"Now?" he asked.

"Uh-huh. I can't wait."

A full-blooded Plains Cree from Duck Lake, Saskatchewan, Ghost Keeper had been raised in a one-room shack on a Native reserve. His mom had struggled to provide him with the necessities of life, and there hadn't been five cents left over to spend on the white man's material baggage. Instead, she had guided him through timeless traditions, sending the boy out on spirit quests so he would be forced to face up to himself and nature.

His journey from there to here would fill a series of novels.

"Open it," said Brit as the Cree gazed down at the present the Mad Dog set before him.

Unwrapping the gift as meticulously as he had exhibits back when he'd worked in the forensic lab, Ghost Keeper bared a square box with a lift-up lid.

"Brace yourself," the Mad Dog cautioned.

"Whoa!" the Cree exclaimed.

"You're looking at the Rolls-Royce of nine mils, pal. Y'ever seen a Europellet popper like that? Even unmodified out of the box, the P210 will shoot sub-two-inch clusters at twenty-five yards. When accuracy is paramount, it's the closest thing to perfection in a pistol. That's why it's a fixture at European prize shoots. One thing about the Swiss, they know their precision engineering. Hey, it's a SIG. What more do I need to say? Reach in, pick it up, and heft it in your hand."

Ghost Keeper did just that.

"I polished it," Brit said, "especially for you."

The blue gunmetal gleamed, as did the wooden grips.

"It's a beauty," the Cree said, "but I can't take it. Who knows how many grand this set you back."

"You *must* take it," Brit pressed, "so I can sleep. How many times have you saved Eddie's life? If it comes to that again, I want you to have the best sharpshooter around."

"But the cost . . ."

"Are we friends?" the Mad Dog asked.

"No question."

"It's a miracle, considering my dad. He did his damnedest to make me into a racist like him. And until I met you, he'd succeeded. When he died, I inherited some cash he'd squirreled away. You don't spend much when you're a trapper in the Yukon woods. My dad's money bought that gun, and that makes me feel good. You can't deny me the satisfaction of righting that wrong."

"Explain it to me," Joe said over a late dinner in Chinatown. "I fought a war so my offspring would have America to call home. We Hetts have fought wars for that since the Revolution. I think it's damned ironic that my only grandkid now swears allegiance to the Crown."

"That depends," Jackie said, "on how you see the Revolution."

"How do you see it?"

"As a western. The British got in the way of America's yearning to tame the wild frontier."

"That's not how I learned it."

"Sorry, Red, but I don't believe in the cherry tree. It's one of those lies they feed us in school."

Joe took a mouthful of chicken chow mein and slurped up a loose noodle. Then he turned and wagged a chopstick at Chuck like a schoolmarm about to rap a troublemaker's knuckles with a ruler. "See what happens when your kid's born here?"

"You're the one who bought the ranch and taught her to ride. She loves horses. Don't blame me."

Joe turned back to Jackie, who was munching on a spring roll. "So be a Texas Ranger and live near us."

"There's not much left of them but the hat, the belt, and the boots. A hundred Texas Rangers—that's hardly the last frontier. But umpteen thousand Mounties all the way to the North Pole? Besides, I look damn good in the uniform."

"So what's wrong with the cherry tree?"

"It didn't happen, Red. 'George,' said his father to young George Washington, 'do you know who killed that beautiful little cherry tree yonder in the garden?' 'I cannot tell a lie, Pa,' George confessed. 'You know I cannot tell a lie. I did it with my hatchet.'"

"Your point?" said Joe.

"That tale's pure fiction. It was made up by a guy named Parson Weems."

"So?"

"So if it's a lie—and we know it's a lie—why's that bullshit fed to every kid in grammar school?"

"For the moral."

"What moral? That lying is okay? Seems pretty strange to me that a lie is used to tout a tale that decries lying."

Chuck laughed.

Joe joined him. "Ya got me, kid. So tell me <u>why</u> the Revolution is a western."

" 'Go west, young man, and grow up with the country.' Isn't that the story of America? Europeans crowded onto shrinking land set sail for the New World and the freedom of the West. Unfortunately for those of us in the Thirteen Colonies, the

French and their Indian allies held all the land from Quebec down the Ohio Country to Louisiana. That's why we fought the French and Indian War—so we English Americans could push west. But no sooner had Britain won the Battle of Quebec than King George gave the Indians all the land to the west in the Proclamation of 1763, thus closing the frontier to colonial expansion. The only way to press west was to overthrow the king, and the Crown's taxing us to pay for the French and Indian War provided a righteous excuse. The upshot? The American Revolution. And that, dear Granddad, is how the West was won."

"I don't see," Joe said, "why that makes you a Mountie."

"Almost three hundred million Americans," Jackie said. "Now *we* have too many people crowded onto shrinking land. Thirty million Canadians have a country bigger than the States. That's why *Dances with Wolves*, *Unforgiven*, and *Brokeback Mountain* were shot here. To experience the *real* West in the twenty-first century, you gotta venture north to the last frontier."

"Benedict Arnold," said Joe.

"I'm no traitor. As you said this morning, I'm still an American at heart. But hey, this dual citizenship thing is cool. I'm like Zorro and the Lone Ranger, the heroes of those westerns Dad grew up on. Corporal Jackie Hett of the Mounted is my secret identity."

After dropping off Chuck and Joe at the convention hotel, Jackie headed home to her apartment overlooking English Bay. It felt good to have her dad and Red here with her; it was the first time the three of them had gathered together in Vancouver. Chuck had flown up several times, but without her grandfather. As Jackie drove through dwindling nighttime traffic, she recalled her excited phone call to her dad in New Mexico late last year.

"Hello?"

"Guess who's talking?"

"I know your voice, Jackie."

"It's *Corporal* Jackie now, dear old Dad."

"Congratulations, Corporal! Climbing the ranks, huh? And 'dear' is good enough. Let's can the 'old,' shall we?"

"Guess what?"

"There's more?"

"I'm now in Special X. That's the big enchilada, Dad. The Special External Section. Not only do I get to travel for cases with links outside the country, but Special X goes after all our home-bred serial killers too. Not bad, huh?"

"Are you going to switch to 'eh'? I wish your mom were still alive to share the pride I feel."

"And there's more."

"When it rains, it pours," her dad said. "Though not very often here."

"There's gonna be a Red Serge Ball next month. Will you be my date?"

Chuck laughed. "Me? Dear *old* Dad? I'm sure there's some young buck who'll gladly take you."

"Sure," said Jackie. "But that's not what I want. I want *you* to see who I am."

No dance is more formal than the Red Serge Ball, so as soon as Chuck's plane landed, they went to rent him a tuxedo. Her dad told the shop to outfit him in duds "as classic as James Bond wears," and he soon preened before her, dressed to kill in formal black. Tall and taut from a constant can-do fight against middle-age spread, with a handsome face that time and sun had creased to ruggedness, Chuck mugged for the mirror with a sketchy British voice—"Hett. Chuck Hett."— while the fitter fluttered around him to make adjustments here and there.

Finally, the store owner sidled in to close the

deal and, like a valet addressing his lord and master, told Chuck, "I don't know what affair you're attending, sir, but I guarantee you'll be the best-dressed person there."

Jackie kept a straight face, but inside she was howling.

"Well?" asked the corporal on the night of the ball. "How do I look, Pa?"

When Chuck turned to face her, his jaw dropped.

Though his daughter generally eschewed makeup, tonight Jackie had done herself up to the nines. Her flaming red hair and emerald eyes had never looked better. Her "gown" was unlike any Chuck had seen before: a navy blue floor-length skirt topped with the Mounties' scarlet tunic. Her hourglass figure was cinched with a gold-and-blue belt, in the center of which gleamed a bison-head buckle. Insignia glittered on the collar and shoulder epaulets of her tunic. Stitched to her right biceps was her new corporal's chevron, and down at the cuff of her left sleeve was the badge of an RCMP marksman. She held black gloves and a black purse in one hand and her Stetson in the other.

"You've come a long way, baby," Chuck said, "since the test of manhood."

The test of manhood was a secret from the days when Jackie was a young girl. The Hetts lived near a creek then, and as Chuck and Jackie strolled along it one day, they came across a fallen tree that spanned the water.

"Stay here, Pumpkin," Chuck said, "and don't move an inch. You are about to see a feat that you'll remember forever. Your dad is going to pass the test of manhood."

His arms outstretched like an acrobat on a tightrope, Chuck scaled the challenging log and, placing one foot in front of the other, began to walk across.

"Look, Daddy," Jackie said thirty years later, mimicking her little girl sweetness, "I can pass the test of manhood too."

"Phew," said Chuck, "did you give me a fright. There I was in the middle of the log, and suddenly I had my daughter standing behind the crook of my knees. I imagined you taking a tumble and washing away to the sea, and me going home to tell your mom that there'd only be two for dinner."

"As I recall, I had no trouble getting back."

"No, you swiveled on one foot and pattered off, while I was left quaking at the knees and barely able to keep my balance for the long journey back."

"You promised me a Barbie."

"Did I?" said Chuck.

"You promised me any Barbie I wanted if I didn't tell Mom."

"I'm surprised I didn't offer you the deed to our house," he said. "She'd have killed me for being so stupid. Many a time, I overheard her saying, 'Would you look at that dunce with his daughter? He's got his back to the street. The kid could run out and get hit by a car, and he wouldn't even notice. That's why dads shouldn't be trusted to watch their kids.' "

"Good old mom."

"If she could see you now. You look like a million bucks, kid. Red suits you."

"It clashes with my hair."

"Not to me."

"You know what, Dad?"

"What?"

"I never snitched on you."

So off they'd gone to the Red Serge Ball. Walking in to that sea of red, spurs, and medals, Chuck had felt like an Antarctic penguin let loose in a crowd of dashing cavalrymen. The men wore the same red tunics as Jackie, but they had banana pants, each blue leg lined with a yellow stripe. As the wine flowed, and the band played, and he and his daughter danced the night away, Chuck began to imagine that he'd crashed Queen Victoria's jubilee. Jackie was in her element, the belle of the ball. And as they swirled around the floor, Chuck gave her a wink.

"I understand," he said.

Red will be a tougher nut to crack, thought Jackie, riding the elevator to her suite.

In family terms, he was the last frontier.

As the elevator opened, she gasped, "Oh no! The cat!"

Jackie had no need for an alarm clock beside her bed. Every morning, at six sharp, Batman sat on her chest, staring into her eyes and meowing loud enough to make the houseplants quiver. Of late, her animal had begun to pack on weight, though, so yesterday Jackie had eliminated his bedtime snack.

To remind herself to feed the starving feline in the morning, she'd stuck a Post-it Note to the kettle, where she'd be sure to see it when she brewed her coffee. But that morning, running late to pick up Chuck and Red, she'd bought her caffeine at a drive-thru on her way to the airport, and therefore—Negligent owner! she thought—Batman's meal got missed.

With guilt in her heart, she opened the door, and there crouched Batman, chewing something yellow on the kitchen floor.

He was eating the Post-it Note.

Fireworks

October 31, Now

Viewed from the sky, the lower mainland of British Columbia resembles Neptune's trident. The waterways that make up the three prongs are Burrard Inlet and the north and south arms of the Fraser River. Yesterday, after leaving Jackie to her work at Special X, Chuck and Joe had driven downtown to check into their hotel and then had set off with Jackie's map to the Mud Bay Airport. Now, alone in his daughter's car, Chuck took the same scenic route around the tip of Point Grey, the chunk of the city between the inlet and the north arm, to the bridge that led to Highway 99 and the border.

On reaching the highway, the retired USAF colonel sped through the soggy darkness for Boundary Bay, following the slick asphalt ribbon around that bight of the Pacific and its tiny neighbor, Mud Bay. Just north of the border, along the top of Mud Bay, Chuck left the highway for a country road that led him through misty farmland to the water's edge.

A sign was picked out of the blackness by his headlights. "Mud Bay Airport."

Airfields don't come any dinkier than this. An old military hangar squatted in a field, flanked by rows of huts just large enough to house single-engine planes. Aircraft lined the triangular runway: two open lanes for takeoffs and landings, and a closed taxiway. If you were cheap, you parked your plane on the grass. If you weren't, you paid extra to park on the ramp. The airport administration building was a double-wide trailer.

Flying on a wing and a prayer.

It wasn't the USAF.

"We don't get many colonels here," the airfield operator had said yesterday as he perused Chuck's pilot's license and his impressive flying record.

"I'm out to pasture."

"Our F-16 is in the shop. I've only got single-engine prop planes at the moment."

"That'll do," Chuck said, grinning. "Three of us are going to circle the harbor for the Halloween fireworks."

"Don't get shot down."

"I won't."

"The unbroken rule is that we take renters up for a familiarization run. But for you—"

"Let's do it by the rules."

It didn't matter to Chuck how he got up into the blue—well, gray, actually, since this was Vancouver—so long as he did. It was fun to be at the controls of such a small plane; it took him back to the thrill of his first solo flight. Later, on the ground, they completed the paperwork, and the owner explained the procedure that Chuck would follow for his Halloween flight.

It had been drizzling on and off all day. So sodden was the weather that it threatened to put a damper on Halloween. But the grave waits for no man, so ghouls and goblins were out in force.

Ninjas too.

The ones lurking in the shrubs that flanked the gate.

Kamikaze watched the two headlights grow brighter as they approached the chain-link fence that supposedly secured the Mud Bay Airport. Damp, dark, quiet, and eerie, that was the atmosphere out here, which made it the perfect spot for what the yakuza had planned.

His plan.

The one he had sold last night to Genjo Tokuda.

So far, everything was going better than he'd hoped. His letter to his father after the failed meeting in Stanley Park had sketched a scheme of revenge that required a skilled Japanese pilot. He hadn't expected the yakuza to bring the kamikaze pilot they did, and he was doubly elated when Chuck and Joe Hett had unexpectedly led him here.

What were the odds of the Americans planning a flight too?

Perhaps not that remote, since both Hetts were pilots.

Still . . .

He had staked out the international arrivals chute at the airport so he would know if Genjo Tokuda had taken the bait. Coincidentally, Kamikaze had also been there for the arrival of his prospective victims, one of whom got into a shoving match with a bodyguard for the *kumicho*.

Tokuda was here.

That meant the meeting was on.

So Kamikaze had decided to take advantage of the coincidence and tail the Hetts instead, to make sure he could find them when it was time to strike.

From the airport, they had gone to the White Spot for lunch. From the restaurant, they had driven to Special X. Leaving Jackie at work, the men had checked in to the hotel, before heading off to the totem pole museum on the cliffs of Point Grey. Finally, having followed the highway down here, they'd taken what had to be a familiarization flight.

Once they'd left the airport, Kamikaze had walked in.

And sure enough, on the counter in plain sight was the paperwork that told him where the Hetts would be tonight.

Banzai!

Shifting to Park with the engine still idling, Chuck swung open the driver's door. The beams of the headlights struck no slashes of rain between the windshield and the gate. As he strode to the fence to punch in the access code, Chuck—for the umpteenth time since leaving the hotel— wondered if he should scrub the flight because of the weather. Joe had been held up by a dress rehearsal of the veterans' ceremony and Jackie had been delayed at work, so Chuck was to get the

plane himself, then fly a short hop northwest to
the Mounties' Air Services runway on Sea Island,
where he would set down and pick them up.

The access code opened the gate to the field.

While he was pushing it wide enough to admit
his car, Chuck glimpsed movement at the corner
of his eye and heard the splash of footfalls from
the shrubs on his other flank. But before he could
react, something slammed against his skull and
his consciousness faded to black.

Dressed from head to foot in black, the four
yakuza were invisible in the shadows. The one
who darted to the idling car to take the wheel
remained a silhouette even when illuminated by
the headlights. Once the filaments dimmed down,
the other three pounced on the unconscious man
like vultures going for a feast.

"The ring," said Kamikaze. "That'll do. Hack
his ring finger off at the palm."

By the glow of the parking lamps, the hoods
shackled Chuck Hett like a courthouse prisoner,
cuffing both hands to a belt around his waist and
closing his ankles in leg irons. One stuffed a rag
into the knocked-out man's mouth and secured it
with a gag. The Claw tugged Chuck's ring down
to the knuckle and tied off the blood flow to that

finger. Then the thug chopped off the finger with a knife as the trussed-up man's cry of pain got stifled to a mewl.

"Roll him," said Kamikaze.

From the bushes, one of the yakuza fetched what appeared to be a rolled-up sleeping bag. Unbuckling the straps, he flapped it out and let it settle down on the roadway like a picnic blanket. Chuck was thrashing as hard as he could to burst free, but his effort was no match for the manhandling by the muggers. They stretched him out on the sleeping bag, then wrapped him up like a sausage roll. To finish him off, the Claw buckled the straps back around the bag.

"Let's go," said Kamikaze.

The four thugs and their victim all crammed into Chuck's car. The Claw tossed the bloody finger, still wearing its ring, onto the dashboard in front of the driver. As the vehicle passed through the gate that gave access to the airfield, a security guard came around the corner of the administration building, rubbing his eyes as if he'd just woken up.

"Squash him!" Kamikaze said.

The Claw translated.

The driver flattened the gas pedal, and the car lurched forward. It hit the guard so hard that the ninjas could hear the crack of breaking bones. There was a thump and a heave as the tires passed over his torso, then out jumped the Claw with his *yubitsume* knife to slash his throat.

The plane was on the ramp, fueled and ready to go. The car crept up beside it and the ninjas climbed out. Three of the four lifted Chuck to the copilot's door, which Kamikaze held open until they'd maneuvered him inside. Once they had him sitting in the right-hand seat, they strapped him in with the seatbelt and shoulder harness to keep him from slumping onto the controls. That done, the yakuza pilot climbed into the cockpit.

The fact that he was dying of cancer could be deduced if you examined his skin, but jaundice doesn't stand out as starkly with Asians. All his life, the man had served Tokuda faithfully, and this death would be far more honorable than wasting away in pain.

"From your *kumicho*," said Kamikaze, handing the cancerous pilot a white scarf.

The man wrapped the *hachimaki* around his brow.

Cracking the seal on a bottle of sake, the Claw poured a cup and passed it up.

The pilot drank.

"*Hissatsu!*" said Kamikaze.

"Hissatsu!" echoed the pilot.

Then he closed the door, waited for his ground crew to vacate the ramp, started the engine, and keyed the mike.

The runway lit up.

Every airport in the world publishes information in what is called a flight supplement book. Basically, these books describe the operating procedures that make each runway function. That's how the pilot knew to punch the button on the microphone five times within eight seconds to activate the runway lights. Lashed to the seat beside him, Chuck blinked when the stygian airfield lit up along the takeoff and landing strips and the joining taxiway.

Leaving behind this ramp of sleeping aircraft, the plane taxied out to the button at the end of Runway 12—which, like all runways in the world, was numbered according to a magnetic compass. Once the engine had revved up to takeoff speed, the pilot powered down the runway and lifted up into the sodden black velvet sky above Mud Bay.

Chuck wondered where they were going, and what the kidnappers had planned for him.

It could hardly be ransom.

So what could it be?

The plane banked to the west in a wide circle,

passing the tip of Point Roberts in the United States and heading straight for the Lions Gate Bridge.

The night sky was already ablaze with pyrotechnics—not from the professionals in English Bay, but from people's backyard fireworks. *Boom!* The sky lit up with multi-burst barrages of green, white, and red stars; orange-tailed comets; and bright silver glitters. Like a Second World War battlefield, the land on both sides of the harbor was alive with explosions—buzz-bomb bottle rockets, colorful Roman candles, and the fountains of whooshing volcanoes.

Now the plane was slowing down to reduce the slipstream effect of forward motion and the spinning propeller. Leaving the aircraft to fly itself, the pilot reached across Chuck to unlock the right-hand door. Then he unbuckled the shoulder harness and seat belt, and pushed Chuck against the open exit.

Before jettisoning his human cargo, the Japanese pilot ignited a hand-held propane torch. He applied the flame to the end of a magnesium ribbon that was jutting from the stuffing of the sleeping bag, and it began to burn along its carefully measured length like the fuse on a stick of dynamite.

Then Chuck was shoved out the door.

Many a time had the colonel stared down death

in the cockpit of a plane, and he knew there was always the chance that he would die plummeting to earth without a parachute. His final thoughts were of Jackie—Oh, how he loved his daughter!—but even those were cut short when the magnesium fuse set off the thermite that had been stuffed between the layers of the sleeping bag.

Thermite is a mixture of iron oxide, commonly known as rust, and powdered aluminum. Because it carries its own oxygen source, it doesn't require oxygen to burn, which is a useful characteristic at high altitudes. When it burns—as it was doing now around Chuck's body—it burns at 4,500 degrees Fahrenheit. Criminals use it to melt steel to open safes, while combatants use it to burn through heavy armor and fireproof barriers.

The flash of white that was Chuck plunging out of the night sky, his skin barbecuing while his insides cooked, was so brilliant, even in comparison with the Halloween fireworks, that watchers below thought they were gazing up at a meteor shower or a shooting star.

Down . . .

Down . . .

Slam!

Chuck hit . . .

Just before the plane.

Floating Chrysanthemums

Okinawa, Japan
April 6, 1945

Pearl Harbor was nothing like this!

The knights of *bushido* had launched the opening attack of the Pacific War to bring glory to Japan, and all had yearned to see the Rising Sun at high noon. But now, these modern samurai teetered on the knife-edge of shameful defeat, with Okinawa the last island in the path of the Yankee avengers before they set foot on Nippon's sacred soil. As it had during the Mongol invasion of 1281, survival of the Chrysanthemum Throne depended on the Divine Wind's sinking the enemy's fleet, which was now hovering just 240 miles south of the home islands and 550 miles from Tokyo itself. Surrender was unthinkable, so the call went out for pilots willing to make the ultimate sacrifice. These men—these kamikaze—would be sent on a mission from which they'd never return, in planes fueled for a one-way trip and loaded down with five hundred pounds of explosives.

"If in doubt whether to live or die, it is always better to die."

"One life for many."

"Death simultaneously with a mortal blow to the enemy."

"To die while people still lament your death; to die while you are pure and fresh; this is truly *bushido*."

So many young men had applied to die for their emperor that there weren't enough flying coffins to meet the demand. Some showed their commitment by writing their applications in blood. They were sent off in aircraft so obsolete they looked like paper planes. Some of the planes were designed to drop their landing gear on takeoff so it could be picked up and reused for other suicide runs.

What greater glory is there than to give your life for your country? To die for your emperor, a god in human form, and in so doing become a god yourself? If you perish as a kamikaze, you'll be revered as a hero at the Yasukuni Shrine. The desperate odds only enhance your death, for the more obvious the futility, the greater the glory of your sacrifice. And why die in the coming invasion when you can sink an American ship and take all those Yankees with you?

"Hissatsu!"

And so they gathered in secret at a vast network of underground hangars, tunnels, and barracks scattered about Formosa and Kyushu to launch a great kamikaze offensive—code-named Ten-Go (Heavenly Operation).

"If I go away to sea, I shall return a brine-soaked corpse."

That was their anthem.

The strategy was simple: The Japanese troops on Okinawa—more than a hundred thousand of them—would dig in and pin down the invading Marines in a costly war of attrition. Anchored just offshore, the ships of the American fleet would be forced to act as bodyguard and lifeline for their troops inland. They would be sitting ducks for a series of mass-formation kamikaze attacks.

Wipe them out, and there'd be no invasion of Japan.

"Hissatsu!"

So now they stood among their bomb-laden planes, these young heroes in their baggy flying suits, with aviation helmets sheathing their heads and goggles pushed up on their brows to bare their eager faces.

To prepare himself for his watery sepulcher, each pilot wrote farewell letters and poems to loved ones at home. "I have been given a splendid opportunity to die. I shall fall like a blossom from a radiant cherry tree."

Some enclosed relics, like a lock of hair.

Then, to emulate the samurai, each pilot was given a folded white scarf to tie around his head. The *hachimaki* would keep his eyes clear of sweat and hair. Around his waist was knotted a thousand-stitch sash, a belt pieced together with one stitch from each of a thousand women to symbolize union with the kamikaze.

Then came a final salute and, for "spiritual lifting" before liftoff, a purifying cup of sake.

"Floating chrysanthemums," they were called, the men who flew the successive waves of Ten-Go. "Purify your heart and be cheerful," each human bomb told himself as he took flight. "Every deity and the spirits of your comrades are watching intently."

As he began his dive toward his offshore target, each pilot would shout at the top of his lungs:

"Hissatsu!"

"Sink without fail!"

"Hell birds!" yelled the Yankee lookouts, to warn their shipmates as the suicide squadron zoomed in.

From the high, thick walls of Shuri Castle, a fifteenth-century fort that had been home to the feudal kings of Okinawa, Genjo Tokuda watched the battle rage at sea. Five days ago—April Fool's Day for America—the fleet had disembarked four divisions of soldiers and Marines. Because no opposition had met them on the beach or in the fields of white winter barley and colorful flowers, the Marines had turned north while the army headed south.

It was time to spring the trap.

One low and one high, the first pair of kamikazes came screaming out of the clear afternoon sky. The ships below opened up with everything they had: five-inch guns, 40mms, 20mms, even rifles. Shining like single grains of rice, both planes rode the Divine Wind through the storm of steel, the edges of their wings cutting through the assault like swords. The sky filled with so much ack-ack that daylight disappeared in a million black puffs. Down, down, down came the plane from above, trailing a banner of smoke and flames as it took hit after hit. Suddenly, the Zero exploded in a ball of fire, and what was left showered down on a Yankee ship.

Meanwhile, the other plane skimmed across the churning sea as spouts of water spewed up from low-level shots. Like a surface torpedo zipping through the air, the kamikaze struck a destroyer amidships at the waterline. The impact crumpled the fuselage like a scrambled egg, popping the cap off its fuel tank and hurling it a hundred feet into the air. The exploding bomb blew a huge hole in the destroyer's hull, which set off its stores of munitions and oil products. A geyser of gas from the plane's ruptured tank ignited with a whoosh, sending flames high enough to char sailors on the bridge, fifty feet above.

The warship was dead in the water.

Damage enough.

Then the bow drifted one way and the stern the other.

The destroyer was cut in two.

Now the sky was scattered with many grains of rice. Explosions from the battle brought Japanese defenders to the mouths of their hillside caves. The men with Genjo Tokuda let out a cheer. Swords and bayonets were raised in triumph behind the ramparts of Shuri Castle.

The Special Attack Squadron hit the Yanks with a vengeance. One after another, in wave upon wave, the planes rushed in, like giant bullets fired from a massive machine gun in the sky. Most blew apart and crashed into the water, but that was no triumph if even one got through. A shell exploded underneath a kamikaze's belly, lifting it clear of the masthead below, but its bomb went down the destroyer's forward stack and turned it into a giant blowtorch.

"He did it!" roared a soldier in Shuri Castle.

Tokuda swept his binoculars from ship to ship to ship, focusing in on the faces of the men under attack. Not since the days of grappling hooks and hand-to-hand swordplay on men-of-war had sailors faced such a personal ordeal. Every Yank was afraid the kamikazes were aiming for *him*.

Pandemonium was rife on the targeted ships. Here, there, and everywhere, plummeting planes slammed home. Deck guns were firing so furiously that their barrels glowed. Tracers by the thousands tore through the puffs of flak as—*bam, bam, bam, bam*—gunners kept up an unflinching barrage. Tokuda watched as a wheel bounced off the wreckage of one plane and decapitated a flak thrower.

"Sayonara!" he shouted.

Fire crews struggled to douse the raging infernos. On the ships with lost power and useless hoses, the Yanks were forced to lug water in bucket brigades. Men shored up bulkheads, plugged leaks, and jettisoned anchors, torpedoes, and other weight to try to save their sinking wrecks. Medics rushed to help the severely injured, and some got burned to death in fire traps. Decks grew so hot that men ran to the toilets to cool their feet. Those catapulted overboard or forced to abandon ship dog-paddled frantically to stay afloat in a sea of sludge, oil, and blood. Castaways got crushed by downed planes or squeezed between the hulls of rescue boats. Many were drowned by high seas, and the worst of the burned survivors simply gave up, wriggling out of their life jackets because they could no longer stand the agony of salt in their wounds.

"Die, Yankee, die," cursed Tokuda.

Pilots killing themselves in order to kill Yanks—this was a new kind of warfare the Americans couldn't comprehend. It was written all over the dumbfounded faces Tokuda saw in his binoculars.

Were these diving madmen religious fanatics? Drunks? Drug addicts? Hypnotized robots? What macabre evil subverts human nature and turns men against their instinct toward self-preservation?

It's alien to Western values.

It's inhuman.

It's weird.

It's *bushido*, thought Genjo Tokuda.

Even more spectacular were the night attacks in the weeks that followed. The greatest seaborne battle in the history of warfare climaxed off Okinawa. Almost three hundred ships were hit and five thousand Americans killed by floating chrysanthemums sacrificing themselves to defend the Chrysanthemum Throne.

Twilight was the best hour for kamikaze raids. Radar warnings did little to help the Yankees see. The prelude—a chorus of air-raid sirens from the ships—signaled to the Japanese that it was time to scramble to the hillsides to witness the fireworks. The sight reminded Tokuda of Ryogoku, a Tokyo district known for its annual pyrotechnics over the Sumida River.

"Hell birds!"

All eyes scanned the sky.

When the sirens blared, the searchlights of the ships went on and began trying to pick out the oncoming suicide wave. Out blinked the non-essential lights of the fleet. The kamikazes thundered in with a metallic roar and were met by the booms of pom-pom guns flashing on the sea. Anti-aircraft fire gushed into the sky, lighting it up like a Roman candle. Bursts of flak above, high-caliber explosions below—what a magnificent festival the battle was tonight. It seemed inconceivable that anything could penetrate such a barrage, but just then a single plane hurtled down like a brilliant meteorite from space.

"Keep going!" Tokuda urged.

And keep going it did, slamming into a munitions ship as an oily fireball of bombs, fuel, and the pilot himself. A multi-colored fan of flames lit the horizon, and a thunderclap shook the island. Burning fiercely, the ship split in two, then sizzled in billows of steam as both sections sank with the crew.

The soldier beside Tokuda fell to his knees.

"Well done. Thank you." He worshipped toward the sea.

"Each soldier will kill at least one American devil."

That was the order from Lieutenant General Mitsuru Ushijima, the officer in command on Okinawa.

And to make sure the Yanks got the point, Radio Tokyo broadcast propaganda using the American nicknames for the Japanese strongholds of the Shuri Line, the eight-mile arc that spanned from Yonabaru, on the east coast, through the town of Shuri to the port of Naha, on the west coast.

"Sugar Loaf Hill . . . Chocolate Drop . . . Strawberry Hill," teased the propagandist. "Gee, these places sound wonderful! You can just see the candy houses with their white picket fences and the candy canes hanging from the trees, their red and white stripes glistening in the sun. But the only thing red about those places is the blood of Americans. Yes sir, those are the names of hills in southern Okinawa, where the fighting's so close that you get down to bayonets and sometimes"— the announcer paused—"bare fists."

And so it was.

American GIs and leathernecks died by the thousands in a drive to give meaning to Lieutenant General Simon Bolivar Buckner, Jr.'s, toast about walking "in the ashes of Tokyo." Three thousand more crumbled from "battle fatigue"—

nervous breakdowns that sent them to hospital. But still the Yanks kept coming. It was a relentless tide from blockhouse to blockhouse, pillbox to pillbox, bone vault to bone vault, across Cactus Ridge and then Kakazu Ridge, where twenty-two of thirty tanks were destroyed by mines, anti-tank guns, artillery, and mortar fire. The Americans withstood a banzai counterattack and kept on the move, as the fighting grew more hellish per man, per yard, per however you want to measure it.

Their gains averaged 163 yards a day.

The defenders let the rumbling tanks pass through their concealed positions, then they cut down the supporting troops with flank fire, attacking the armor with satchel charges and flaming rags that forced the crews to bail out to be spiked by bayonets. "You can't bypass a Jap," the Yanks were heard to yell by those who grasped English, "because a Jap doesn't know when he's bypassed."

Pocked with caves and strongly held by the defenders, the slopes of the Shuri Line became known as forbidden land. It was here that the Yanks—exposed to the big guns and mortars on the heights of Shuri Castle—had the most hellish time. Ishimmi Ridge, Dakeshi Ridge, Wana Ridge, and Wana Draw—they were the battlefields by mid-May. On Ishimmi Ridge, the defenders had two hundred isolated GIs pinned down in a last stand. For seventy hours, the Yanks had battled without sleep. Riflemen got blown to bits by mortars or were struck in the head by machine-gun fire. Blood was everywhere—in the weapons, on the still living, splattered all around. The dead lay where they fell, putrefying in the broiling heat. Wounded men, groaning because the morphine was gone, were propped up with rifles in their hands. Their grenades depleted and short of ammunition, the few unscathed GIs searched their dead buddies for cartridges and clips, and laid out all the bayonets for the hand-to-hand fight that was sure to finish them off.

The Marines on the ridge above Tokuda's cave were ground down to human wreckage. You could smell the battle line before you could see it. Amid bandages, blood, and mangled flesh, men writhed in agony and died, whole chunks ripped out of them. Now was the time for a banzai charge, so Tokuda drew the samurai sword his father had given him at the start of the war. He wormed through the bowels of the cave toward the jagged oval of daylight ahead, and that's when he heard—*rumble, rumble, rumble*—the sound of one . . . then two . . . then three Sherman tanks nearing the hillside.

"Corkscrew and blowtorch."

That's what the Americans called the new technique they had developed to kill the Japanese in their caves.

One of the tanks was armed with the usual 75mm cannon. It made up the corkscrew part of the "blowing" party. As Tokuda closed on the cave's exit, a blast from the cannon hurled a shell down the tunnel. Narrowly missing Tokuda as it screamed past, the shell exploded with such force that it slammed him into the rock wall. The guns of the other two tanks had been adapted to squirt a mixture of gasoline and napalm. These flame-throwing tanks were the blowtorch team. The last thing Tokuda saw before it all went black was a tongue of yellow fire streaming past his right flank, and the last thing he heard was his own shriek of pain as that half of his face got cooked alive.

Thunder God

Vancouver
October 31, Now

Three days a week, Chief Superintendent Robert DeClercq was up before dawn for a six-thirty fencing workout with an old Hungarian master. Swordplay is ideal for keeping the body in shape. The classic fencer's position—weight balanced between flexed legs, the hand with the foil feinting, thrusting, and parrying—mimics a yoga stance. And because swordplay is performed at lightning speed, it requires quick reactions and superb hand-eye coordination.

Three days a week, days he didn't fence, the chief met the forensic pathologist, Gill Macbeth, after work for swordplay of a different—but no less vigorous—kind.

DeClercq was in as good a shape as he had ever been.

"What do you think of that?"

"Nevermore," said Binky as the Mountie left the bedroom to wend his way out to the hot tub on the deck.

"A *lot* more," DeClercq taunted, "if I have my way."

"Ditch him, Gill," Binky said. "He's not good enough for you."

"*Srrit . . . srreeew!*" whistled Gabby as Macbeth came naked out of the bedroom.

"Where's the Viagra?"

"Ruffle my feathers, baby!"

"Your birds need a new shtick," complained DeClercq.

"They have one," Gill said, "for Halloween."

The West African gray parrot and the green-winged macaw shared a roomy aviary-cum-solarium in the cedar-and-glass architectural marvel that Gill—thanks to a generous inheritance—called home. On her way to the fridge for a bottle of champagne, she peered in at Binky on his perch and quoted:

"Be that word our sign of parting, bird or fiend!"
  I shrieked, upstarting—
"Get thee back into the tempest and the Night's
  Plutonian shore!
Leave no black plume as a token of that lie thy
  soul hath spoken!
Leave my loneliness unbroken!—quit the bust
  above my door!
Take thy beak from out my heart, and take thy
  form from off my door!"

                    Quoth the Raven, . . .

"Nevermore," said Binky.

DeClercq laughed. "Binky's a bad omen. But he doesn't look like Poe's raven to me."

"I'll paint him black," said Gill.

While the cop fetched a pair of champagne flutes from the bar, the pathologist slid back the glass door to the deck, where a pool and a hot tub overlooked the Lions Gate Bridge and Stanley Park. As Macbeth stepped out into the chilly autumn night, her skin puckered with goosebumps and her nose wrinkled from the smell of cordite wafting up from the fireworks on the beach.

Pausing in the doorway, Robert felt the embers of lust getting stoked again. Gill had bent over the hot tub to crank the knob, and now, as steam rose from the bubbling water, she circled around to the far side and stood face to face with him, her sexy silhouette outlined against the panorama of all those city lights.

What a woman! thought DeClercq.

When the lights shine on her, the stars shine on me.

With her eyes smoldering with mischief, she made a show of stepping into the tub. One foot, the other foot, and a shimmy down into the water as her convex hips, her concave waist, and her breasts sank beneath the frothy foam.

"Want to play footsie?"

"You bet," he said.

She held the bottle of champagne above the water. "Let's pop the cork and see how high it'll fly."

"People who live in glass houses shouldn't—"

Suddenly, a blinding explosion seared the night sky beyond her, and a fireball plummeted to the earth.

"What was that?" exclaimed Gill, standing up and splashing water as she looked behind her.

"Whatever it was—" the cop began, but he didn't finish the sentence.

From the aviary, Binky finished it for him.

"Nevermore," squawked the bird.

* * *

"He got chocolate raisins!"

"Lucky me."

"He won't share, Daddy!" bawled the wicked witch.

"Share with your sister, Stuart."

"All gone," mumbled the Frankenstein monster through a mouthful of marbles.

"Big jerk!" cried the witch.

"Dad, she snapped off one of my neck bolts!"

"Sarah—"

"Daddy, he broke my witch's hat!"

Pete knew he shouldn't take his eyes from the road, but he chanced a peek in the rearview mirror. Sure enough, one of the two collar bolts beneath the green face of the monster had been snapped off, and the pointed hat of the wicked witch drooped like erectile dysfunction.

"You're a deadbeat dad," Alice had bitched when he'd phoned last week to tell the wickedest witch of all that his child-support check would be late. "If the kids end up on crack, I'll blame you. Get off your lazy ass and *be* a dad for Halloween."

So to shut up his ex-wife, Pete had taken both brats out to trick-or-treat, and once they'd bagged enough candy to rot their teeth and launch their future dentist's bills to the moon, he'd caged them in the back of the car and set off for the North Shore to finish his daddy duties with a bang of fireworks.

His eyes returned to the road.

If not for the inadequate causeway bisecting Stanley Park and crossing the entrance to the harbor as the Lions Gate Bridge, the mountainside population would be larger. Decades ago, when the Guinness family built the bridge to their British Properties, three lanes would have seemed an extravagance, a freeway from one woodlot to another. But now, unless you drove the long route around the harbor, this was the only crossing that connected the bedrooms of the North Shore with the downtown office towers.

"He got chocolate peanuts!"

"Crybaby!"

"He won't share, Daddy!"

"That's enough!" Pete was fed up with the antics of these urchins on a sugar high. He scowled at them in the rearview mirror, and that's when he was blinded by a light from above just a second before—*craaack!*—the windshield bowed under the weight—

Pete shrieked in horror!

Of a black skull mottled with charred meat.

On reflex, he wrenched the steering wheel

toward the oncoming lane, causing a head-on collision, the first in a chain reaction of collisions along the bridge, which ended in a twenty-car pileup and dozens of injuries.

It was an honor to die as a Thunder God.

In the closing months of the war, the Japanese had developed what they hoped would be the ultimate kamikaze weapon: a piloted glider bomb called the *ohka*, the "cherry blossom." Manned by a pilot facing certain death, the *ohka* would be carried to its target on the belly of a mother plane, then set free like a baby coming down the birth canal. As the *ohka*'s three rocket engines accelerated to over 550 miles per hour, the pilot—honored as a Thunder God—would guide it straight toward an enemy ship.

"Hissatsu!"

Kaboom!

And you went to Yasukuni Shrine as a god.

Technically, this old prop plane qualified the yakuza pilot as a kamikaze, not a Thunder God. But his uncle had guided an *ohka* to its target during the war, and was forevermore revered by his family, so now the cancer-ridden pilot fantasized that he was a Thunder God too.

Having dropped his dead weight onto the Lions

Gate Bridge, Tokuda's henchman targeted his propeller at the billowing sails out on the harbor. Then, pushing the controls forward to turn his plane into a dive bomber, he gave it full throttle.

The Thunder God descended in a power dive.

Sgt. Dane Winter was striding up the street when a woman walking toward him raised both hands to her face like Munch's *The Scream* and cried, "My God, no!"

His plan was to hike across downtown to False Creek and up over Burrard Bridge to the south shore, where he'd follow the creek-side walk to his condo. Jackie had been caught in a delay at work, so he'd told her to let Chuck drive her car to Mud Bay Airport to pick up the plane. Dane would drive her down to the convention center to meet up with Joe after his rehearsal. From there, Jackie and Joe could drive Dane's car to the Mounties' airport on Sea Island, and Chuck could pick them up there for the fireworks.

"What about you?" she had asked.

"I'll walk home," he'd said. "The exercise will do me good, and I can pretend I'm out trick-or-treating like when I was a kid. That solves your problem."

So that's what they had done. Joe and Jackie

had driven off, while Dane spent half an hour touring the convention center. How he wished he could have hooked his grandfather up with Joe. Think of the war stories those two vets would have shared!

Now he was walking home.

The shock etched into the woman's face prompted the Mountie to whirl around just in time to see a miniature version of 9/11 unfold before his eyes. A single-engine plane came dive-bombing out of the sky and rammed into the convention center, hard enough to shiver its pilings and shake the canvas sails that lined its length like a typhoon hitting a windjammer. The plane exploded on impact, and flames blew back from its tail. One wing was blown off and propelled into the air. The sergeant caught the registration letters as it pinwheeled down to the street.

"Lewis. Special X."

"Rusty," Dane said into his cellphone as he dashed toward the crash site, "a plane just struck the convention center. I'm on the scene. I need a registration checked with Transport Canada."

"Shoot."

"C-DKYZ. I want the name of the registered owner and the airport the plane calls home."

Why?

By the time DeClercq and Macbeth had dried off, got dressed, and rushed out to the chief's car, the traffic along Marine Drive and up Taylor Way was completely stalled. That left them no option but to hoof it.

All the way down Sentinel Hill to the grid-locked approach to the bridge, DeClercq and Macbeth were busy on their cellphones. He was directing the Mounted's response to what bore the hallmarks of a terrorist attack, while she was informing ambulance crews to carry in their stretchers from wherever they were bottlenecked. It would be hours before vehicles on the Lions Gate Bridge could move an inch.

Boom!

Boom!

Boom!

The show must go on, so as the pair huffed up the incline to the crest of the bridge, where the beams of the piled-up cars shone in all directions, the storm overhead fractured into pyrotechnic shards. The blasts turned the blood on the bridge redder, and the sky, as if torn asunder by the fireworks, opened up and poured down rain.

Boom!

Boom!

Wee-ooh! Wee-ooh! Wee-ooh! . . .

The night was full of screaming sirens, some responding to Halloween hijinks and others to the plane crash, but up here the screams were human. Screams from injured drivers trapped until the Jaws of Life could extricate them. Screams from pedestrians pinned to the bridge by cars that had jumped the sidewalks. Screams from those laid out on the roadway and receiving first aid. And screams from two trick-or-treating kids—one the Frankenstein monster, the other the wicked witch—being hauled from the back seat of a smashed-up car at the hub of the carnage.

A car with a driver slumped at the wheel and a body smashed on the windshield.

"Daddy's hurt!" wailed the witch, the dye in

her black rat's nest of backcombed hair trickling down her anguished face.

"Is he dead?" cried the monster, struggling to break loose from the hold of the good Samaritan who had pulled him out of the car.

The bawling witch was going into hysterics.

Weaving his way to the wreck, DeClercq crouched down to face the traumatized pair.

"Hello. My name is Robert. I'm the policeman who's going to see to your dad. Are you hurt?"

"Daddy's hurt!" the witch sobbed, then she threw herself into the chief's arms.

"Are you okay, son?"

"Yes," the monster sniveled, shivering from shock and his rain-soaked clothes.

"What's your name?"

"Stuart."

"And your sister's?"

"Sarah."

"Where's your mom?"

"At home. We don't live with Dad."

Over the girl's shoulder, DeClercq caught sight of several uniformed cops and ambulance workers sprinting through the curtain of rain from the North Shore. He forked his fingers at two of the constables and motioned them over.

"Sir?" said the female, recognizing him.

"Stuart, Sarah, I want you to go with this constable. She'll phone your mom and get you home. I'll take your dad to doctors at the hospital."

The female cop scowled. She obviously thought baby-sitting duties were beneath her.

"Get over it," DeClercq warned beneath his breath. "And find your heart."

His eyes dropped to her name tag, and her flinch said that she knew she'd just blown any chance she might have had of joining Special X.

The male constable caught on. "I'll take them, sir," he said.

"No. She'll do her duty. We don't need shirkers here. We have a crime scene: the hood of this car. Find a way to build a tent to preserve forensics. And pass me your flashlight."

The chastised officer took both kids by the hand and gently tugged them away.

Crawling into the back seat of the car, the chief reached forward to check the neck pulse of the driver. Nothing. The head-on collision had caved in his face. No airbags.

DeClercq switched on the flashlight.

What a mess!

At 1,600 degrees Fahrenheit, it takes an hour to cremate the human body. This cadaver had burned for only as long as it took it to plunge from the plane, so while the body squashed on the windshield was charred black on the outside, it was as pink as ever within.

The beam of the flashlight caught something strange. Preserved in the mash of internal organs in a way that reminded DeClercq of a fossil caught in amber were the brittle, charred bones of one scorched hand. It struck the Mountie that one of the fingers was missing, and he recalled yesterday's discussion with the Japanese diplomat about *yubitsume*, the yakuza finger-cutting ritual.

But this wasn't a pinky.

It was a missing ring finger.

What, if anything, did that mean?

Then the flashlight beam picked out something else. Patches of iron were stuck to the corpse, which was also dusted with white powder of some sort. From those clues and the brilliant glare he'd seen in the sky at Macbeth's, DeClercq deduced that whoever had taken this dive had been wrapped like a mummy in something that bound thermite to his flesh.

The chief had seen thermite used to weld railroad tracks in place, and he also knew that it had been used during the Second World War to purify uranium for the Manhattan Project.

These were the residues.

Okay, the Mountie said to himself, think this through.

Someone seeks revenge against a fingerless man. No one dumps a body this publicly unless he's making an important statement. So up goes a plane with a human thermite bomb aboard, and down comes the charred victim onto the Lions Gate Bridge. Then whoever committed the crime crashes the plane into a convention center that's playing host to Pacific War vets.

Why? wondered DeClercq.

"DeClercq."

"Chief, it's Dane. I'm at the crash site."

From the hump of the Lions Gate Bridge, the chief superintendent had a bird's-eye view of the sergeant's location. He gazed southeast along the seawall walk, over the figurehead of the *Empress of Japan*, and past the Nine O'Clock Gun to Canada Place.

Vancouver's answer to the Sydney Opera House, the landmark on the south shore of Burrard Inlet was Canada's pavilion for Expo 86. Seen from afar, it resembled a sailing ship, with its bright white fabric sails billowing along what appeared to be its hull but was in fact a pier extending into the harbor. The Pan Pacific Hotel soared at its landward stern. A domed IMAX theater was the figurehead at its prow. And in between was the convention center, whose long docks were home base for cruise ships doing the Alaska run. Tonight, however, those docks were bare, and instead of sea traffic, a kamikaze plane had struck Canada Place amidships.

"How bad is it?" DeClercq asked.

"It could be worse," said the sergeant. "The plane was too light to do major damage. It slammed into the west side of the main meeting hall and broke apart. The pilot hurled out of the cockpit and smashed in through the jagged glass. I'm standing over the upper half of him. The lower half must be back in the plane. A smear of blood runs across the floor. Tonight was only a rehearsal, so the hall was all but empty. The only person dead is the Japanese pilot."

"Japanese?" said DeClercq.

"Yeah, there's one of those kamikaze scarves around his brow. And guess what? During his flight from the cockpit to this final resting place, he must have lost his prosthetic finger. I'm staring at a missing pinky, Chief."

* * *

No sooner had Dane punched off than his cellphone jangled.

"Sergeant Winter."

"It's Rusty Lewis. Transport Canada has tracked the plane."

"I'm listening."

"It's from a small airfield down near the border. I can't get hold of the owner, but it's called Mud Bay Airport."

"Corporal Hett."

"Jackie, it's Dane. Where are you?"

"Air Services. It's nuts here. They're waiting to respond to a crash downtown. Chuck won't be able to land."

"You've spoken to him?"

"No. They're keeping the airwaves clear."

"I don't know what it means, but there's something you've got to know. The plane that crashed tonight was from Mud Bay Airport. Chuck wasn't the pilot. I'm looking at the guy as we speak. He's Japanese. And he's missing a finger."

"Yakuza?"

"Looks like that to me. We can't reach the airport owner, so we don't know who rented the plane. If you're out of contact with Chuck, you'd better get down to Mud Bay. A worst-case scenario would be that he got hijacked for his plane."

Whup, whup, whup . . .

As the RCMP Eurocopter approached the blacked-out airfield, the pilot kicked in FLIR—forward-looking infrared—to pick up any heat signatures. That would tell them if there were bad guys lurking about.

"Body heat," the pilot told Jackie through the headphones. "Only one. In the open. On the ground."

"Check it out," said the corporal.

Not Dad, she prayed.

As the helicopter traversed the airfield, a string of lights flashed red-blue, red-blue on the roofs of the patrol cars that were speeding down the rural road to secure the airport's perimeter.

"Light him up," Jackie said, and a spotlight knifed down, pooling around a man sprawled in a bloody puddle near the gate.

"There!" said Joe, pointing. "In the shadows."

The pilot keyed the chopper's mike to switch on the airport's ramp and runway lights, and there, beside the line of buildings, with its doors open, sat Jackie's car.

"Set us down," she said.

The overhead rotor blew waves of rain out in concentric circles, so the pilot jockeyed the Eurocopter far enough away from the car to preserve forensic clues. As cops from the patrol cars swarmed toward what appeared to be a run-over security guard, Jackie jumped from the cockpit and sprinted to her car.

By now, she knew that a body had been dumped on the bridge, and that the ring finger seemed to be missing from its right hand. So the instant her flashlight beam glinted off her dad's signet ring—a ring that bore the insignia of the U.S. Air Force—she knew her father had died a death too horrible to comprehend.

The ring was still on his finger.

And the finger was on the dash.

"Find anything?" Joe called from a decent distance away. Her grandfather knew better than to traipse across a possible crime scene.

There was no need for Jackie to reply. The moment she turned to face him, the old man could see the answer in the pain around her eyes. She was tough, but he was tougher, for Joe was a veteran of both the Depression and the Pacific War. So when he held his arms wide open to embrace her, Jackie swiftly closed the gap between them. Both Hetts, however, knew that no matter how hard they clung to each other, that gap would always be there, for the generation connecting them had been snatched away.

"Why?" Jackie choked. "Why kill Dad?"

"Wrong place, wrong time," Joe mumbled flatly.

"No!" she replied, gritting her teeth. "There must be more. Why? Why? *Why!*"

Hickam's Flag

Potsdam, Germany
July 16, 1945

On May 8, 1945, less than a month into Harry S. Truman's presidency, Nazi Germany surrendered.

So that left the "Japs."

How Truman felt about the "Japs" was a matter of record. "I think one man is just as good as another, so long as he's honest and decent and not a nigger or a Chinaman," he once wrote. "Uncle Will says that the Lord made a white man of dust, a nigger from mud, then He threw up what was left and it came down a Chinaman. He does hate Chinese and Japs. So do I. It is race prejudice I guess. But I am strongly of the opinion that negroes ought to be in Africa, yellow men in Asia, and white men in Europe and America."

In his hatred of the Japs—Truman called them "savages, ruthless, merciless, and fanatic"—the president wasn't alone. The sneak attack on Pearl Harbor—Roosevelt's "date which will live in infamy"—had enraged America to its racial core. Hitler's war was white on white, but the fight with Japan was different. The Japs were the Other; comic books portrayed them as bucktoothed yellow monkeys. Some GIs in the Pacific War collected scalps or ears as trophies.

Admiral William Halsey told men going into battle, "Kill Japs, kill Japs, kill more Japs. The only good Jap is a Jap who's been dead for six months."

The motto of the U.S. Marines was: "Remember Pearl Harbor—Keep 'em dying."

The commander of the Tenth Army at the Battle of Okinawa, General Joseph Stilwell—also known as "Vinegar Joe"—wrote, "When I think of how these bowlegged cockroaches have ruined our calm lives it makes me want to wrap Jap guts around every lamppost in Asia."

As Truman put it, "When you have to deal with a beast, you have to treat him as a beast."

That's why the American flag that flapped at

the meeting of Truman, Churchill, and Stalin in Potsdam, Germany, in July was the same Stars and Stripes that had flown from the flagpole at Hickam Field during the Japanese sneak attack.

Remember Pearl Harbor.

Truman did.

And this was the man who would decide whether to drop the atomic bomb on Japan.

They called it Truman's Little White House, this grimy yellow-and-red lakeside villa in Babelsberg, between bomb-blasted Berlin and the site of the Potsdam Conference. Yesterday, after a week at sea on the *Augusta*, the president had docked at Antwerp, Belgium, then flown in for his first showdown with Joseph Stalin. As luck would have it, Stalin was delayed for a day, so Truman and James Byrnes, his secretary of state, toured Berlin, sightseeing instead of strong-arming. That night, after they'd returned to the villa for drinks and dinner, Henry Stimson, the secretary of war, arrived with a coded telegram. A subsequent cable carried much the same message:

To Secretary of War from Harrison. Doctor has just returned most enthusiastic and confident that the little boy is as husky as his big brother. The light in his eyes discernible from here to Highhold and I could have heard his screams here to my farm.

"Big brother" was the world's first atomic device. It had been exploded that pre-dawn at Alamogordo Bombing Range, two hundred miles south of Los Alamos, in New Mexico's desert.

"Little boy" was code for the uranium bomb to be dropped on Japan.

"Highhold" was Stimson's home near Washington.

"My farm" was the Virginia spread of Stimson's assistant, George Harrison.

The medical terms in the telegram bamboozled those who manned the Potsdam communications center.

They thought that the secretary of war—who was seventy-seven years old—had just become a dad.

From the moment Truman assumed his role as U.S. commander in chief, after the death of President Roosevelt on April 12, 1945, his focus was on Russia. On April 13, the day after he was sworn in, Truman was advised that Churchill was upset with the Russians. They weren't living up to their agreements in Europe, and hadn't been since the Yalta Conference.

Now it was time for the president to meet Generalissimo Stalin in conquered Germany. The location chosen was Potsdam's Cecilienhof Palace, the estate of the former kaiser. Before leaving, Truman told the world what he hoped to achieve: "We've got to teach [the Russians] how to behave."

To that end, the Americans had made the conference coincide with their first test of the atomic bomb. With the test a success, Truman had an ace up his sleeve for his negotiations with Stalin. The time was nigh for a little atomic diplomacy. As Truman liked to say, whenever he had the upper hand, "If you can't stand the heat, get out of the kitchen."

Behind the scenes, however, another man called the shots: the "assistant president," Jimmy Byrnes. Byrnes had spent thirty years in the House and the Senate, and sat on the Supreme Court, and served Roosevelt as director of war mobilization, and seemed to be the man to step into FDR's shoes . . . until he lost the vice-presidency to Truman at the Democratic Party's 1944 Chicago convention. In fact, when the "old Missouri farmer"—

as Truman liked to call himself—had first arrived in the Senate in 1935, it was Byrnes who took him under his more experienced wing.

Truman looked up to Byrnes, and Byrnes looked down on Truman. He regarded his new president as a political nonentity with no abilities to speak of and no knowledge of how to conduct foreign policy—or much else, it appeared. Byrnes saw Truman as an accident of history, and not a good accident. So of course, Truman made Byrnes not only his secretary of state, but also his chief adviser on the question of whether to drop the bomb.

And now it was "bull bat time."

Bull bat time was a phrase politicians used for a night of drinking, playing poker, and discussing matters of state. So after Stimson brought news of the explosion of the bomb, Truman and Byrnes filled their glasses with Jimmy's best bourbon and took a congratulatory stroll to see the moon and the stars reflect off Griebnitz Lake.

"We *did* it," Truman said.

"We sure did," Byrnes agreed.

The men clinked glasses and downed a slug of whisky as a toast to the bomb.

"So how should I play this with Uncle Joe tomorrow?" asked Truman.

"Hard ball," Byrnes replied. "When you sent Hopkins to Moscow, what'd you tell him?"

"I told him to use a baseball bat, if he thought that was the proper approach to Stalin. Just crack him over the head."

"That's good advice," said Byrnes. "We've got blue chips on the table. The Russians are planning world conquest. Force is the only thing they understand. The atomic bomb will make Stalin more manageable in Europe. It'll bully him. A combat display against the Japs will impress the Russkies with Uncle Sam's military might. We'll be able to dictate our own terms at the end of the war. There's only one way to play this. Give 'em hell, Harry."

July 17, 1945

"That SOB!" Truman fumed over drinks the following night. "Did you see how he tried to push me around, Jimmy?"

"You stood your own, Harry. You bossed the meeting."

"When we had pictures taken, did you see how Stalin stood on the step above me? The balls of that guy! And they call me the 'little man.' Hell, I'm five-feet-eight. Stalin's got to be five-five. Five-six, tops. He thinks he's the 'big I am'? Well, I've got news for Uncle Joe. In time, he'll see how big *I* am."

July 18, 1945

Truman and Prime Minister Winston Churchill met for lunch to compare notes on Stalin. The president wrote in his diary: "P.M. & I ate alone. Discussed Manhattan (it is a success). Decided to tell Stalin about it. Stalin had told P.M. of telegram from Jap Emperor asking for peace. Stalin also read his answer to me. It was satisfactory. Believe Japs will fold up before Russia comes in. I am sure they will when Manhattan appears over their homeland."

July 20, 1945

Fortified by the muscular success of the atomic bomb, Truman stood up to the Russians—as Churchill saw it—"in a most emphatic and decisive manner."

Then Truman wrote to his wife, Bess: "We had a tough meeting yesterday. I reared up on my hind legs and told 'em where to get off and they got off. I have to make it perfectly plain to them"—Stalin's Russians and Great Britain—"at least once a day that so far as this President is concerned Santa Claus is dead and that my first interest is U.S.A., then I want the Jap War won and I want 'em both in it. . . . They are beginning to awake to the fact that I mean business."

July 24, 1945

Late in the day, at the end of the Big Three session, Truman walked around to Stalin's chair and, aided by his interpreter, said casually, "You may be interested to know that we have developed a powerful new weapon of unusual destructive force."

Stalin smiled blandly and showed no special interest.

"I'm glad to hear that," the Russian said. "I hope you make good use of it against the Japanese."

Later, as they were waiting for their cars, Churchill asked Truman, "How did it go?"

"He never asked a question," the president replied.

"Ike's against dropping the bomb."

"Why, Harry?" Byrnes asked, topping up his bourbon.

"According to what he told Stimson, the Japs are already defeated. At the moment, they're seeking a way to surrender with a minimum loss of face. Ike has grave misgivings about shocking world opinion by using a devastating weapon that's no longer mandatory to save American lives."

"The Pacific isn't Eisenhower's theater. He's supreme commander in western Europe."

"That's another problem. MacArthur's supreme commander in the Pacific, and he also thinks the bomb's unnecessary from a military point of view. Know what he told his staff when he learned that the Japs had asked Russia to negotiate surrender with us? 'This is it. The war is over.' "

"I don't see MacArthur here at Potsdam to make the decision. And we won't consult him."

"He'll be livid, Jimmy."

"There's much more at stake here than Japan, Harry. We've got to stop the Russkies from gobbling up the globe. What's that story you told me about your granddad and the Injuns?"

"Solomon Young ran a wagon train from Independence, Missouri, to San Francisco. The redskins bothered the other trainmasters, but they didn't bother him. He scared 'em. My granddad let the Indians know that he had the guns and the ammunition, and that he'd shoot them if they gave him any trouble."

Byrnes raised his glass. "You gotta let your enemy know you got the guns. The Russkies have to *see* the bomb explode in Japan. They'll know there's an ominous bulge in our pocket after that. And any time we want to use atomic diplomacy, I can say to Molotov—or to Stalin—'You don't know Southerners. We carry our artillery in our hip pocket. If you don't cut out all this stalling and let us get down to work, I'm gonna pull an atomic bomb out of my hip pocket and let you have it.' In all future disputes with the Reds, we can stand by our guns."

"In eastern Europe."

"And Asia. Stalin says Russia will enter the war against the Japs on August 8. If they do, he'll demand concessions in the East. Mongolia, Manchuria, and Korea will gradually slip into Russia's orbit, then China and, eventually, Japan. But drop the bomb before that and we won't need the Commies. They'll have no bargaining chips."

"That's a lot of lives," said Truman.

"Jap lives, Harry. Think of the *American* lives we'll save."

"The joint chiefs say invading Japan will cost forty thousand U.S. dead. It's not like Okinawa.

The geography's different. And before long, there won't be a Jap city standing."

"That's all the more reason to strike now. If we're gonna scare the Russians, the bomb needs a virgin background against which to show its strength."

"That's a lot of lives," Truman repeated.

"How many American lives does General Marshall think invading Japan will cost?"

"He says half a million."

"Well, there you go. That's the figure we'll use."

"We'd better warn the Japs."

Byrnes shook his head. "They had Pearl Harbor. This will be *our* surprise attack. If we warn the Japs the bomb will be dropped on a given city, they'll bring in our prisoners of war and use them as shields."

"Should we give 'em a demonstration? Let the Jap military see our guns?"

"What if the bomb's a dud and fails to explode? That'll play into the hands of Jap hard-liners, and we'll look like fools. Plus, gone will be the element of surprise."

Truman swirled his whisky and downed a slug.

"So that decides it?" said the president.

"Tomorrow we give the order."

"Okay, Jimmy. The bomb drops unless the Japs fold and negotiate surrender."

"Negotiate? That doesn't sound like 'unconditional' surrender to me, Harry."

July 25, 1945

Today, the order went out:

TO: General Carl Spaatz
Commanding General
United States Army Strategic Air Forces
1. The 509 Composite Group, 20th Air Force will deliver its first special bomb as soon as weather will permit visual bombing after about 3 August 1945 on one of the targets: Hiroshima, Kokura, Niigata and Nagasaki. . . .
    2. Additional bombs will be delivered on the above targets as soon as made ready by the project staff. . . .

Truman recorded in his diary: "This weapon is to be used against Japan between now and August 10th."

July 26, 1945

In the end, it all came down to the emperor. That was the only condition Japan tried to negotiate.

"Unconditional surrender" was a slogan that Truman had inherited from Roosevelt. At a press conference in Casablanca after FDR met with Churchill in January 1943, the American president told reporters, "Some of you Britishers know the old story. We had a general called U.S. Grant. His name was Ulysses Simpson Grant, but in my, and the prime minister's, early days, he was called 'Unconditional Surrender' Grant. The elimination of German, Japanese, and Italian war power means their unconditional surrender."

The term was a war slogan. The words were propaganda designed to stimulate support from other nations and to help energize the war effort at home. But as soon as Truman came to power, he embraced Roosevelt's slogan as if it were gospel in a VE day speech to the American people. "Our blows will not cease until the Japanese military and naval forces lay down their arms in unconditional surrender," he vowed.

Now, as Japan tried to surrender, it was time to issue the Potsdam Declaration.

Everyone knew that Japan would not agree to any deal that threatened the status of the emperor. To his people, Emperor Hirohito was a god, the soul of Japan made incarnate. The country would fight to the last man if he was jeopardized.

At Potsdam, Churchill tried to reason with Truman.

"It's best to leave the Japanese some show of saving their military honor, and some assurance of their national existence," the PM argued. "The emperor is something for which they're ready to face certain death in very large numbers, and this might not be so important to us as it is to them."

"After Pearl Harbor," Truman said, "I don't think the Japs have military honor."

The secretary of war agreed with Churchill.

Let Japan keep the emperor.

"I heard from Byrnes," Stimson said later, "that they"—Byrnes and the president—"preferred not to put it in."

Consequently, the Potsdam Declaration demanded unconditional surrender from the enemy. "The alternative for Japan is prompt and utter destruction."

Without an assurance regarding the emperor, the Japanese rejected the ultimatum.

On August 6, Truman was sailing home on the

Augusta with—in his words—"my conniving secretary of state" when they received word that Hiroshima, a target still undamaged by the conventional air war, had been obliterated by an A-bomb.

Truman issued a statement. "The Japanese began the war from the air at Pearl Harbor," he declared. "They have been repaid many fold. . . . If they do not now accept our terms, they may expect a rain of ruin from the air, the like of which has never been seen on this earth."

On August 8, Russia declared war on Japan.

On August 9, Nagasaki was devastated by an A-bomb.

On August 10, Truman wrote in his diary: "Ate lunch at my desk and discussed the Jap offer to surrender which came in a couple of hours earlier. They wanted to make a condition precedent to the surrender. Our terms are 'unconditional.' They wanted to keep the Emperor. We told 'em we'd tell 'em how to keep him, but we'd make the terms."

On August 14, the day Japan surrendered but kept its emperor, the flag flying over the White House was the same Stars and Stripes that had flown in the attack on Pearl Harbor.

Hickam's flag.

*   *   *

Time magazine named Harry Truman its "Man of the Year." Alongside his cover photo, the magazine ran an image of a fist as mighty as the hand of God clenching lightning bolts in a mushroom cloud.

That autumn, a new sign appeared on the president's desk at the White House.

One side read: "I'm from Missouri."

The statement on the other side referred to a practice common in Wild West poker games. A knife with a buckhorn handle marked the player whose turn it was to deal. If a player declined the deal, he'd pass the "buck" to another player.

The expression on Truman's sign meant, If there's a decision to be made, I'm the man to make it.

The sign read: "The buck stops here."

Yasukuni Shrine

Vancouver
October 31, Now

Genjo Tokuda unsheathed Kamikaze and carried the sword out to the deck of the house at the top of the British Properties. There, he assumed the stance of a samurai warrior, just as his father had taught him to do so many decades ago in that Zen garden fronting his family's Shinto shrine.

"Banzai!" the old man cursed at the dark, slicing the *katana* down as if to cleave the distant chaos on the hump of the Lions Gate Bridge. Then he slashed down again to bisect the still-smoking pier that had been torpedoed by the kamikaze plane.

That felt good.

The *kumicho* shivered.

Through all those years, from 1945 to now, Tokuda had yearned to exact tonight's revenge.

First, the bridge.

Then, the pier.

And next, the Sushi Chef . . .

Back in 1945, Genjo Tokuda had seen out the war as a prisoner in a U.S. POW camp. Hospitalized for the burns and deep wounds he had suffered on Okinawa, he—unlike his commanders in that cataclysmic battle—had been denied the honorable death of a heroic samurai: hara-kiri.

Instead, he was demeaned.

Through a veil of morphine that quelled the agony racking his body, he glimpsed—through the half of his face that wasn't a reddish scar—someone watching him from the foot of his hospital bed. The soldier—a muscular man with a shaved head and hateful eyes—was dressed in khaki from cap to boots.

"Okinawans are hurling themselves off suicide cliffs," snarled the Yank. "Know why?"

His enemy's body language conveyed what he meant, but Tokuda didn't reply.

"Because they think we rape and torture those we capture. Know why?"

Again, no reply.

"Because they were told by Nips like you that to join the Marines, a leatherneck like me has to kill his own mother."

Silence.

"Know what?"

The drugged samurai waited.

"You fuckers are fucking right!" the jarhead said, and he spat on Tokuda's bed.

"Good morning, Monkey Man."

Tokuda forced open his eyes.

"I don't know your name," the jarhead said, " 'cause they found no papers on you. So I'll call you Monkey Man, since that's what you are to me. You like cartoons?"

Today, the Marine was dressed in sage green. His bloodshot eyes tattled that he had spent last night in the bar, and he had nicked his face twice while shaving.

Tokuda wondered if henceforth his own facial hair would be only half a beard.

"Here's Bugs Bunny."

His tormentor held up a frame from the film "Bugs Bunny Nips the Nips." It showed the rabbit battling it out on a Pacific island with a short, bucktoothed, slant-eyed "Jap" in big, round glasses. The Marine dropped the cartoon onto the bed.

"No? What about Popeye?"

In the next cartoon, a squinty-eyed sailor clenched a corncob pipe in his teeth and had rolled up his sleeves to bare an anchor tattoo on his huge forearm. "Let's blast 'em Japanazis!" read the caption, and beneath was an ad for the U.S. Treasury: "A 25¢ war stamp buys 12 bullets."

"Get it?" said the Marine.

Tokuda got more than the jarhead thought, for he had seen similar cartoons about the war in Europe, except those were directed at Hitler's Nazis, not the German people. In the Pacific, however, U.S. hatred got spewed at all Japanese, who were viewed as a subhuman race of animalistic demons.

"You're a sap, Mr. Jap," jeered the next cartoon in bamboo script. His wrists going limp to illustrate his taunt, the Marine mimicked Popeye, calling Tokuda a "yellow-skinned Japansy."

One by one, the cartoons fluttered down onto the bed like autumn leaves. In "Jap Trap," a mousetrap had crushed the neck of a rat-like Japanese soldier. In those titled the "Tokyo Kid," a snaggle-tooth monster with drooling lips clutched a bloody dagger in its clawed fist and sneered in pidgin English at American factory workers.

The jarhead aped, "Tokyo Kid say . . ."

> *Oh so happy*
> *For honorable scrap*
> *Busting of tools*
> *Help winning for Jap.*

In the next one, the same degenerate monster cowered in fright.

"Tokyo Kid say . . ."

> *Boom planes*
> *Saved from*
> *Box of scrap*
> *Make so very*
> *Unhappy Jap.*

* * *

Then it was over.

August 15, 1945.

The first time Japanese nationals ever heard their emperor's voice, it came by radio from a phonograph record that had been smuggled out of the palace in a laundry basket of women's underwear. That thwarted an attempted raid on the Chrysanthemum Throne by a thousand outraged officers who were intent on heading off dishonorable surrender by assassinating Emperor Hirohito.

"The enemy now possesses," intoned the Son of Heaven, "a new and terrible weapon with the power to destroy many innocent lives. . . . It is according to the dictates of time and fate that we have resolved to pave the way for a grand peace for all the generations to come by enduring the unendurable and suffering what is insufferable."

In short, this time the Divine Wind had *not* saved Japan.

By then out of hospital and caged behind barbed wire, Tokuda had vowed to follow the Way of the Warrior, as had his heroic commanders at the Battle of Okinawa. In the code of *bushido*, surrender shames one's family. Hara-kiri by sword is the warrior's honorable death, and according to what Tokuda had heard . . .

General Ushijima was headquartered in a cave that snaked through a prominent coral formation at the southern shore of Okinawa. The flat summit was defended by Japanese snipers, mortar men, and machine-gunners. Below the jagged pinnacle, the cave had two outlets: one facing land, and the other above the sea.

Backed by flame-throwing tanks spewing five thousand gallons of napalm, the Yanks captured the crest of the hill on June 20. A surrender demand was rejected by Ushijima, and his men then launched counterattacks to push the enemy back. Explosives sealed the mouth of the cave on the inland slope.

At 10:00 p.m. the next day, Ushijima and General Cho—the patriot who gave the "no prisoners" order in the Rape of Nanking—sat down to an elaborate meal of miso soup, fish cakes, canned meats, rice, cabbage, potatoes, pineapple, and tea, washed down with sake and a bottle of fine Scotch. As they dined, headquarters staff sang "Umi Yukaba," a solemn poem from ancient times of sacrificing life for the emperor.

At 3:00 a.m. on June 22, the moon was in the sky and dappling on the sea. Inside the cave, General Ushijima was dressed in full uniform, and General Cho wore a white kimono. In preparation for death, the soldiers exchanged last poems.

General Ushijima's:

We spend arrows and bullets to stain heaven and earth,
Defending our homeland forever.

General Cho's:

KAMIKAZE

The devil foe tightly grips our southwest land,
His aircraft fill the sky, his ships control the sea;
Bravely we fought for ninety days inside a dream;
We have used up our withered lives,
But our souls race to heaven.

"Well, Commanding General Ushijima, as the way may be dark, I, Cho, will lead the way."

"Please do so," replied Ushijima, his voice serene. "I'll take along my fan, since it is getting warm."

By candlelight, the morbid procession walked toward the cave's seaward exit, passing the staff, who'd drawn up in a line to pay their last respects. On the back of his kimono, General Cho had brush-stroked, in large characters, the words "With bravery I served my nation, / With loyalty I dedicate my life." Behind him, Ushijima cooled himself with flutters of an Okinawan *kuba* fan.

The moon, by now, had sunk into the western sea. Mist scaled the cliff from the brine below. Dawn had yet to break on the horizon. Ten paces out from the cave, at the lip of its ledge, a white sheet spread over a quilt created a ritual seat. There, both men knelt and exposed their abdomens. Sensing movement below, the Yanks up top threw down a few grenades. Neither general flinched.

Both bowed in reverence toward the eastern sky. An aide handed each man a hara-kiri dagger with half the blade wrapped in white cloth. Behind Ushijima stood the adjutant, grasping his *katana* sword with both hands and poised to strike. The general also held his dagger in both fists, then . . .

"It's too dark to see your neck," the swordsman said. "Please wait a few moments."

With the first flush of dawn, Ushijima plunged the blade deep into his belly. Barely had the samurai shout escaped from his throat when the razor-sharp sword beheaded him. As the corpse lurched forward onto the sheet, Cho performed the same ritual, and was himself done in by another flash of steel. With that last honorable duty to their emperor done, both spirits would be immortalized at Yasukuni Shrine.

Mine too, thought Tokuda. As soon as they set me free from this accursed camp.

He wished he had his *daisho*.

His samurai swords.

Both had been with him when corkscrew and blowtorch had burned him alive.

And when he'd come to, both were gone.

*   *   *

"Lookee, lookee. Come see me."

The jarhead strutted back and forth on the other side of the barbed-wire fence, a pair of samurai swords stuck through his belt.

The Marine taunted, "Tokyo Kid say . . ."

> *Yank play poker*
> *Hand win swords*
> *That make Jappy*
> *So-o-o-o unhappy.*

Tokuda recognized both swords as his own.

"Got another cartoon for you," gloated the Yank. He spiked a grim photograph onto the barbed wire, pinning it to the perimeter of the POW camp. The snapshot, taken by U.S. forces, showed the dead bodies of Ushijima and Cho with what appeared to be blood at their temples.

"Japansies," the picador jabbed. "They violated the samurai code. The cowards shot themselves because they didn't have the guts to take it like men."

"Lie!" Tokuda spat in Japanese. "You faked that to demean their families!"

"Sorry to say, Monkey Man, but we gotta part ways. They're shipping me out to Ginza for the occupation. I don't know your name, but I want you to know mine. So if your kids ever ask you, you'll be able to tell 'em, 'The Marine who whupped my yellow ass in the Pacific War was Lance Corporal Eugene Kerr.' "

The jarhead turned away, but then turned back.

"Nice cutlery. I'll take good care of it. I'll use it in my backyard to pick up dog shit."

So now he had a reason to live, instead of a reason to die. The thought of his father's *daisho* being dishonored like that shamed Tokuda to the core.

With the signing of Japan's surrender aboard the USS *Missouri* on September 2, Japanese soldiers not wanted for war crimes were released from confinement. Nameless and with half his face scarred beyond recognition, Genjo Tokuda was sprung from that U.S. prisoner-of-war camp. He made his way to the bombed-out Ginza district, where he struck a deal with the tattered remnants of the local yakuza for help in regaining his honor. If they would locate Lance Corporal Eugene Kerr for him and aid in the recovery of his father's *daisho*, he would kill any five men they wished executed as payment.

What was there to lose?

Before long, a thug known to his gang mates as the Claw reported that they had found Kerr. In the company of Tokuda, the yakuza waylaid the Yank in an alley one night as he staggered drunkenly home from a poker game. The samurai burgled his digs to recover Tokuda's swords. The next morning, MPs found Kerr's body, but they never found his head, which had been cleanly sliced from his shoulders by the sweep of a razor-sharp blade. They did, however, find his eyes, which had been clawed out before his death and left to stare up from the filth on the alley stones.

Every year, on the anniversary of his corkscrew-and-blowtorch disfigurement in the Battle of Okinawa, Genjo Tokuda sipped sake in honor of his family from a bowl mounted in the jarhead's skull.

Jarhead.

What a fitting description.

The Kamloops Kid wasn't as lucky.

As Genjo Tokuda tightened his grip on the Tokyo yakuza, turning the black market into a profitable endeavor, he kept track of the fate of his former Hong Kong cohort. For beating Canadian prisoners to death, Sergeant Inouye was tried and found guilty of war crimes. At first, his Canadian citizenship saved him. That conviction was overturned because Canada couldn't try a Canadian for war crimes. But eventually, his Canadian citizenship doomed him. The Kamloops Kid was tried and convicted of treason, and in 1947, he was hanged at Stanley Prison.

With time, Tokuda sensed he was safe from prosecution. America needed Japan as an ally in the Cold War, and in 1948, Truman granted amnesty to all Japanese soldiers not already imprisoned for war crimes. His past a dead issue, Tokuda revived his real name.

Over the years, he occasionally recalled the pretty Canadian nurse he'd won in a card game and raped at St. Stephen's during the fall of Hong Kong. Magnanimously, he had let her live while so many others died, and he wondered what had become of her in the post-war years.

With the emergence of his unknown son, that question had been answered.

A man's reach should exceed his grasp, Tokuda had read somewhere; so he had thought just weeks ago that dissatisfaction would be his fate. True, he was one of Japan's richest titans. But what was fortune to an old man with no family to inherit his wealth? The Pacific War had wiped out his family tree, and the wounds he'd suffered on Okinawa had left him a eunuch. True, he had forged his yakuza hoods into a force to be feared. But after his retirement, that strength had turned to flab. Gone were the days when a samurai would spill his guts for *bushido*—as the author Yukio Mishima had in 1970—and in place of honor came street punks with no moral ethics, like that "Japansy" he'd had beheaded for missing the Stanley Park meeting. True, he had used the yakuza to wreak vengeance on America, by flooding its youth with speed and sapping its economy. But that wasn't *personal* vengeance against the *actual* killers who had slaughtered his family and dishonored their Shinto shrine.

Now, however, he was standing on his pinnacle overlooking Vancouver, sword in hand, as those who had once seemed out of reach were finally drawing closer to his bony grasp.

Tokuda had a son.

Sired by the rape of that nurse.

A son who was morally fit to inherit his father's earthly wealth.

A son who desired to live by the code of *bushido*.

A son who yearned to become a twenty-first-century samurai.

A son who wasn't afraid to worship at the Yasukuni Shrine, where Japan's 2.5 million war dead—including those so-called war criminals executed by the occupiers—were honored as deities.

A son who, even as Genjo Tokuda slashed at the city with his samurai sword, was down there in that spread of glittering lights, hunting for the bait that would hook one of the *actual* killers of their ancestral family. An American killer who was fated to suffer the same excruciating pain he had once inflicted on this vengeful *kumicho*.

Slash . . .

Slash . . .

Slash . . .

Special 0

"Cascade Consulting," read the sign out front of a nondescript building in the Mayfair Industrial Park, just this side of the Forensic Psychiatric Hospital at Colony Farm. Cascade Consulting's business was nebulous, but whatever it was, it required cars to come and go all night. Luckily, the building was situated next to the Trans-Canada Highway, on the north bank of the Fraser River. So wherever the cars were coming from and going to at such ungodly hours, the reps had several routes to choose from.

Question?

What did Cascade Consulting do?

If a door-to-door salesman walked in off the street, he'd be met by a receptionist skilled at thinking on her feet. She might call the boss out for backup, and he would then say, "We don't need photocopy supplies at the moment," or whatever was necessary to get rid of the salesman. If you asked a local cop what Cascade was all about, you'd be met with a shrug. That's because the building was on a jurisdiction line between two forces, and anything near a boundary gets less police attention. What's more, when cheap patrolmen wandered in to ask, "Any chance cops get half price here?" they were advised that the business was strictly client-based.

Whatever that meant.

In fact, there was only one way to pierce the veil, and that was to do what this cop was doing now. At four o'clock in the morning, before the break of day would smudge the horizon, he wheeled his aging Mercedes-Benz into the parking lot, climbed out, crossed to the building, pulled open the door, and said to the night guard at the desk, "DeClercq. Special X. Here to see Oscar."

"ID?" the guard asked.

The chief superintendent flashed his bison-head badge.

"Oscar's waiting."

The guard buzzed him in.

For reasons that no one can now recall, "Oscar" is the in-house name for Special O. That's "O" as in "observation," the physical surveillance trackers of the RCMP. Special O is so secretive that it might as well not exist. Oscar is "offside" to other officers because it also investigates for the anti-corruption unit of Internal Affairs. Only the brass—the so-called white shirts—know where Oscar has its office.

White shirts like DeClercq.

The cop who greeted him inside the door to the inner sanctum was Corporal Nick Craven. Blond-haired, blue-eyed, and in his mid-thirties, Nick had once worked at Special X, but he later abandoned urban life to police the rural Gulf Islands. "Be careful what you wish for," the Chinese say, and so it had been with Craven's dream of idyllic country policing. Out in the wilds, he had run afoul of a psychopath named Mephisto, and that rotten luck had cost him an ear and one of his hands. Disillusioned, Nick had recently returned to the city, where he had taken a posting with Special O.

"Is everyone here?" DeClercq asked.

"Roger. I called in the old guys. Who knows how many years in O are gathered in this room."

"Good. This will be dicey, so experience will count."

Craven led DeClercq to the front of the war room. Although coffee was being guzzled by the gallon, the faces before them were still as puffed and red-eyed as you'd expect in a team that had been rousted from sleep and told to muster fast. There was no mystery about why they were here. Anyone who had to ask would not be in Oscar. Many of the faces were non-white, for it was an asset in O *not* to look like the stereotypical Mountie.

O's job was to blindside the bad guys.

"You know who I am," the chief said, "so let's get down to work. Two days ago, a gang of thugs flew in from Japan. One was the hood of hoods in Tokyo's yakuza."

DeClercq withdrew several blown-up passport photos from his carryall and began pinning them on a spread of corkboard that mimicked his Strategy Wall.

"Genjo Tokuda, the godfather. In his eighties. He looks like Two-Face in a *Batman* movie."

The next tough had an ugly facial mole.

"This one's the Claw. Tokuda's enforcer. He gets that nickname from his penchant for gouging out eyes. There have been several Claws over the years."

Soon, a rogues' gallery lined the wall.

"No criminal records, and we all know why. Japan's economic bubble burst under the squeeze of corruption. And now Tokuda has his tentacles in here."

"Why?" asked a watcher.

"I don't know. Tokuda's the right age to have been embroiled in the Second World War. It's possible he's here for some kind of revenge. Last evening, a kamikaze plane slammed into a Pacific vets' convention, and indications are that Tokuda's to blame. Old men his age obsess over tying up loose ends."

"Where do we find him?"

"There's the rub," said DeClercq. "The Japanese planted a bug in his bags before he left Tokyo. They told us, *after* the gang had arrived, and provided a GPS device to track the bug. The luggage went to a hotel, but the thugs who brought it did not. They vanished and are probably holed up in safe houses."

"A bug scanner?" Craven said.

"That's most likely how they found it. We initially assumed they had come here for business reasons—money laundering, drugs, human trafficking—so we didn't think a clock was ticking. When they disappeared, we began to think we might be wrong. Since then, we've been trying to pick up their trail before calling Oscar."

The clock on the wall threw seconds into the room.

"As it turned out, a clock *was* ticking, and last night the bomb went off as a kamikaze run. So now I need Oscar's help to *find* them as well as track them."

"They'll be armed," someone said.

"We'll need an ERT package."

"The call's already gone out, Chief," Craven replied.

If ever there was a throwback to the last frontier, it was Sgt. Ed "Mad Dog" Rabidowski. As the son of a Yukon trapper, he could take the eye out of a squirrel with a .22 at one hundred feet before he was six. Now when he went hunting on his days off, it was for elk on Pink Mountain or grizzly bears at Kakwa River. On days at work in the city, he hunted for bigger game, like punks threatening standoffs against the emergency response team. In this age of modern redcoats recruited from universities, the Mad Dog harked back to that era when hard-knuckled, sharp-shooting action men policed the wilderness from the vantage point of a saddle. With jet black hair and eyebrows, a droopy mustache, and a permanent scowl, he was the cop DeClercq used to answer the age-old question, "What does the rational man do when confronted by the barbarian?"

He fights fire with fire.

He unleashes the Mad Dog.

Before the phone had finished its first ring, Rabidowski was wide awake.

"Uh-huh?" he grunted into the receiver, hoping not to disturb his sleeping wife.

Having listened to the caller, he swung out of bed, wrapped a robe around his muscular frame, and padded off down the hall to the guest bedroom. The second the door cracked open, Ghost Keeper snapped awake too. Yesterday, they had decided they would take the Cree's birthday gift— the SIG nine mil—to the range for an early morning shoot, so he had bedded down here.

"Shoot's off," the sergeant said. "That plane that crashed into the pier? Oscar just called, requesting an ERT package. Time to mount up."

Robert DeClercq made a point of never—repeat *never*—eating breakfast in a joint that wasn't one of a kind. He was making a valiant last stand against franchising, a battle that was about as winnable as Custer's last stand. At least he knew that he wouldn't be served rubber eggs or that slop they make with synthetic stuff. He was at an age when he viewed life as too short not to demand the little joys of existence, like food that a chef cooked *just for you*.

Call him a rebel.

"Thanks for meeting me so early."

"I'm an early riser," said Yamada, the diplomat who had warned Special X that Genjo Tokuda had brought his gang to Vancouver.

Despite its unappetizing name, the Greasy Spoon was DeClercq's favorite morning eatery. It was a typical mom-and-pop establishment, except that mom and pop were a pair of gay men. Pop—he was actually dubbed that—whipped up gourmet fare in the kitchen while Mom—he was dubbed that too—worked the front room, berating diners who didn't eat every scrap on their plates. Politically correct the Greasy Spoon wasn't; instead, it offered a flamboyant shtick that worked all the way to the bank. Even at this early hour, "the Spoon" was packed.

"You didn't bring your 'sister'?" asked DeClercq.

"She's at the consulate, waiting for instructions. The message you left with our answering service said that you require a new memorandum of understanding from Tokyo, ASAP."

"I do."

"So she's ready to process it."

"Hello, handsome," said Mom, sashaying up to the table as fey as could be. "And who's this sexy bugger? In case you want to know, I get off at three."

"That's soliciting."

"So what'll you have?"

"The blueberry pancake."

"Oooo, sidestep the question." Mom rolled his eyes.

"Pancake?" said Yamada.

"They're huge," cautioned DeClercq.

"How huge?"

"This huge," interjected Mom, reaching down to give DeClercq's waist a gentle pinch. "You have to pass a chub test before I'm allowed to place the order."

"Don't order the breakfast sausage," warned the chief.

"You're testing me, aren't you?" said Yamada.

"How so?" asked DeClercq.

"Choosing this place for breakfast."

"It serves the best eye-opener in town, and we both have to eat."

"You think I'm a buttoned-down diplomat with Japan's obsessive-compulsive focus on cleanliness."

"You won't find a restaurant cleaner than this."

"It's run by gays, and gays help make up its clientele."

"So?"

"So you wonder if I'll be afraid of the cutlery. Or worried about the health of the chef."

"That would be Machiavellian. Why would I do that?"

"For the same reason I called Lynda West my sister when we met in your office the other day."

"Your *half*-sister," said DeClercq.

"I was testing your reaction. Your gullibility."

"To see if I was a flat-foot who would dismiss it as beyond the realm of possibility? Your father was an American occupier posted to Japan. So was Lynda West's. But what are the chances of one man fathering both a mixed-race diplomat and a white woman who end up working in the same consulate?"

"Not too slim?"

"No," said DeClercq. "It's not impossible for

that to be the reality behind your so-called joke. Before dismissing it, I'd need to know if there were facts you were hiding from me."

Yamada bowed slightly. "But why test you?" the diplomat asked.

"To see if I'm sharp enough to deal with Tokuda."

"And why test me?"

"To see how diplomatic you are. How expedient. To test if you're Machiavellian enough to help me deal with Tokuda."

Yamada bowed again.

"We see eye to eye, Chief Superintendent. This restaurant reflects the real world, not some germ neurosis. So you will see me eat breakfast as heartily as you."

"That's diplomatic."

"And expedient."

"Because the Special External Section handles all cases with links outside this country, political wrangling is a major part of my job. When something goes wrong, there's always finger pointing, so memorandums of understanding are how I cover my ass."

"Of course. MOUs are shields."

"I have an MOU from you that covers the GPS tracker. Japan's jurisdiction over it ends at Canada's border, but technically, this was still a Japanese intelligence file. In a run-of-the-mill case, we'd have tracked Tokuda on the sly until he left Canada, and he would never have known that we were on his tail."

"*Was* a Japanese intelligence file?" Yamada picked up the hint.

"Tokuda came here to smash that kamikaze plane into our convention center last night. That turns the case into a Canadian criminal investigation, and given that it's the yakuza that Special X is up against, Japanese nationals will be in the line of fire. I need a new memorandum to cover my ass."

"How broad an understanding?" asked the diplomat.

"Carte blanche from Tokyo to deal with Genjo Tokuda in any way I see fit."

Crowded Womb

In the hours before the sun came up, Lyn Barrow thought back to dialogues she'd had with her half-brother.

"How did that happen?" her brother had asked.

"Good question," Lyn replied.

"I thought we were brother and sister, born a year apart."

"So did I."

"But we're actually *twins*?"

"That's what Mom told me," said Lyn.

"I assumed that she'd had sex with some Asian guy just before the fall of Hong Kong. Then I was born in Stanley Internment Camp, after she was captured."

"And I assumed that she'd had sex with some

British prisoner while in Stanley Camp, and as a consequence, I was born in captivity a year or so after you."

"What's your first memory of me?"

"I can't recall," said Lyn. "You were always just *there*. I thought you were my sister."

"I hated that!"

"What? Being dressed in girl's clothes?"

"Yes."

"Be thankful. That's probably why you're alive. Had the others in camp known you were the son of a Japanese soldier, you might've been killed and eaten for revenge."

"You're joking!"

"That's what every mother feared would happen to her kid. And if it came to that—cannibalism to keep from starving to death—who better to consume first than the Japanese boy?"

"Mom told you that?"

"Yes. That's why she started the rumor that you were her illegitimate daughter by a Chinese lover. Many called her a whore, but it kept you alive. Girls have lower status in the Far East. And whites can't tell the nationality of an Asian face."

"You were Mom's favorite. She didn't want me. That's why she's confiding in you."

"She's dying," said Lyn. "It's the drugs. Morphine has her revealing stuff that she's kept locked inside."

"Like what?"

"Mom finally told me the name of my dad. He wasn't a captive in Stanley Camp. He was a British officer in the hospital where she nursed."

"What was his name?"

"Captain Richard Walker. They had sex in a closet that Christmas morning, just before the Japanese stormed the building."

"What happened to him?"

"He was killed by one of the Japanese soldiers. He was bayoneted in front of Mom."

"No wonder she's crazy."

"Don't say that!"

"Face it, Lyn. Can you remember a time when she wasn't in and out of the loony bin?"

"You hold that against her?"

"Sure I do. You weren't the one they abused in that foster home after the war. *I* was the Jap, remember? The one the old guy burned with his cigarette. The one the old lady locked in the crawlspace under the stairs. You heard me screaming. Alone and scared to death. We'd never have gone into foster care if Mom weren't nuts."

"You wouldn't blame her as much if you knew the whole truth."

"Which is?"

Lyn struggled with the pros and cons of revealing what Viv had told her.

"What?" pressed her brother.

"Mom was raped."

"*Raped!*"

Lyn nodded sadly. "That same morning—Christmas. At St. Stephen's. And the man who raped her was the Japanese soldier who bayoneted my dad."

"You mean . . . ?"

"Yes. Mom was raped by *your* father. We were both conceived on Christmas Day, during the fall of Hong Kong."

"How is that possible?"

"Apparently, it's not that uncommon," Lyn said. "There are several cases documented on the Internet. In a normal single birth, an egg from the mother is fertilized by a sperm from the father to create an embryo that travels down the oviduct and lodges in the womb. That single cell then develops into a baby.

"With fraternal twins, two eggs from the mother's ovaries are fertilized by two sperms from the father to gestate two embryos. Unlike identical twins, which develop when a single cell splits in two, fraternal twins have different DNA. Identical twins are always of the same sex. Fraternal twins can be brothers, sisters, or one of each, like us."

"I'd say we're more different than most."

"Of course," said Lyn. "Because ours was a crowded womb. Mom released two eggs in the way that usually results in twins. But one egg was fertilized by a sperm from my dad—Captain Richard Walker—while the other was fertilized by a sperm from your dad—the Japanese soldier who raped her."

"Did Mom tell you his name?"

"Yes. Corporal Tokuda. She heard another Japanese soldier call him that when the corporal used his samurai sword to decapitate a baseball player."

"*Decapitate!* Are you saying my father was a war criminal?"

"I'm just telling you what Mom said."

"Did she know anything else about Tokuda?"

"Just the name of his sword. The other soldier—those imprisoned in Stanley Camp called him the Kamloops Kid—told the captives that if anyone tried to escape, Corporal Tokuda would return to the camp and hack off their heads with his sword, Kamikaze."

* * *

That first exchange, Lyn now recalled, had led to a second one.

"I found him," her brother had said a week or two later, waving a page of scribbled notes in his hand.

"Who?" Lyn asked.

"Corporal Tokuda."

"How?" she inquired.

"Through British colonial records. After Hong Kong fell in 1941, government bureaucrats interned in Stanley Camp began keeping detailed statistics on births. Twenty-two babies were born in 1942, about twenty of whom were conceived before the Japanese attack. Ten were born in 1943. Thirteen in 1944. And six up to August 1945."

"There's a record of you?"

"Yes. That many births worried both the British and the Japanese. More mouths to feed, and more pressure on limited accommodations. In October 1943, the Japanese threatened to segregate males from females if there were any more births."

"Sex in the camp disturbed them?"

"Marital sex was okay. What bothered the Japanese command was promiscuity."

"Why 1943 and not before?"

"Women were giving birth to babies when their husbands weren't in Stanley Camp."

"So the Japanese did the math?"

Her brother nodded. "Guess what they did to stop it? The commandant decided that any woman who didn't register the name of her child's father would work as a prostitute."

"That's incentive."

"I'll say. Fail to register my dad, and Mom would have had to bed all the Japanese troops."

"So she named Corporal Tokuda?"

"After that information was passed to the Japanese forces, they must have given the British registrar Tokuda's first name, since it's penciled into the camp's birth records."

"What was his first name?"

"Genjo."

"How did you find this out?" Lyn asked.

"I queried Britain's Public Record Office, and they checked their War Office and Colonial Office papers. Then I went looking for a Genjo Tokuda on the Internet."

"And found him?"

"Most likely. A Genjo Tokuda was in the Japanese Imperial Army in Hong Kong in 1941. After the war, he lived under another name until the occupiers declared an amnesty for war criminals. By then, he was active in the Tokyo yakuza."

"He's a gangster!"

"Not anymore. He's in his eighties."

"You're not thinking of contacting him, are you?"

"I have to, Lyn. I want to know who I am. I feel like I've lived my entire life in no man's land. How often have I heard you complain about not knowing your father? If you knew he was alive, wouldn't you feel compelled to seek him out?"

"Not if he was a gangster. What if he doesn't believe you're his son? That's a good way to get yourself killed."

"I'll be careful. He lives in a tower above his old headquarters in Tokyo. I'll write and offer a blood sample so he can test my DNA."

But things hadn't gone according to plan. Just days ago, her brother told her that his father hadn't shown for a meeting he'd set.

"I thought he'd at least fly someone in to collect the sample of my blood. According to what I've read, he doesn't have an heir. Chances are that I'm his son. How could he not care?"

Her brother was downcast. "Rejected by Mom. Rejected by Dad. At least I'm not rejected by you."

"We've been through a lot together, and you've always been there for me."

"I love you, Lyn."

"And I love you. Forget about Tokuda."

But he hadn't forgotten. While their mother lay dying in the hospital, he'd tried again to make contact with his father. And that second time, he'd succeeded. Tokuda had come to Vancouver, and earlier tonight, father and son had finally met. What the gangster and her brother had talked about was a mystery to Lyn. For the first time since they were children, he was keeping secrets from her. But that was okay with her, because she had a secret of her own.

Lyn knew how her brother's mind worked. He had an obsessive need to understand who he was and where he came from, and she had used that to achieve her own ends. She'd told her brother his father's name because she knew he'd go to the ends of the earth to find him. And he hadn't disappointed her. He'd saved her the work of tracking her quarry, and had even brought the prey right into her backyard. Now all she had to do was strike.

Their mom was dead.

Her rapist—and the killer of Lyn's dad—was in Vancouver.

He was the cause of all her family's suffering.

Her mother's insanity.

Her brother's abuse in foster care.

And *her* own wretched life, which had been spent shouldering the burden of both their ordeals.

"Will you see him again?" she'd asked her brother.

"Lyn, I'm going with him to Japan. I want to learn the code of *bushido*—the way things used to be—and he's going to teach me."

"Don't be absurd!"

"Oh, I'm deadly serious. My father is a samurai, the last of his kind. I want to learn everything I can from him before it's too late. You know, all my life, I've felt as if I were shit on someone's shoe," he explained. "But no longer. I'm going back to a time when men were *men* and people lived with honor."

"And when is all this meant to happen?"

"Tomorrow." He shrugged. "I don't want to waste any more time before I can *prove* to my father that I'm fit to be his son."

Good, thought Lyn.

Today it will be.

I'll use my brother as a Trojan horse and sneak right past the men guarding Tokuda.

The Big Bang

Tinian, Mariana Islands
August 6, 1945

The crewmen of this huge plane didn't realize it, but they were about to change the world in what would soon be one of history's three most famous aircraft, behind the *Kitty Hawk* and the *Spirit of St. Louis*.

"Tower to Dimples Eight-two. Clear for take-off."

At 2:45 a.m., Colonel Paul Tibbets thrust four throttles forward and sent the sixty-five-ton *Enola Gay* down Runway A at the world's largest airfield. Fire trucks and ambulances were parked every fifty feet along both sides of the airstrip, ready to respond if something went wrong. With twelve men, seven thousand gallons of fuel, and a single five-ton bomb onboard, the lumbering machine carried an overload of fifteen thousand pounds. If something did go wrong, there'd be hell to pay.

The runway ended at a cliff, where the ground gave way to black sea. The men were heading for Iwo Jima, over six hundred miles and three hours away. In the spacious area behind the cockpit, Sergeant Joe Hett was busily at work, as were the navigator, the radioman, and the flight engineer. Back of them, just below the long, padded tunnel that ran over the bomb bay, linking the front and rear compartments, there was a round, airtight door that accessed "Little Boy."

Like the others, Joe wore a survival vest with fishhooks, a drinking-water kit, a first-aid package, and emergency food rations. A parachute harness with clips for both his chest chute and a one-man life raft were cinched over green overalls and covered by a flak suit that would provide protection against shrapnel. Strapped to his waist was a Colt .45. His only identification was the dog tags around his neck.

As a precaution, Col. Tibbets also carried a small metal box with twelve capsules of cyanide.

At the first sign of trouble, he would hand them out so that each man—should he find himself on the verge of capture—could choose between the lethal poison and a bullet to his brain. The other alternative was no alternative at all. When they saw the bomb aboard the *Enola Gay*, the Japs would be determined to learn its secret, by whatever means necessary.

But that secret was something even the crew didn't know.

That something big was up was obvious. On December 17, 1944—the forty-first anniversary of the Wright brothers' first *Kitty Hawk* flight—the 509th Bomb Group had been assigned, under Tibbets's command, to fly special single-bomb B-29s. But only Tibbets knew why. High-altitude drops were practiced back home in the States until the group was deployed to Tinian, an island in the Pacific. Before long, the 509th had become the butt of jokes and the object of sneers by other fliers, who gave the crews a hard time because of their lack of combat blooding.

Finally, General Curtis LeMay—old "Iron Ass" himself—had issued the order for Special Bombing Mission No. 13. "The bomb you're going to drop is something new in the history of warfare," the men had been told. "It is the most destructive weapon ever produced. No one knows exactly what will happen when the bomb is dropped from the air. That has never been done before." At midnight on August 6, they had gathered in the crew lounge at the Tinian airfield. Declaring that the weapon they were about to deliver had the potential to end the war, Tibbets had said, "Do your jobs. Obey your orders. Don't cut corners or take chances."

Then a truck had driven them to the *Enola Gay*.

Joe's first impression when he saw the scene at the runway was that he was Clark Gable at the Atlanta premiere of *Gone with the Wind*. The plane was lit up by klieg lights and mobile generators, and a crowd of about a hundred—including reporters and film crews—milled around the bomber. Had the MGM lion stuck its head out of the cockpit and let loose a roar, Joe would not have blinked.

"This way!"

"Smile!"

"Look serious!"

"Look busy!"

Reporters shouted as flashbulbs burst in the already blinding glare. Then, after one more group photo, Tibbets had shut down the carnival with a simple order to his bombing crew: "Okay, let's go to work."

One by one, the men had clambered up the ladder to the hatch behind the *Enola Gay*'s nose wheel, and now all were en route to hit Japan.

With what kind of bomb? Joe wondered.

As the plane burrowed through the inky night, Tibbets gave the tail gunner permission to test his weapons. The gunner had a thousand rounds to defend the bomber against attack. He fired off fifty shots in a jarring burst, filling the fuselage with the rattling noise of war and his turret with the stench of cordite and burnt oil. The tracers arced into the sea.

"Judge going to work," Tibbets radioed back to Tinian's tower at 3:00 a.m.

As agreed, the tower didn't respond.

Time for the explosives expert to arm the bomb. There had been too many B-29 crashes at the airfield to chance detonating the weapon on takeoff. But now that they were safely in the air, the expert could get to work. He swung open the circular door and, followed closely by his assistant, lowered himself through the hatch that fed into the bomb bay.

Curious, Joe left his battle station and stuck his

head into the hole to watch this critical stage of the mission. The "gimmick"—a term used for the bomb—was clamped to a special hook and dangled over the long doors of the bay. The bomb was about ten feet long and twenty-eight inches in diameter. Four thick cables like umbilical cords ran from it to a control panel in the area aft of the cockpit, where the ordnance man could monitor the "gimmick" like a doctor does a woman in labor.

With their backs to the open hatch, the demolitions team looked like a pair of mechanics working on a car. The ordnance man stood ready to pass tools to the explosives expert while he carefully placed gunpowder and an electrical detonator into the open casing. Then, after sixteen turns had tightened the breech plate, he sealed the armor, and Little Boy was armed. That's when Joe noticed the antennae sticking out of the nose.

What were they for?

Before the two men climbed out of the hold to check the circuits on the monitoring console, the beam of the flashlight swept forward into the dark of the bay. In Joe's imagination, he saw this torpedo-like "fish" streaking through the water in Pearl Harbor, a moment before it slammed into the guts of a battleship.

Then he recalled that *Life* photo of him—outrage flashing in his eyes—shooting up at the Zero as it skimmed over Hickam Field. He knew that day had—relentlessly, inevitably—brought him to this one.

He couldn't put it any better than "Iron Ass" LeMay, the man in charge of this mission, who'd said:

"We're going to bomb them back into the Stone Age."

Half an hour before the plane was scheduled to reach Iwo Jima, at 5:52 a.m., Tibbets unstrapped himself from the pilot's seat, handed the controls to his co-pilot, and went back to spend a few moments with each of the crew. When he got to Joe's station, the elevators gave a distinct kick to the *Enola Gay* as "George," the automatic pilot, began to fly the bomber.

"Red, have you figured out what we're doing this morning?"

"Colonel, I don't want to get put up against a wall and shot," Joe replied jokingly, referring to the unwritten commandment that the crew keep their mouths shut.

"We're on our way now. You can talk."

Joe knew that the plane was carrying some sort

of new superexplosive. "Are we hauling a chemist's nightmare?" he asked.

"No, not exactly."

"How 'bout a physicist's nightmare?"

"Yes," Tibbets confirmed.

Joe recalled a phrase he'd once read—though with little idea what it meant—in a popular science journal. "Just a question, Colonel," he said now. "Are we splitting atoms?"

Without responding, Tibbets returned to the cockpit. Switching off "George," the pilot began the climb to nine thousand feet, the altitude at which the *Enola Gay* would rendezvous with two Superfortresses, the *Great Artiste* and *No. 91*. Outside the cockpit, to the east, a waning moon appeared in the banks of cloud. Ahead, the sky was deep blue with cirrus wisps as night gave way to dawn. By the time the bombers met up over the porkchop-shaped island of Iwo Jima, the world was an iridescent pink.

With the *Enola Gay* in the lead, the three B-29s formed a loose V heading up the "Hirohito Highway" to Japan.

It was 5:05 a.m., Japanese time.

An hour and a half later, the ordnance man again swung down into the bomb bay to unscrew three green plugs in the middle of the weapon and replace them with red ones.

Tibbets used the intercom to address the crew.

"We are carrying the world's first atomic bomb," he said, using the word "atomic" for the first time.

Several men gasped.

One let out a long, low whistle.

"When the bomb is dropped, we'll record our reactions to what we see. This recording is for history. Watch your language, and don't clutter up the intercom."

Dead air hung in the fuselage, then Tibbets came back on.

"Red, you were right. We *are* splitting atoms."

"It's Hiroshima," the colonel announced after hearing the weather report. The *Straight Flush*, one of three weather scouts patrolling over different cities, had gazed down on Hiroshima from six miles up through a gap ten miles wide in the clouds. Sunlight shone through the hole like a spotlight, as if to say of the target, "Here it is!"

Fifty miles out from ground zero—the Aioi Bridge—the world's first atomic bomber was lined up to drop its deadly cargo.

In the nose, the bombardier leaned forward against the headrest that had been specially designed for this drop.

"IP." Initial point, the navigator reported.

"On glasses," Tibbets ordered through the intercom.

The crewmen had Polaroid goggles like those worn by welders, and they knew that the knob at the bridge of the nose should be turned to the setting that let in the least amount of light. By slipping them on, nine of the twelve were plunged into darkness. The pilot, the bombardier, and the radar monitor still had work to do. Before putting his goggles on, the airman who was keeping a log of the mission scrawled, "There will be a short intermission while we bomb our target."

Thirty seconds to go.

"Hiroshima coming into view!" shouted the bombardier.

"Stand by for the tone break—and the turn," warned Tibbets.

Eyes glued to his viewfinder, the bombardier spied dark buildings hunkered down on the fingers of land that reached into the deep blue of Hiroshima Bay. The six forks of the Ota River flowed brown and muddy. Roads across the city were metallic gray. A gossamer haze shimmered over the 300,000 souls below, but the bombardier could still make out the T-shaped Aioi Bridge as it moved inexorably into the crosshairs of his bombsight.

"I've got it!" he yelled.

He turned on the tone signal that filled the ears of the crew with a low-pitched, continuous hum, telling them that the B-29 had entered the automatic synchronization of the final fifteen seconds of the bombing run.

At eight-fifteen, the bay doors snapped open and Little Boy dropped from its hook. When the umbilical cords ripped away, the tone signal in the plane was instantly killed. The abrupt lightening of the bomber bounced it ten feet up in the air.

"Bomb away!" came the shout from the nose as Tibbets swung the *Enola Gay* into a steep, right-hand power dive to hightail it out of there before all hell broke loose.

Forsaking his bombsight, the bombardier gazed down through the Plexiglas to watch Little Boy drop. The gimmick wobbled a bit until it picked up speed, then it vanished earthbound with a sonic shriek.

Inside the gadget, a timer tripped a switch. Juice zapped from the batteries toward the detonator.

At five thousand feet above Hiroshima, a barometric, height-detecting switch activated a small radar set. Its transmitter bounced radio waves from the ground to the strange antennae that Joe had noticed on the bomb. The radar readings flipped the final switch in the chain at just under two thousand feet above the city, closing the circuit that sent electricity to the detonator.

Bang!

Forty-three seconds after the drop and almost six miles down from the *Enola Gay*, the bomb's detonator ignited the explosive powder in its casing. That blast propelled a five-pound atomic "bullet" of uranium 235 along the six-foot barrel of an internal cannon, where it rammed into the "target," a seventeen-pound hunk of uranium 235 fixed to the muzzle, to produce "crit," critical mass.

BWAMMMMMMMM!

This atomic explosion!

Seen from the bomber, the brilliant dot of purplish-red light above Hiroshima might have been the Big Bang that created today's ever-expanding universe. God only knew how many people were fried in the next few seconds, as a searing fireball blasted out for miles. Like an overexposed photograph, the sky was filled with a bright white light. Inside the plane, the crew members were protected by their dark goggles. As near as Joe could tell, Hiroshima had ceased to exist.

Joe could *taste* the intensity.

It tasted like lead.

In place of the city, the crew got a glimpse of hell. Firestorms raged across the land, and a gigantic, funnel-like column of air—a physical manifestation of the explosion itself—rose up at the speed of sound. Its core was hellfire red. The smoke was purplish gray. Someone yelled something unintelligible, and the *Enola Gay* was slammed by the ear-splitting din that shells make when they blow right beside you.

"Flak!"

"The sons of bitches are shooting at us!"

"There's another one coming!"

As the intercom was overwhelmed by pandemonium, a few of the crew were thrown from their seats in a bone-jarring crash. Whatever had hit them a moment ago now hit them again, bucking the bomber up from its flight path.

"That wasn't flak. Stay calm," Tibbets announced. "That was the shock wave bouncing back from the ground. There won't be any more. Let's get our recordings going."

Eleven miles from Hiroshima, the Superfortress

began to orbit the devastated city. As the men waited to express their thoughts for posterity, they peered out at a huge mushroom cloud. The monstrous black plume was shot through with flames, the head billowing out for miles as it roiled up past the *Enola Gay* at thirty thousand feet and continued to rise.

"My God," someone whispered. "What have we done?"

Stunner

This isn't happening to me! How dare someone do this to Dad! Let me get my hands on him for five minutes! Life will be gray without Dad in it! Wrong place, wrong time! That's how it is! Denial, anger, bargaining, depression, acceptance: the five stages of grief were colliding in Jackie's battered heart and mind like boxcars slamming each other in the midst of a train wreck.

Her initial concern had been Joe. He didn't look well. Though he tried to put on the brave face of his generation—the Depression and the war steeled men like Joe to overwhelming loss—the health problems of an old man undermined his will. She and her granddad had leaned on each other for support through the midnight hours, but soon it was obvious to Jackie that Joe was struggling to shore up his crumbling front for her sake.

"Red?" she said as they drove away from Special X.

"Uh?"

"Your face suits your name."

"It's my blood pressure."

"You need sleep. I don't want you having a heart attack or a stroke on me."

"I need my pills."

"Where are they?"

"Back in the hotel room."

"Let's go get 'em. Then I'll take you home with me. Unless you'd rather be alone?"

"Would you?"

"To be honest, yes. I feel a desperate need to run. If I don't work this tension out, I'll explode."

"Go do what you gotta do."

So having dropped her granddad off at the hotel, after extracting a promise that he'd take something to help him sleep, Jackie went home, changed into her running gear, then drove Dane's car to the North Shore and parked in a cross street that ended at the seawall. Along False Creek, or around Stanley Park, or here at the foot of the mountains, this city had a multitude of oceanside walks.

From Dundarave Pier, Jackie began jogging east with the wind at her back. The tide was high and waves were crashing over the stone wall, drenching her with spray if she timed the ebb and flow wrong. Within the hour, dawn would ignite the horizon, flushing the sky beyond the Lions Gate Bridge and the lonely cone of Mount Baker in Washington State.

Splash . . .

Splash . . .

Splash . . .

Puddles spewed out from her runners.

The surest way to keep her emotions under control was to concentrate on trying to make sense out of what had happened. That she was officially off the case was a certainty, for no one knew better than the chief how personal involvement in a murder could cloud your judgment. DeClercq had run gauntlets like this when his first wife and his daughter were murdered, and again when his second wife got caught in crossfire. Having learned the hard way, he'd insist that Chuck's murder was investigated by cops with cold minds.

Still, she'd rather play the cop and try to do

something useful—like come up with a motive to pass on to Special X—than break down under emotional stress and cry her heart out for her dad.

Splash . . .

Splash . . .

Splash . . .

When she heard that a Japanese pilot had intentionally crashed a plane into the Canada Place convention center, Jackie's reaction was that of any North American in the post 9/11 world: "It's got to be terrorists."

But that thought had forced her to ask, "Why would Japanese terrorists attack Vancouver?"

Japan, to her mind, wasn't a hotbed of international terrorism. Of course, there had been that Sarin gas attack on Tokyo's subway system in 1995, when twelve people died and six thousand were injured. But that was an act of *domestic* terrorism by a religious cult trying to hasten the apocalypse. That sort of craziness could spawn in any country.

For a 9/11 parallel, you had to go back to 1972, the year three members of a terrorist cell called the Japanese Red Army landed at Tel Aviv's airport and opened up with machine guns on a group of Christian pilgrims to the Holy Land, killing twenty-five and wounding eighty.

Still, why Vancouver?

Sucking in deep breaths of ocean air as she ran through the tunnel of night, Jackie thought back to the headlines she'd read on the day after 9/11.

"Kamikaze Terrorist Attacks."

"Kamikaze Blitz on the U.S.A."

At the time, that was a forgivable connection to make. During the Pacific War, Americans had reacted with disbelief to the Japanese kamikaze attacks. Sure, they'd been raised on Nathan Hale—"I only regret that I have but one life to lose for my country"—but kamikazes actually *meant* it, and that scared the hell out of most Americans. So it was only natural to equate the human bombs of the Al-Qaeda attacks with the kamikazes of the past.

The similarities seemed striking.

Both the attackers of 9/11 and the kamikazes volunteered to sacrifice themselves for sacred beliefs. Both thought that they were inflicting divine punishment on their enemies. Both prepared themselves spiritually for the carnage to come. Both thought that their gods were watching over them, and that death had its own rewards. The Al-Qaeda crews were told to shout "Allah is great!" as they struck, for that's believed to incite terror in the hearts of infidels. And the kamikazes were told to yell *"Hissatsu!"* at warships as they crash-dived.

There was, however, a big difference.

The targets, Jackie thought now.

Splash . . .

Splash . . .

Splash . . .

At both Pearl Harbor and Okinawa, the Japanese had aimed their planes at military targets: the warships, airfields, and armed soldiers of their enemy. Sneak attacks have always been a legitimate tactic in war—fighting men refer to them as "the element of surprise"—so America had the wherewithal to defend itself.

Not so with 9/11.

That involved the indiscriminate massacre of civilians.

So what to make of this?

Here, the plane had slammed into a ship-shaped conference center hosting military vets from the Pacific Theater. Quasi-civilians, but vets at heart. So did that qualify as a terrorist attack?

It has to be a long-simmering grudge, thought Jackie.

A vendetta by a Japanese vet—or his relatives—with a wound still festering from the Pacific War.

A kamikaze attack required a plane.

Mud Bay Airport had poor security.

And her father—a Pacific vet himself—was simply in the wrong place at the wrong time.

Splash . . .

Splash . . .

Splash . . .

Ironically, the rising sun was just about to conquer the overcast horizon beyond the Lions Gate Bridge and the torpedoed convention center. Having reached Ambleside Park at the foot of Sentinel Hill, with Gill Macbeth's home at its crown, Jackie stopped running east and turned around. Across the water and against the distant lights of Point Grey, she glimpsed the black silhouette of Siwash Rock, just offshore from Stanley Park. Unlike the sandstone that had once surrounded it, this volcanic chimney had withstood erosion from the relentless sea to become one of the prominent landmarks of Vancouver.

It was no use.

She couldn't hold back.

One look at Siwash Rock and Jackie burst into tears for her dad.

The way Jackie heard it, the story went like this.

Thousands of years ago, said a Squamish Indian

chief, there was a noble and upright warrior whose wife was about to give birth. According to his religion, "clean fatherhood" was most noble and upright. That's why the warrior and his wife walked down to where the sea met the shore of what is now Stanley Park.

"I must swim," the warrior said.

"I must swim too," said his wife.

It was a custom for both parents of an unborn child to swim until their flesh was so clean that there was no scent for the creatures of the wilderness to pick up. The scent of a human is fearsome to forest animals, and it was believed that parents would be fit to have their child only if there was no reason for such fear.

And so they swam in the turbulent waters of the narrows, just off Prospect Point.

Before the woman waded ashore and vanished into the forest, she said to her husband, "Come to me at sunrise, and you'll not find me alone."

On and on, the warrior swam so he would be spotlessly clean for his child's first look at the world. The law of vicarious purity held that only a child unhampered by uncleanness at birth would have the opportunity to live a clean life.

But as he swam, a great canoe manned by four

giants representing the deity paddled into the narrows.

"Get out of our way," the giants ordered, for if their oars touched a mortal, they would lose their powers.

Ignoring them, the warrior kept on swimming.

"Move ashore," they commanded.

The swimmer refused. "I won't stop," he declared. "Nor will I go ashore."

"You dare defy the deity?"

"For my child to live a spotless life, I'll defy anyone, including the deity himself."

As the giants debated what to do, they heard the cry of a newborn child in the forests of Stanley Park. Because the warrior had placed his child's future above everything else, the deity decreed him to be an example for all men to come. As the warrior's feet straddled the line where sea met land, the giants raised their paddles and transformed him to stone.

That's why, today, the petrified image of *T'elch* stands as an erect and enduring sentinel at the entrance to the harbor. Like a noble-spirited and upright warrior, Siwash Rock is a monument to a man who kept his own life clean so that Clean Fatherhood would be the heritage of generations to come.

*　　*　　*

From now on, Jackie knew the sight of Siwash Rock would remind her of her dad.

All cried out and running with the wind in her face, Chuck's daughter focused on the revolving beam of the lighthouse ahead, which winked just this side of DeClercq's waterfront home. Suddenly, Jackie was tired and ready for sleep.

Splash . . .

Splash . . .

Splash . . .

Not a soul had passed her during her pre-dawn jog. Not in this kind of weather. But as Jackie closed on the finish line in front of the cul-de-sac where she'd parked Dane's car, she saw the first fellow runner of dawn come around the corner. He was bundled up in waterproof gear that she thought unsuitable for jogging, and his face was hidden by the hood. As they crossed paths, she nodded and said, "It's all yours." Then, an instant after she discerned Japanese features in the cowl, the jogger karate-chopped her with the edge of his hand and, stunned, Jackie lost consciousness.

Black Rain

Knock, knock . . .

A pause.

Knock, knock . . .

Again.

In his dream, Joe Hett awoke to knocking on his door, an insistent rapping that was a harbinger of official business. Throwing back the covers, he swung out of bed, slipped into his slippers and tugged on his terry-towel bathrobe, then shuffled through his house to confront whoever was at his door.

Knock, knock . . .

"Hold on," Joe said in his dream, sliding off the burglar chain and thumbing back the lock. When he swung wide the door, he came face to face with two uncomfortable men in USAF uniforms.

"Colonel Hett," said the Southerner with the higher rank, "I regret to inform you that your son, Captain Chuck Hett, was killed in combat in Vietnam."

Knock, knock . . .

"Jesus Christ!"

Joe's eyes snapped open and he jerked bolt upright in bed. His heart pounded in his throat and cold sweat beaded his forehead. For an instant, he was relieved that it had only been a dream—that Chuck had not been killed in Vietnam—but then it sank in that his son was dead all the same.

Throwing back the covers, Joe swung out of bed. Slipping into his slippers, he pulled on his bathrobe and cinched the belt around his waist. Then he shuffled across the hotel room to the door and undid the various anti-burglary devices.

Knock, knock . . .

"Hold on," Joe said, as he had in his dream, and he opened the door to two men dressed in the red serge uniform of the RCMP.

"Colonel Hett," said the Mountie with the higher rank, "I'm Chief Superintendent Robert DeClercq. This is Sergeant Dane Winter. We have reason to believe that your granddaughter, Corporal Jacqueline Hett of my section, Special X, has been kidnapped."

"Jesus Christ!" said Joe.

Joe himself had been a part of U.S. Air Force "notification teams," and he knew the drill by heart. The dead or missing member's commander or an officer of equal or higher rank would arrive at the door with a chaplain and a doctor or nurse, if available. The brass would be in USAF dress blues: matching coat, trousers, and tie, with a lighter blue shirt. Metal rank insignia would glitter on the coat, and a service cap would be tucked under one arm.

What threw him here was the color.

Both Mounties wore scarlet, and each had a weaponless Sam Browne, riding breeches, high boots, and brown leather gloves. Rank and insignia pins and medals gleamed on their chests. And of course, each held the Stetson hat.

"I know what you're thinking," DeClercq said.

"You do?" said Joe.

"You wish you were home so America could handle this."

"No disrespect intended, Chief Superintendent, but history doesn't condition us to have confidence in Redcoats."

"Do you want this uniform to instill confidence in you? Or do you want it to instill purpose in us?"

Joe was plumbing for any sign that he could trust this Horseman. Earlier, Jackie had said to him, "DeClercq's the sharpest cop I know. We can leave the manhunting to him." But she was talking about tracking down a killer after Chuck was already dead. This was his beloved granddaughter alive in some thug's clutches.

Still, he found what he was looking for in De-Clercq's bearing. Usually, a passing of the burden occurs at times like this. The notification officer has tragic information that he must pass on to somebody else. As soon as the news is delivered, the weight of the burden shifts. The officer can do little to comfort the upset recipient, and the bearer of the bad news finds relief in having discharged his duty.

But not here.

For what Joe sensed was that the Mountie was *taking on* a burden, as if the effect of his news on Joe was the effect on him too. And then the colonel recalled something else Jackie had said: "He'll track down whoever killed Dad as much for *himself* as he will for us."

"She's your granddaughter," DeClercq said, "but Corporal Hett is under *my* command. We have a call to arms in the Mounted for ordeals like this: 'A member is down.' You have my promise. I'll not leave her behind."

The old man nodded. That's what he had to hear. The last thing he thought he'd be doing in his eighties was girding himself for battle. But if this was where the battle was, this was where he'd fight it. Old though he might be, Joe still had the right stuff. He had steeled himself in the Pacific so many decades ago, and he found the fortitude to do it once more.

"Fill me in," he said.

"After she dropped you here last night, we think Jackie went for a jog," the chief began. "She parked Sergeant Winter's car in a cul-de-sac off the North Shore seawall, and it was later found abandoned by the local police. The same MO we saw with your son."

"Jac can take care of herself. We trained her in self-defense from the time she was a girl."

"We think that she was waylaid by professionals. And that this hood is behind it."

DeClercq showed the colonel a photo.

"I had a beef with this guy at the airport," said Joe.

"We know. His name is Genjo Tokuda. He's a retired godfather of Tokyo's yakuza."

"What's he doing here?"

"I think we just found out. I thought your son died because he was in the wrong place at the wrong time. But Jackie's snatching is too great a coincidence."

"And the kamikaze attack?"

"Crashing the plane into the Pacific vets' convention was designed to blindside us while the real target is in play. Grabbing Jackie—like the murder of your son—is a means to that end."

Joe stared at the photo. "He's about the same age as me."

"Tokuda was in the Pacific War. We checked," said Winter.

"Stationed where?"

"China. Hong Kong. The South Pacific. And finally, Okinawa."

"That's a long time to hold a military grudge."

"It's more than that."

"How so?"

"You served in the 509th Group, Colonel. Jackie told me you flew in the *Enola Gay*."

Joe took a deep breath and slowly exhaled.

"You think Tokuda holds the same grudge that Tokyo's governor gave voice to after 9/11?"

"What's that?" asked DeClercq.

"The governor said that September 11 was nothing like the kamikaze attacks in the Pacific War. He said it more closely resembled the indiscriminate attacks on Hiroshima and Nagasaki."

The colonel glowered at the photo. "I think you're right," he said. "Tokuda wants *me*."

Hiroshima, Japan
August 6, 1945

The all-clear siren had sounded at 7:31 a.m. to tell the war-weary citizens of Hiroshima that it was safe to come out of their shelters for the day and go to work. By a quarter after eight, as rush hour got under way, the streets were bustling. Seen from above, Hiroshima resembled a human hand. Its fingers poked into the bay where the commander of the Japanese fleet had waited for the first triumphant radio reports from the forces attacking Pearl Harbor. Already, the cruel August sun beat down on the deep blue sea and the six brown finger-forks of the Ota River. Within the clusters of wooden houses with their black-tiled peaks and rooftop vegetable gardens, people lit ovens to cook breakfast or read the *Chugoku Shimbun*. Outside, the byways were abuzz with people in trolleys, people on horse carts, people on bicycles, and pedestrians. In a throwback to the days when the Imperial Cavalry had trampled all before it, officers at Hiroshima Castle rode to work on horseback. At the moment, a prince on a white stallion cantered across the Aioi Bridge.

Six miles above the city, in the *Enola Gay*, that bridge moved into the bombsight that was aiming Little Boy.

Hiroshima Castle sat on the palm of the hand. The four-hundred-year-old moated citadel was the command center of the Imperial Army. In its shadow stood several armaments factories and the *Gaisenkan*, the "triumphal hall" from which so many soldiers had embarked and to which so few would return. In the cells of the castle, American prisoners ate bowls of mush. With forty thousand Japanese troops in residence, the yard outside was full of men doing calisthenics.

The strange thing is that no one heard the blast.

A noiseless flash of light—whiter than any white most Japanese had ever seen—cut across the sky like a sheet of sunlight. In that first millisecond, the fireball was more than a hundred million degrees Fahrenheit. Those close to the blast were vaporized. Some left behind permanent shadows where their own bodies had shielded brick and concrete. The ghost of a painter up a ladder, about to dip his brush into a paint can, was etched on the face of a building. A coachman, hand up and whip in the air, and his horse were cast as silhouettes on a bridge. In the hospitals, all the X-ray plates were exposed.

Within seconds, 78,000 died and 51,000 were injured. Death took a quarter of the population, and a third of the casualties were soldiers. At Hiroshima Castle, just nine hundred yards from the epicenter, stone columns were rammed straight down into the ground.

The castle vanished.

The heat flash ignited fires a mile away. The eyes of those caught gazing up as the weapon exploded melted into their sockets and dribbled down their cheeks. Steel doors and stone walls glowed red. The asphalt pavement turned to tar.

Hiroshima had been built to burn. Ninety percent of the closely packed houses were constructed of wood, and seventy thousand buildings instantly went up in flames. The raging firestorm consumed everything in its path. The dome of the Museum of Science and Industry was stripped to its steel frame. Burned-out cars, trucks, and trolleys and crumpled bicycles tumbled along the streets. Any trees left standing were black and bare of leaves, their limbs stretched heavenward as if begging for mercy. So intense was the heat even a mile away that men's caps were etched into their scalps, kimono patterns were tattooed on women's bodies, and children's socks were fused to their legs.

The bomb caught them going and coming. First came the explosion. Morning commuters were snatched off the streets and hurled through the air. Workmen were buried alive. Water mains snapped, and glass shards shot in all directions. Atop Mount Futaba, an officer whose uniform was torn off by the blast extended his sword as the signal for his dead anti-aircraft crew to open fire.

Then came the implosion.

Tongues of fire licked up through the dust-choked miasma, and the seething mass at the purple-red core of the explosion sucked in super-heated air. Uprooted trees and airborne doors, roofs, and strips of matting got lost in a whirl-wind. The boiling mushroom cloud blotted out the sun, plunging Hiroshima into atomic darkness.

Within the hour, black rain began to fall.

Oily, gooey, and inky with radioactive soot, drops of moisture the size of marbles teemed down onto the blazing ruins from nine o'clock on. In some parts of the wasteland, it rained for more than an hour, splattering gobs of uranium waste around with vengeful abandon.

Panicked people screamed that the Americans were showering Hiroshima with gasoline as a prelude to torching it and setting fire to those still living.

Was that the plan?

Were they to be burned alive?

Or was this their fate?

Were they being gassed?

For there was the odor in the air, the "electric smell" produced by nuclear fission.

At that moment, only one thing was certain:

Two billion American dollars will buy an awful lot of bang for the buck.

Captain Mitsuo Fuchida—the pilot who had led the attack on Pearl Harbor—got no reply from the airport tower as he flew toward Hiroshima. Everything had been fine yesterday afternoon when he took off, but now there was a strange mushroom cloud billowing over the city. Only as he came in to land did he grasp that all that remained of Hiroshima was fire, smoke, and rubble.

The airport was more than two miles from ground zero, but it too had succumbed. The shock wave had blown the windows out of runway buildings. It had shattered the glass of cockpits that faced the city and caved in fuselages until they looked like crescent bananas.

In his immaculate white uniform, gloves, and shoes, the stunned captain walked toward Hiroshima. At the entrance to the airport, he ran into an exodus of mangled refugees, a long line of living corpses fleeing from hell. Their hair scorched to the roots, their faces blotted by raw burns, some with mouths unable to stretch wide enough on for food, they hobbled toward him on makeshift crutches or leaned on one another for support.

As he pressed on toward the devastated city, Fuchida was met by one grotesque tableau after another.

Blackened and bleeding, her skin dangling in shreds, a stumbling mother clutched a dead baby to her breast.

Completely naked, his clothes scorched off, a blind man dragged his wife by the hand, unaware that she had abandoned him back along the road when the flesh of her arm had sloughed off like an elbow-length glove.

"Itai! Itai!"

It hurts! It hurts!

So many times did Fuchida hear those words

that eventually—at least in his mind—the agony seemed to fuse into one shrill shriek.

Soon, the living gave way to the dying and the dead. Pus-oozing people sat on the ground, retching and waiting for death. On the waterfront, corpses floated in and out with the tide. Cadavers clogged the gutters, and bodies blocked the streets. Sick, blistered horses hung their heads off bridges. Hiroshima reeked like a charnel house. And near the city center, a whole square mile had simply disappeared.

Wandering through the ruins, Fuchida shook his head.

"Tora! Tora! Tora!" had sunk to *this*!

Hibakusha, they called them.

"Survivors of the bombing."

The lucky ones were those killed outright. For them, death came in the blink of an eye. But those still around were ticking time bombs, for radiation had damaged their cells. The first stage of what would become known as "radiation sickness" included nausea, headaches, diarrhea, malaise, and fever.

About two weeks later, the second stage took hold. Hair blanched white, then fell out altogether. Pale and shaky, weak and tired, the afflicted couldn't concentrate. And what had been a low-grade fever spiked as high as 106.

The blood disorders set in a month after the blast. This third stage saw people grow so anemic that they might as well have been ghosts. Almost all the nurses and doctors were dead, so agony became sheer torture. Gums began to bleed, and blood spots the size of grains of rice and hemorrhages as big as soybeans appeared. Women had miscarriages, and menstruation ceased. Men became sterile. Finally, many began convulsing and vomiting up blood. Often, their gagging went on for ten days straight before they collapsed and expired.

Hiroshima was the ancestral home of Genjo Tokuda and his family. His father, his mother, his sisters, his brother, his wife, and his only child— a four-year-old boy—had all survived the initial blast of the bomb dropped by the *Enola Gay*. They would have to wait for radiation sickness to kill them slowly.

By the time the American conquerors released Tokuda from their prisoner-of-war camp, all but his wife were gone. He went home to Hiroshima, only to find that she was in the final stages of bleeding out. He stayed with her until she gagged to death in his arms. Then he laid her to rest with the remains of the last child he would be able to sire, for radiation and the damage done to his genitals by the American flame-thrower on Okinawa had rendered him sterile as well.

That day, standing amid the ashes of what had once been his family's Shinto shrine, where his father had taught him the Way of the Warrior and bequeathed him the two samurai swords, Genjo Tokuda swore a sacred oath to the *kami* gods.

Before he too was laid to rest, he would see that the killers who'd manned that bomber—the *Enola Gay*—suffered the same pain that he was suffering now.

Sushi Chef

Fish.

She could smell fish.

Not fishy fish, like fish that's about to go bad, but fresh fish, of the sort served at a sushi bar.

Sushi.

Yum!

Who'd have thought?

When Jackie was a girl, she had hated fish. Luckily, her mom and dad were meat-and-potatoes people who'd had no affinity for fish either, so she'd never been forced to eat the wretched stuff.

Vancouverites, however, were mostly fish fans—well, what would you expect, it being the West Coast and all?—so once Jackie had been posted here, she'd found herself repeatedly supping on teriyaki cooking in the company of a sophisticated school of raw-fish freaks.

"Go on. I dare you."

"Yuk," she told her first patrol partner.

"Don't know what you're missing."

"A bellyful of worms."

"It takes more than ten years of training to qualify as a sushi chef. It's an art, Jackie."

"Gimme a break."

"*If you knew Sushi like I know Sushi, oh, oh, oh what a treat . . .*"

Hett laughed.

"Close your eyes and open wide."

"Then what? 'Lie back and think of England'? Wasn't that Queen Victoria's advice for losing your virginity?"

"I double dog dare you."

"Oh! Since you put it like that . . ."

And so it had gone, until at last she'd chanced a nibble of salmon. And now—a full-fledged sushiite—she ate just about anything harvested from the Pacific.

Still, how could this smell be sushi?

Surely she sniffed the sea?

For the last thing Jackie remembered before someone had doused her lights was going for a pre-dawn run on the seawall to calm her jittery nerves and clear her overwrought mind.

This had to be the ocean.

She struggled to open her eyes.

And damn, if Jackie *wasn't* sitting by a sushi bar.

As near as she could tell, this sushi bar was built into the lower level of a mountainside house. Beyond the threshold, steps ascended under a veil of overhanging towels, and Jackie could look down on Vancouver through bamboo blinds on the windows. The pale wood interior was hung with paper lanterns, and graced with floral arrangements and bonsai trees.

With her mouth gagged and her wrists and ankles lashed to the limbs of an executioner's chair, Jackie looked toward the square bar in the center of the room. A *tsu*—a sushi expert—always sits at the counter so he can see his food being prepared. And so it was with Tokuda, whom the kidnapped Mountie recognized from both her grandfather's run-in at the airport and the photo pinned to DeClercq's Strategy Wall. As she eyed the octogenarian, who was relishing the dishes set before him by his personal sushi chef, Jackie wondered if he was making a point by sitting sideways at the bar so she would have to face his ugly scar.

She knew enough about sushi to comprehend that the *itamae*—the "board man"—was a master chef. He patrolled his sushi bar like a boxer does the ring, stepping lightly from side to side in a white kimono tunic that was belted at the waist. Around his brow was tied a white *hachimaki* scarf of the type worn by kamikaze pilots. The tunic was spotless. His hair was cut short, and his fingertips had been scrubbed to ensure the level of cleanliness demanded by his art.

Slice . . .

Slice . . .

Slice . . .

The glittering blade of his sushi knife had been shaped on natural stone, and he slashed it across the cutting board with flourishes that were deft, swift, and uniform. The knife was honed on one side only, so it left each layer of fish—cut slightly on the bias—with dissimilar surface textures. Swinging his arms and pivoting his torso as if this were a floor show, the *itamae* reduced a hairy crab and an ominous coil of purple octopus tentacle to bite-size pieces that went onto small beds of glutinous rice and were dabbed with *wasabi*.

Bowing respectfully, the chef served Tokuda a palette of underwater colors: white from squid and yellowtail; blue from mackerel and eel; yellow from sea-urchin roe and *tamago*; red from salmon and tuna.

"*So deska?*" he inquired. Okay?

The yes-man watched his master pop the tidbits into his mouth, the rice side up so his tongue could savor the fish flavor.

"*Hai,*" replied Tokuda.

That pleased the chef no end. Anticipating his *kumicho*'s every need, he poured him a cup of sake from a bottle kept warm in a tub of hot water.

Jackie might have been a voyeur in an exclusive gentlemen's club. To the Japanese, everything to do with fish—catching, cutting, cooking, and making sushi—was men's work, and the yakuza was also a men's organization. Courage is the attribute most admired by gangsters, for if there's a turf war, a yakuza is expected to fight to the death. Because they don't rumble like men, women can't be trusted, and they aren't seen as strong enough to withstand interrogation. They're born to be mothers and to serve the needs of their husbands, and so are forbidden to join yakuza gangs.

Why am I here? Jackie wondered.

Scrape . . .

Scrape . . .

Scrape . . .

The sushi chef was using the heel of his knife to scrape the sinewy meat from the shoulder of a tuna into a fluffy mousse that he then heaped on seaweed with finely chopped scallions and finished off with the raw yolk of a quail egg.

To renew his palate, Tokuda was nibbling *gari*, thin shavings of pickled ginger.

Having served his boss the tuna, the chef was reaching for a pot of mild green *sencha* tea when the old man finally decided to acknowledge Jackie's presence by swiveling a quarter-turn around on his stool.

If looks could kill, thought Hett.

"Hai," said the chef, as if to an unspoken order. Raising a counter leaf to exit from the sushi bar, he rolled out what seemed to be a mobile serving tray and pushed it across the hardwood floor to the executioner's chair. The tray had a lift-up cover designed to keep food hot, but today the stainless-steel coffin held a set of gleaming knives.

The chef selected one.

Please, no! Jackie thought.

She was still wearing her rain-soaked jogging suit. With one hand, the *itamae* pulled the collar out from her neck, and with the other, he made a slash down the front of her chest. For a moment, Jackie feared she had been slit from jaw to navel, but the razor-sharp blade had only parted her clothes.

Her sweatshirt gaped open, flashing her bra.

A flick of the blade's tip and that was sundered too.

So cold were the eyes of the sushi chef that he might have *been* a fish himself.

Squeeze . . .

Squeeze . . .

Squeeze . . .

He fondled her breast as if he was checking the ripeness of fruit in a market, or . . .

Oh, God. No!

Checking its bias for slicing.

Suddenly, a closed-circuit TV on the wall to Jackie's right came to life. A security camera caught the image of an approaching car. Tinted windows hid the faces of the occupants, but someone within must have punched a remote control. The camera watched as the garage opened to swallow the car, and after the door closed, the screen went dead.

Tokuda said something in Japanese. One of his words was *"musuko."*

For an extradition hearing, Special X had once sent Jackie to Japan, so she knew that word translated as "son." She wondered if Tokuda was saying that his son had arrived in the car. It had to be *his* son, for the old man got up, shuffled out of the sushi bar, and disappeared up the stairs beyond the toweled threshold.

No way would he be doing that for someone else's son.

Did that mean this was it?

My turn to die? wondered Jackie.

Meanwhile, the groping chef still had hold of her breast. From the way he eyed it—just as he'd eyed the fish—Jackie sensed that his mind was focused on presentation. Was the grate she'd noticed beneath the chair waiting to drain her blood? Would her pink flesh be reduced to slices on beds of glutinous rice? Would she be the guest of honor at some wartime cannibal feast?

Red had once shocked her with tales of Japanese troops who'd run amok on the southern arc of their conquest, eating Australian soldiers and then, after their food ran out, killing and eating each other.

Was this a vestige of that?

Or was this even worse?

Jackie was trained to unearth the motives buried within twisted minds.

What if this was revenge?

Revenge against whom?

Red?

If so, what revenge would be the most diabolic of all?

Forcing pieces of her down the gagging throat of her captive granddad?

Prisoner of War

So it all came down to lies.

When Chuck and Jackie were both kids, Joe had read "The Emperor's New Clothes" to each of them. Now, as he exited the convention hotel and headed west along the seawalk bordering Coal Harbour, his mind rewrote that Hans Christian Andersen tale.

Once upon a time, there was an emperor named President Truman. A haberdasher by trade, he concerned himself with outward appearances. In every news photo, Truman seemed to be a well-dressed, dapper little guy. The emperor was definitely a dandy, a man prone to flaunting fancy clothes in public.

A front man, thought Joe.

Unfortunately, the emperor fell in with a scheming tailor. A backroom puppet master by the name of Jimmy Byrnes. The tailor told the emperor that he'd make him a new suit of clothes from a special atomic material that would be invisible to the most foolish and unpatriotic of his subjects.

But not to me, thought Joe.

For there was no greater patriot than Red Hett, whose bloodline ran back to the American Revolution.

And so the emperor donned his atomic suit and paraded in front of his awestruck subjects, all of whom—Joe included—oohed and aahed at his magnificent ensemble, for they all feared being branded foolish and unpatriotic.

But as the parade made its way through the streets of passing time, a youngster on the sidelines saw through the atomic lie and cried out, for all to hear, "The emperor is naked!"

Suddenly, those who had shared in the lie could no longer overlook the evidence before their eyes, and soon a chorus of voices began to say, "The emperor *is* naked!"

But not, of course, the emperor himself.

To admit publicly that he couldn't see his own atomic clothes would expose him as the most foolish dupe of all. So until his dying day, Truman—like that emperor in Andersen's tale—had continued parading about naked, in the hope that patriots would see truth where he himself knew there were only lies.

Patriots like Joe.

How could I have been so naive? he wondered now.

"On that trip coming home from Potsdam," Truman had nakedly lied, "I ordered the atomic bomb to be dropped on Hiroshima. It was a terrible decision. But I made it."

Hook, line, and sinker, Joe had swallowed the lie. Japan was given the chance to surrender, and because the Japs didn't take it, they got what they deserved. The bomb was a military necessity. It saved hundreds of thousands of lives that would have been lost in the invasion of Japan. The bomb was a weapon of last resort against an enemy determined to fight to the death.

Bullshit, thought Joe.

They were never given the chance.

So we'll never know if the bomb was a necessity.

But *I* know that *I've* got innocent blood on my hands.

And so does Tokuda.

And he's determined to make me pay with the innocent blood of *my* family.

Damn you, Byrnes!

Joe should have seen the lie when there was no mention of Japan's emperor in the Potsdam Declaration. He knew that forcing the Japs to give up their emperor as part of their "unconditional surrender" was the same as forbidding Americans to worship God.

When the post-Hiroshima surrender conditions made it clear that they *could* keep their emperor after all, it should have been obvious to Joe that the bomb was a *setup*.

But he was cut from the patriotic cloth of his generation, and back then it was assumed that America never did wrong. As Lillian Hellman had once said, "It is considered unhealthy in America to remember mistakes, neurotic to think about them, psychotic to dwell upon them." Wrapping himself in the Stars and Stripes, Joe had embarked on the post-war peace exactly as Truman advised: "Never, never waste a minute on regret. It is a waste of time." He had started a family and seen his service through; he had weathered the tumult of Vietnam and retired with his illusions intact.

That's how John Wayne did it.

And so had Joe.

It was only when he began preparing his address for the vets' conference that Joe had actually read Truman's secret Potsdam diary. Discovered in 1979, seven years after the president's death, the diary set forth the reasons for his decision to drop the bomb.

July 25: Truman's order went out. "The 509 Composite Group, 20th Air Force will deliver its first special bomb as soon as weather will permit visual bombing after about 3 August 1945 on one of the targets: Hiroshima."

July 26: The Potsdam Declaration.

Which meant that the decision to drop the bomb wasn't made *after* Japan was asked to surrender.

It was made *before*.

And Joe had done the killing.

Instead of being a weapon of last resort, the *Enola Gay*'s atomic bomb was destined to drop, and the man who was really behind that decision—Jimmy Byrnes—had done everything in his power to see that destiny fulfilled.

"My God! What have we done?"

Who was the crewman who voiced that in the plane?

Too many unanswered questions tumbled around in Joe's troubled mind.

Would Japan have surrendered if the Americans had agreed to preserve the emperor?

Was Japan already too exhausted to fight on?

Would Russia's entering the Pacific War have been the tipping point?

With Japan surrounded, would a naval blockade and conventional bombing have done the job?

Why wasn't the bomb dropped on troops massing on the southern island of Kyushu, instead of on a city so low on the list of military targets that it had yet to be attacked with conventional weapons?

If targeting innocent civilians is the MO of terrorists, does that make the atomic bombing of Hiroshima a war crime?

Ask New Yorkers, thought Joe.

Whatever the answers to those vexing questions, the aftershocks of Hiroshima were crystal clear:

America is the only country to have used a nuclear weapon.

And Japan is the only country to have suffered one.

And now the bomb had spawned a more ferocious atomic monster than any encountered in 1950s Japanese horror films. Joe was embroiled in a nightmarish rendition of "Revenge is a dish best served cold." It had already cost him his only child, and it threatened to cost him his sole grandchild too. That would be the end of the long line of Hetts who had answered the call to serve their country, and Joe would be left to die alone.

Or maybe not.

Perhaps there was more?

Wasn't it more likely that this enemy from half a century ago was killing Joe's family as a warm-up to the end-game: the annihilation of the atomic bomber himself?

Then so be it, thought Joe.

Take me on, Tokuda.

That's why Joe was out here on this foggy sea-walk, feeling dumbfounded by how radically different the weather was from what he enjoyed in the Southwest. The rain overnight had dissipated to a Scotch mist, and that must have warmed the air above a cooler sea, for the ocean exhaled a lazy, pearl gray cloud. The thicker it got, the more the fog felt like a living entity. Clammy fingers brushed his skin, and the heavy air filled his lungs like smoke. Traffic he couldn't see rumbled past, along with the disembodied voices of invisible people. Joe advanced slowly through this shadowy gloom, confused and disoriented by what he imagined was a real London pea-souper, and he felt a little like Sherlock Holmes being stalked by Moriarty.

Footsteps.

Coming toward him.

Tires.

Whispering behind.

Shoulders hunched against the chill, Hett walked with his hands stuffed in his pockets.

A figure loomed up in the fog.

Car doors swung open beside him.

They took the bait, Joe thought as he punched on the cellphone in his pocket.

Then hands grabbed him.

And he was snatched off the seawalk.

"They've got him!" Craven said. "The cellphone's on."

His words went out from a "control" car crawling through the fog on the downtown byway that ran parallel to the street that skirted the seawalk. Because Special O did double duty investigating bad cops for Internal Affairs and watching bad guys for the Mounted, it was literally kept at arm's length from the rest of the force. Consequently, Oscar had something no other section could boast: its own cipher channel.

A cipher channel is secure.

For your ears only.

And every wired ear on air was working this target.

"Got 'em," confirmed the "I guy" from the passenger's seat beside Craven. The Special I cop had been selected because he was of Japanese heritage and fluent in several Asian languages. In complicated tails like this, there'd often be a specialist in the lead control car. Today, it was the Asian tech from Special I. At other times, especially in cases involving a foreign jurisdiction, it would be a cop from a visiting agency who knew their target's lifestyle. He could then feed Special O quirks: "That's typical. No big deal. He likes to go for a rub and tug back home too."

If Special O—the watchers—was the eyes of the RCMP, Special I—the electronic buggers—was the ears.

"They've turned off Coal Harbour Quay. The signal's going south on Cardero."

The I guy was gripping a gadget that looked like a remote control for a model airplane. In fact, it was a trap that captured cellphone signals. Around the city, towers fight to "pull" cellphone signals. The closest tower to your phone wins the signal, but the weaker ones track it too. Because more than one tower has a fix, the gizmo in the I guy's hands could use triangulation to map the point of intersect and locate the phone within one or two car lengths. With so many cellphones around, the trap required proximity. It picked up every signal in the vicinity and displayed each number on its computer screen. In this case, Special I had supplied the phone in Joe Hett's pocket, so the I guy knew which number to stalk.

"Quite the receiver," Nick Craven had said before the colonel was snatched.

"Yeah," said the I guy. "We're always a step ahead. The bad guys use a device like this to clone phones. That's how they steal your signal and stick you with the bill."

"But not like that one, eh?"

"No. It's state of the art. But tech stuff changes so fast these days that by the time you and I stop talking, this signal trap will probably be obsolete."

But now they were moving; they were on the hunt.

And that was Cardero Street up ahead.

"There," said Craven.

"Yeah, that's them. The signal is coming from the vehicle passing in front of us."

Through the blur, they could just make out a car passing from the harbor on the right to the left-hand downtown core. As if on cue, the rear window lowered as it cut across Hastings—their intersecting street—and something got tossed out.

"Houston," said the I guy, "we've got a problem."

"I'm an old man," Joe had said, "and I'm not afraid to die. I faced down that fear a long time ago, at Pearl Harbor. But my granddaughter is all I have left, and she's too young to die, so I'll sign whatever you need signed for me to be used as bait."

That was back in his hotel room earlier this morning, when he and the Horsemen had forged a battle plan.

"It's complicated," DeClercq had said. "A lot can go wrong."

"Enough's wrong *now*," Joe had replied. "And something must be done! They killed my son. They'll kill Jackie. Get me near them and I'll take the fuckers with me."

"I've been in your shoes, Colonel."

"So I hear. And you did just what I'm proposing to get *your* daughter back. Do we have a deal?"

The danger with technology is that it cuts both ways. If there had been time, they might have planted a tracking device in one of Joe's teeth or injected a microchip into his body. The Japanese, however, are the top dogs of high-tech, and the yakuza would definitely be armed with the best signal scanners around. If they found Joe wired with a chip, they'd kill him then and there.

And Jackie too.

So in the end, Joe had ventured out without the bells and whistles. The only electronic signals he emitted were those that were part of everyday life. And now that he had been snatched off the quay and hauled into the car, the American was a low-tech prisoner of war.

"Search him."

Or at least Joe figured that's what the thug with the mole on his cheek had barked in Japanese, for no sooner was the command given than there were paws all over him. And of course, the first item these goons found was the cellphone in his pocket.

Easy come, easy go.

By now, the redcoats had their fix.

"Walk with your hands in your pockets," Joe had been told by an Asian cop with a section called Special Eye. He figured the "eye" was like private eye, and that's what made it special. In fact, everything about the Mounties seemed special to them.

"The moment something happens, punch on the

phone. It'll appear to be dormant, waiting for a call, and I'll be able to triangulate the signal and track you with this."

The eye guy—for that's what they called him—had waved some sort of receiver.

So here sat Joe, sandwiched between two heavies in the rear seat, where he was frisked by the Mole and a punk with a black-and-white samurai tattoo creeping up one side of his neck.

In front, the wheelman turned the corner and crawled away from the harbor.

The street sign read "Cardero."

The tough in the passenger's seat navigated from a glowing digital map.

A chill filled the car as the Mole lowered the back-seat window and tossed out the cellphone.

Crunch!

It was run over by the car behind.

"Double trouble," Craven said. "The target has a shadow. It just ran over the cellphone jettisoned by T1."

"How many in T2?" a voice asked through his earpiece.

"Can't tell, Chief. Tinted windows."

"The phone thrown out of T1—was it on your side?"

"Affirmative."

"Did they make you?"

"I doubt it. The fog's too thick. I couldn't see in. The window's a black hole into the back seat."

"Hastings T-connects with Cardero. That gives you a reason to turn. If they turn on Georgia, your backdoor takes control."

"Roger," said Craven.

As a kid back in the fifties, DeClercq had been a fan of the Hardy Boys. He'd read every Franklin W. Dixon book up to *The Mystery at Devil's Paw* in 1959, when he had opened a Christmas present and—he couldn't believe his eyes—found in his hands *The Hardy Boys' Detective Handbook*, written in consultation with a cop named Captain D. A. Spina of the Newark (New Jersey) Police Department.

Holy cow!

That same day, he had founded the Gumshoe Detective Agency, staffing it with neighborhood kids who were hired out at twenty-five cents a case.

Rover missing?

Don't worry.

The Gumshoes would find your dog.

Billy playing hooky from school?

The Gumshoes would track down the truant.

The success rate was remarkable—"If we can't solve it, you don't pay"—because Robert De-Clercq used all of the Hardy Boys' techniques. From their handbook, he learned how to put together a real fingerprint kit, and how to make casts and "moulages" of shoe prints and tire marks, and how to collect evidence at the scene of a crime, and how to talk the slang of the underworld—like using "do-re-mi" for money and "gun moll" for a babe who carries a criminal's gat—and best of all, how to "shadow" a suspect.

Now, half a century later, that enterprising Gumshoe was sitting in the rear of this mobile command van, with two lives depending solely on his judgment. Who'd have thought that in this age of state-of-the-art surveillance, the watchers of Special O and other surreptitious followers around the world would *still* be using the system laid out on page 246 of *The Hardy Boys' Detective Handbook*?

But they are.

If it ain't broke, don't fix it.

Sitting in the middle of the back seat, Joe turned his head right to glance at Tattoo, the punk who'd come out of the seawalk fog and pushed him into the car.

Tattoo was running a signal scanner up and down his body.

The punk said something in Japanese, and the Mole said something back.

Joe swiveled his head 180 degrees to stare at the kidnapper who'd thrown the cellphone out the window.

For their part, his abductors were glaring at the hearing aids the old man had in both ears.

"I've got the eye," the backdoor said. "Just picked up the fare. I can't see T1 through the fog. But T2's east on Georgia."

"I'm VCB," reported Craven.

Visual contact broken.

"Moving up as backdoor," confirmed the double back.

"Parallels?" DeClercq asked.

"I'll move into double back," signaled one of the outriders.

The terms used by Oscar weren't the same ones the Hardy Boys had used, but the system was. In the "straight-line surveillance system," five cars move as a pack. Whoever's being followed is referred to as the "target." More than one target means they get prioritized. T1 for the primary. Then T2, T3, and so on. Some cases grow so huge that they require a target sheet. Each T refers to a suspect, and if an unknown male appears, he becomes U/M.

Here, T1 was the car with Joe in the back.

T2 was the car working counter-surveillance: yakuza hoods following yakuza hoods to see if they were being followed. That was the "double trouble" mentioned by Craven. T2 was the car that had crushed the cellphone seized from Joe.

Ideally, the five-car pack would work like this:

Target 1
Target 2
Buffer Vehicle(s)
Control
Parallel Backdoor Parallel
Double Back

Craven, who would be in the control car with the I guy and a "foot" (a cop who could hop out and follow on foot, if necessary), would track the target vehicles on a straightaway. As control, he'd be the one "with the eye," and would call the changes. In a straight line behind him would be his backdoor and the double back, and flanking the backdoor would be the parallels (east and west parallels or north and south, depending on direction).

The quickest way to get made is to ride "bare" on the bumper of a target, so the watchers let cover cars slip in between the target and the pack. That way, the bad guys see camouflage in the rear-view mirror.

"Never turn with the target" is the Special O rule of thumb. If the bad guys turn, the control drives straight ahead. The backdoor closes up to fill the control position, then turns the corner with the target while the double back becomes *his* backdoor. One of the parallels changes lanes to become a new double back, and the original control circles the block to take that empty slot.

The target turns, Oscar shuffles. . . .

The target turns, Oscar shuffles. . . .

"Any monkey can do surveillance," they say in Special O. "But to do it well is an art."

It's like ballet. There's constant motion, and the fluid shifting ensures that all roles are covered. Ideally, the bad guys never realize they're being followed, since what's going on behind them seems to change at random.

Ideally.

But not today.

Unluckily for Oscar, the fog was a wild card.

Tossing out the cellphone was an ominous sign. That left only the hearing aids in Joe's ears as fallback. At the moment, they were Oscar's eyes *and* ears, transmitting images and sounds to the command van. Lose them and O would be reduced to physical surveillance. And if that failed in the fog . . . Bye, bye, Hetts.

By dead-end intersecting with Cardero, Hastings Street had given Craven a reason to turn. But no buffer cars had appeared before T2 vanished into the haze, so he had no option but to ride bare on the counter-surveillance car. When both targets then turned left on Georgia, Craven relinquished control to his backdoor and, listening to the shuffle through his earpiece, drove on into the West End.

"What's going on in T1?" he asked the I guy.

The Asian translated the intercepts that were passing from Joe's hearing aids to DeClercq's command van.

"One guy says, 'The scanner shows the hearing aids are giving off signals.'

"Another guy replies, 'Of course. They're electronic.'

"The first guy argues, 'If we toss them out, the old man won't hear her scream.'

301

"The other guy responds, 'Get rid of them. It's not worth the risk. He can't be totally deaf. And she'll be shrieking.' "

"Is that it?" Craven asked.

"The bugs are picking up noise."

"What kind of noise?"

"Static."

"You mean interference?"

"More likely a hearing aid being removed."

"Damn," said Craven.

"The second voice is back. 'Turn here,' it says. 'Let's see if we're being followed.' "

"The last thing we need."

"Now more static."

"The other hearing aid?"

"Uh-oh."

"What?" said Craven.

"The intercepts just died. But I think I heard the second guy say, 'If we're being followed, then I'll claw his eyes out, and you cut his throat.' "

Heads or Tails

How long had it been since *that* came bouncing down the stairs?

An hour?

Several hours?

She had lost track of time.

Her wristwatch was hidden under the sleeve of her sweatshirt, the material lashed to the chair by the bindings around that arm.

So what had gone on up there?

And who'd made those grunting sounds?

Shortly after the mystery car had driven into the garage and Genjo Tokuda had left this sushi bar to greet his son, the Sushi Chef, cocking his head and listening as if something wasn't right, had released his grip on the Mountie's breast and followed the yakuza boss up the steps.

Thump!

What's that? Jackie had thought.

Someone taking a tumble?

Then . . .

Bump . . .

Bump . . .

Bump . . .

Down the stairs it had come, splattering the walls with blood before it hit the floor of the sushi bar and rolled over to Jackie's foot like a bowling ball.

Then she'd heard the grunts.

Punctuated by a muffled voice.

Male or female, the corporal couldn't tell.

Any moment, she had thought, the grunts will turn to screams. But they hadn't. Then finally, the mystery car had exited the garage and, caught by the security camera that fed the screen in the sushi bar, vanished into the first tendrils of mist creeping up the mountainside.

Again, the screen had faded to black.

Then nothing . . .

Nothing . . .

Not a peep from above.

And as time stretched into what her anxiety

computed to be an eternity, Jackie began to wonder if Tokuda had departed with his son, leaving her to stare down at the cold eyes gazing up at her from the Sushi Chef's severed head.

Snaking her way down the mountainside in her half-brother's car, Lyn Barrow wondered how her twin would react when he learned what she had done to his father.

Poetic justice.

Her Way of the Warrior.

Still, she had little doubt that her half-brother would be enraged by this twist of fate.

All his life, he'd been struggling to understand who he was. Now that a relationship with his father was finally within his grasp, she had snatched it from him to meet some needs of her own.

Would her half-brother want to kill her?

Probably.

And if so, what should Lyn do to defend herself?

Fratricide might be the only answer.

Tracking a suspect through the West End was like hunting the Minotaur in the labyrinth.

These days, the West End is a maze of streets.

In the beginning—1862—"the three greenhorns" were Vancouver's first white settlers. That trio had visions of building a big metropolis named New Liverpool on their 550-acre parcel of rainforest. But "the three greenhorns" turned out to be an apt nickname, for their development savvy was sorely lacking. Indeed, a U.S. cavalry raid on an Apache village in Arizona had, bizarrely, turned up a stack of promotional pamphlets aimed at selling their lots.

The coming of the railroad in 1887 had helped the three greenhorns realize their dream, however. Almost overnight, the West End was the place to be. Victorian top hats began constructing mansions with gardens, stables, and ballrooms with floors laid over dried seaweed for "bounce." The area became known as "Blueblood Alley." The end of the Gilded Age turned those castles into rooming houses, and the explosion of high-rise mania in the 1960s helped transform the West End into the most densely populated square mile in Canada.

With all those settlers crammed into cell blocks of two hundred apartments or more, the streets—which had been laid out for horses and buggies—were choked with belching autos. City planners responded by blocking off the most congested intersections with shrubs and benches to deter traffic from veering off the main byways. Today, you need a guide to help you navigate your way through the urban canyons, and that's what the T1 yakuza thugs had in their car.

An electronic guide.

A twenty-first-century scout.

"There," DeClercq had said shortly after the cellphone was tossed out. His finger was pointing at an image that had been captured by one of the fiber-optic cameras in Joe Hett's hearing aids and beamed to the bank of closed-circuit TV monitors in back of the command van. Inside the target vehicle, the captive was craning his head right and left as if to look at the goons flanking him in the back seat. He was actually giving Special O the layout of who was sitting where within the car.

But now the signals were dead and the screens were blank; the hearing aids had also been ejected from T1. The stalking had turned into a game of cat and mouse through the narrow, foggy canyons of the West End.

"If we're being followed," the Special I tech had translated, *"then I'll claw his eyes out, and you cut his throat."*

"I'm eastbound on Robson," the current control reported. "T1 just turned south on Broughton."

"And T2?" DeClercq asked.

"It's turning too."

"Cover cars?"

"Negative. All traffic's going straight on Robson."

"If we go bare on the bumper, the colonel is dead. Backdoor?"

"Here, Chief."

"Turn a block before Broughton and head south on Nicola."

"Roger."

"Control," said DeClercq, "keep on going. Once you're past Broughton, turn south. I want you driving parallel on the other side of the targets."

"Got it."

"Both parallels?"

"Here, Chief," said one of them.

"Ditto," replied Craven. After relinquishing control, he had cycled around to the empty parallel position.

"Head for Davie Street. One at Jervis. One at Nicola. If either target emerges at that end, holler."

"Affirmative."

"Roger."

"Double back?"

"Here."

"Break away and head for the causeway

through Stanley Park. To get to the North Shore, if that's where they're going, they must pass Lost Lagoon. Eye the road and the underpass. If they escape down Georgia or around the lagoon, you'll see them."

"Will do."

"Okay, everyone, listen up. We're tracking the target cars on parallel streets. Because the West End is a labyrinth, that limits their choice of routes. Once they know they're not being followed, Oscar will regroup. How's the fog?"

"Bad, Chief."

"Thicker by the minute."

"Good. That'll slow the targets down to a crawl. As soon as you're in position, pitch the feet."

From his position between Tattoo and the Mole, Joe had sight of one corner of the rear-view mirror. Since they threw out the cellphone, they had been shadowed by what Joe assumed was a counter-surveillance car. But after they zigzagged a block east from Broughton onto what Joe read as Jarhead Street—which had to be wishful thinking, the Marines and all, because he could barely make out the signpost through this gray shroud— the vehicle behind them fell out of sight.

With a jerk, the driver wrenched the lead car

west and accelerated, picking up speed faster than those inside could see ahead.

The Mole said something.

The wheelman checked the mirror.

There was nothing back there for him or Joe to see.

As the navigator called out directions from the digital map, the car weaved through the West End. Judging from the *oooo-wah, oooo-wah* of foghorns grumbling in the haze, they had just one or two blocks more before they would plunge into the sea.

"Chief, it's Winter. Yamada just arrived."

"Does he have the MOU?"

"Yep. Showtime."

"Good. We're going to need it. Bring him in."

Most people who passed the command van and the cluster of similar trucks on the downtown side street wouldn't have taken a second look. Decades of moviemaking in Hollywood North had accustomed Vancouverites to hundreds—more likely, thousands—of similar-looking shoots. "When I hear the thunder of hoof beats, I think horses, not zebras," the old saying goes, and it would be thinking zebras to conclude that the white van was really a mobile cop shop.

The back door opened.

Two men climbed up and in.

The back door closed.

And shut out the world.

The inside of the box could have been the set of a techno-thriller or the monitor room of a network like CNN. DeClercq sat in the director's chair facing a wall of screens, each of which was fed by mobile cameras in the field. The watchers working this case were "wired up," which was actually a misnomer, since each had a microscopic *wireless* plug buried in one ear. Each was also "miked" with a transmission device so sensitive and multidirectional that it captured both nearby voices and background noise. Sergeant Winter was wired up and ready for action, but as commander of this intricate operation, DeClercq had headphones clamped over both ears so nothing distracted his focus.

Yamada bowed.

DeClercq swiveled his chair, releasing an earphone so they could talk.

"The situation is worse than we thought this morning. In addition to killing Colonel Chuck Hett and launching a kamikaze dive at the convention center, Genjo Tokuda and his gang have abducted both Colonel Joe Hett and his granddaughter, Corporal Jackie Hett, whom you met in my office."

"He'll kill them," stated the diplomat.

"I know," said the chief. "We don't know where Corporal Hett is, but we're tracking the car with Colonel Hett in it through the foggy West End."

DeClercq gestured toward the bank of screens, each of which was fuzzy with so much haze that it looked like static.

"Does Tokyo understand that I will do what I have to do?"

"Yes," confirmed the consul.

"Good," said the Mountie, indicating the MOU in Winter's grasp. "Does the memorandum of understanding cover whatever eventualities I might face?"

"Tokyo knows Tokuda."

"Is that a yes?"

"The document can be read that way."

"Then that's how I'll read it. I'm going to turn on the speakers so you can follow along. It's cramped in here, but I'm sure we can find you a seat. Sergeant Winter will explain what we're doing. Please excuse me. I must get back to work."

On one of the screens, a car was taking shape in the fog.

DeClercq flicked on the speakers.

"I'm picking up a fare," reported one of the feet. "Southbound on Jervis. He's inching along."

"That's taxi talk," the sergeant explained. "You'll hear a lot of that. Back in the early days of Special O, all frequencies were open. There were no ciphered channels. Because what they said could be monitored by crooks with receivers, the watchers communicated with cryptic talk that mimicked cabbies working the streets."

"Tricky," said Yamada.

"You'll hear, 'I'm occupied.' Or, 'He's in my pocket.' That means they've found the target. 'I'm dropping off my fare' tells us the target is exiting from his car. 'I'm out of pocket' or 'I'm vacant' means a watcher has lost his target. 'VCB'—or visual contact broken—is what's used if the target is temporarily out of sight. The sort of loss that happens if a truck cuts in. 'VCB vacant' is the worst of all. That means the target is lost and the speaker has no idea where it is."

"The crooks have escaped?" said Yamada.

"And the operation has failed."

The same car that had appeared on the initial screen was slowly materializing on a second.

"I've got the wheels," a new voice reported through the command van's speakers.

"That's one of the younger guys," Winter said, "so no taxi talk. At the moment, Special O is going through a shakeup. The oldsters who go back to day one are nearing retirement. In thirty years on the force, some never left the section. They see themselves as shadows, plain and simple. Taxi talk is their signature, though it's no longer needed, and they don't get involved in takedowns."

"Pros," said Yamada, with respect.

"The new blood is full of piss and vinegar," Winter said. "Like so many people these days, they have short attention spans. Special O is no longer seen as a career assignment. The youngsters transition the section to get good at surveillance, before heading out to mix it up as regular Mounties. And if an O operation results in a takedown, they're champing at the bit to get their hands dirty."

"Amateurs," said Yamada.

"But good for the section. Sure, there's friction, but the dynamic is healthy. The newer guys are giving the older guys a shot of Viagra."

"Team leader?" A different voice.

"I'm listening," replied DeClercq.

"Since I got pitched, I've been walking a dog

down Jervis. Aren't there supposed to be *two* targets?"

"Yes," said the chief.

"One behind the other?"

"Affirmative."

"All I can see is *one* car blocking the road, and all the feet seem to have the eye on it."

The fog and the counter-surveillance car.

Two wild cards.

And reacting to both had broken up Oscar's five-car plan.

The five feet too. The two wild cards had broken up their plan as well.

Normally, pitching the feet worked like this: Each car had both a driver and a rider known as "the foot." The vehicles tailed the target by cycling through their five-car ballet until the target got ready to "lay down the wheels." The moment the bad guys began to park their car, each driver had to surreptitiously pitch his foot so the foot trackers could pick up the tail. At that point, the drivers "buried" their cars, blending into the background while finding parking spots. The others continued the ballet on foot.

The first foot was control.

The second was his backdoor.

The third was double back.

And the last two flanked the backdoor as parallels.

Pitching the feet, like surveillance, was an art. You had to stay far enough back not to be noticed but close enough to switch to leather. And you had to perform both in a way that appeared natural, in case *you* were being watched by a counter-surveillance team.

It was like "Spy vs. Spy" in *Mad* magazine.

The wild cards, however, had undermined that, forcing Special O to pitch the feet from parallel streets, and when none of the watchers had the eye, T1 had slipped away in the fog while T2 fell back to run interference.

It was decision time.

Lives hung in the balance.

With T1 gone, there could be no error with T2 or DeClercq would have the Hetts' blood on his hands.

"Who's *not* VCB vacant on T1?" he asked.

Dead air.

"Is T2 moving?"

"Negative, Chief."

"What's going on inside?"

"Hard to tell. Tinted windows and all. I can see the lit-up screen of a navigation system."

"That's what we're up against. A digital map. T2 can navigate this city on the fly."

"If we lose them, game over," warned one of the feet.

"Okay," DeClercq decided. "Here's what we do."

The plan he laid out was overheard by every ear wired to the ciphered channel.

That's why they paid him the big bucks.

"Take them," ordered the chief.

Fixed Bayonets

The members of the Emergency Response Team—
ERT, to the Mounties—drove Chevrolet Subur-
bans big enough to muscle other cars off the road.
When it came to vehicular takedowns, the goal
was to wrest control, and they didn't want the
bad guys elbowing their bulk on through. Instead,
they tried to hit them hard, cut them off, and
pinch them in, jamming them from both sides.
Hitting them hard was taken very literally—the
bigger the bang, the better—and during those pre-
cious few seconds when the bad guys were
stunned, the Mounties would smash windows
with hand-held battering rams and blow the occupants away the instant they drew guns.

Normally, that was just common sense.

Live and let die.

But today, DeClercq had said, "I want the car in one piece."

An ERT package usually shadowed Oscar from way back, biding time until the command was given to move in. But this was going to be hand-to-hand with fixed bayonets, so the Mad Dog and Ghost Keeper parked their wheels at Robson and Jervis and began to sneak in on foot.

Ordinarily, black was the color of an ERT cop's garb. Pull-down balaclava cap to cover the face. Turtleneck beneath a combat jacket over cargo pants. Tactical vest with movable Velcro pouches stuffed with tear gas, pepper spray, ammo clips, and stun grenades. Nine mil on the hip and a submachine gun in the hands. Still, this was the Great White North, so the team also had winter camouflage. In the white wear the Cree and the Mad Dog pulled on, they looked like ghosts in the fog.

"Ready?"

"Ready."

"Let's do it," Ghost Keeper said.

They called themselves the Assassins, the triad inside T2. All were lean, mean, and hungry, and on their way up in the yakuza. Back in Tokyo, they had jumped at the chance to make their bones for the legendary *kumicho*, Genjo Tokuda. So now here they idled, blocking the street in case any cops were on their tail, while the Claw made a getaway with the old American who was marked for death.

"Anything behind us?"

"Not that I can see."

The Assassin in back was squinting out the rear window.

"The man with the dog?"

"Nothing. He vanished into the fog."

"We'll wait a minute more. Then we'll vanish too."

"I'm north on Jervis, nearing Barclay," Craven said into his mike.

"I'm east on Barclay, nearing Jervis," said a gruff voice in the plug in his ear.

"Hang on."

"You too."

Bang!

They collided.

The impact of the collision spun both Oscar cars around a quarter turn, effectively blocking the hazy intersection just a few car lengths in front of the target vehicle.

"You stupid asshole!" Craven shouted as he staggered out into the mist, holding a hand to his temple.

"Fuck you!" the other driver shouted back, waving a clenched fist as he emerged from his door.

"I had the right of way, dick wad!"

"You were speeding."

"Yeah, sure. In this weather."

"Come here and I'll knock your block off!"

"You and whose army?"

"Just me, you dumb cocksucker!"

And that was it. The street fighters might as well have been rolling up their sleeves as they closed on each other in between their banged-up cars.

Push . . .

Shove . . .

Push . . .

Shove . . .

Craven threw a punch with his good hand.

"Back up," ordered the Assassin in the passenger's seat. "This fight will attract the cops."

Honnnk!

A car appeared in the fog behind them, blocking their retreat down the narrow street.

"Who's driving?"

"Some Chinese bitch I can barely see over the steering wheel," the thug in back answered.

Honnnk!

Honnnk!

Honnnk!

The back-seat thug was trying to wave off the tailgater through the rear window.

Honnnk!

Honnnk!

"Deal with her," ordered the Assassin in front. "The crash scene is drawing a crowd."

The man walking his German shepherd reappeared on the far side of the street. Either he'd circled the block on his regular walk or he'd been lured by the commotion.

Coming up behind the Assassins' car on this side of the street, and passing the bitch who—

Honnnk!

Honnnk!

—wouldn't let up on the horn, were a pair of beefy guys nuzzling each other in what would have been broad daylight were it not for the murk seeping through the swirling haze. Not only did the two have their arms draped across each other's shoulders, but the homos wore identical white jackets, as if to announce to the world that they were on the same team.

That's what happens, the back-seat Assassin thought as he began to open his door, when a degenerate country like this allows butt-fuckers to marry.

Honnnk!

Honnnk!

Honnnk!

Okay, bitch. Either you back up the fucking car, he said to himself as one foot hit the ground and his hand crossed to the shoulder holster just inside his gaping jacket, or I'll back it up with you dead on the floor.

Constable Cynthia Oh of Special O hit the horn again. Her left palm was on the steering wheel, and her right hand gripped the Smith & Wesson in her lap. As the least likely looking cop in the five-car plan—she was, in fact, the fifth wheel—she was chosen to pinch in T2 from behind.

"If they think something's up," DeClercq had warned, "they'll call T1 or Tokuda on their cellphones, and it'll be game over for Corporal Hett and us."

"Yes sir," Oh had said.

"We need that car in one piece, so an ERT Suburban can't ram it. With all this fog, an intersection collision won't be suspicious. But once a car pulls up behind, T2's survival instinct will kick in, and you'll be on your own."

"Yes sir," Oh had said.

"You're far from the stereotype, Constable. You're the best hope we have. I'm depending on you to dispel their suspicions and then open up their car."

"Yes sir."

"Can you do it?"

"Yes sir," she had said.

So here she was—

Honnnk!

Honnnk!

—playing picador, and about to find out if she would get gored.

"It's going down," Craven muttered to the cop he was pushing around.

"Want more?" he shouted to keep up the ruse.

"Tell me when," mumbled the cop who had his back to T2.

Both itched to go for their guns.

The foot across the street was a dog master in the Mounted. A Mountie and his dog, they fit the stereotype. Except that this stubble-faced old fart on the verge of retirement didn't look like Sergeant Preston. He could be—and was—a granddad.

Crouching down, the foot fed the dog a biscuit. Then he unhooked the leash.

With a simple command, the dog would be off for the kill.

The Assassin in the passenger's seat was protected by bulletproof glass. Just beneath the bottom rim of the passenger's window, his index finger curled around the trigger of a Steyr pistol. These three killers were into firearms, and they knew quality.

In the side-view mirror, the Assassin watched the gay men approaching the car. Behind him, the man in the back seat was half in and half out of the interior.

"Watch the queers," the passenger warned as the hit man exited to deal with the bitch.

They never knew what hit them.

The "gay" man closest to the curb had one hand in his pocket and his other arm pointed away across the shoulders of his "lover." From the corner of his eye, the Mad Dog caught enough of a peek inside the gaping jacket of the yakuza emerging from the car to sign his death warrant. As the embracing pair drew parallel with the open door, the ERT cop tapped his partner lightly on the far shoulder.

The other "gay" man flicked his eyes left. Because he was left-handed, Ghost Keeper had taken the inside position, resting his glove on his buddy's curbside shoulder. That flick of his eyes had allowed him to sight along that arm to the glove, which was pointing at the yakuza's head. Instead of a human hand, the glove was filled with the grip and barrel of the SIG P210 the Cree had just received as a birthday gift.

The tips of the fingers were open . . .

Bam!

To let the bullet fly.

The problem with bulletproof glass is that it protects both ways. The Assassin in the passenger's seat was immune to any pistol shots fired by the "queers," but they were also shielded from any return fire he might be contemplating.

Behind the passenger's seat, however, the door yawned open, and even before the goon with the new third eye in his forehead could drop to the curb, the Mad Dog had deftly lobbed a stun grenade into the car.

BAM!

It exploded like an atom bomb.

Inside the car, the din blew both Assassins' eardrums. While the armed thugs were lost in the confusion, the Mad Dog dove headfirst into the back seat. Aiming up to do as little damage to the vehicle as possible, he—

Bam!

Bam!

—shot both Assassins through the head.

Constable Oh shifted into reverse, then retreated down Jervis Street so the yakuza car was free to move again.

Crawling out of the back seat and holstering his weapon, the Mad Dog helped Ghost Keeper shove the curbside corpse back into the car. The inspector jumped into the back seat as the sergeant circled around to the driver's door. Pushing the dead wheelman across the dead passenger's lap so he could squeeze in, the ERT cop tailed Constable Oh through the fog.

In the end, the fog had been a blessing. The takedown was hidden from public view, and the crowd that eventually gathered was dispersed with a simple "There's nothing to see, folks. Just an auto accident caused by the fog and some firecrackers set off by a pair of troublemaking kids. Hey, it's Halloween."

Only one civilian—a pedestrian on his way to the store to buy a pack of smokes—had witnessed the action. The guy was about to call someone on his cellphone when a foot stopped him.

"Sir, what you saw is only part of this crime. If something goes wrong, hostages will die. There will be an investigation to see if there was a leak, and as the only civilian here, you'll be the prime suspect. The call you're making will lead to your standing trial, and chances are you'll spend a couple of years in jail. So for your own protection, I want you to come with me. We'll have a cup of coffee while you record your witness statement. By the time you're finished, the police response will be over, and I'll be witness to the fact that you did nothing wrong. Well, what do you say?"

"Depends."

"Depends on what?"

"Will you buy me a doughnut?"

War Memorial

Tinian, Mariana Islands
August 6, 1945

"The party's on!" the mess officer bellowed when news reached the Tinian airfield that the mission was a success. The 509th's kitchens buzzed with activity as hot dogs by the thousands plopped into cooking pots, and crates of beer and lemonade were put in the fridges to cool, and pies by the hundreds were baked for a pie-eating contest. It would be the biggest "blowout" Tinian had ever seen. . . . A poor choice of words, given the much *bigger* blowout that had rained down on Hiroshima.

The program read:

509TH

FREE BEER PARTY TODAY 2 P.M.

TODAY—TODAY—TODAY—TODAY—TODAY

PLACE—509TH BALL DIAMOND

FOR ALL MEN OF THE 509TH COMPOSITE GROUP

FOUR (4) BOTTLES OF BEER PER MAN—

NO RATION CARD NEEDED

LEMONADE FOR THOSE WHO DON'T CARE FOR BEER

ALL-STAR SOFTBALL GAME 2 P.M.

JITTERBUG CONTEST

HOT MUSIC

NOVELTY ACTS

SURPRISE CONTEST—YOU'LL FIND OUT

EXTRA ADDED ATTRACTION: BLONDE,

VIVACIOUS, CURVACEOUS

STARLET DIRECT FROM ???????

PRIZES—GOOD ONES TOO

Wear Old Clothes Wear Old Clothes Wear Old Clothes

6 AUGUST 1945

WELCOME PARTY FOR RETURN OF *ENOLA GAY*

FROM HIROSHIMA MISSION

At 2:58 p.m., after twelve hours and thirteen minutes in the air, the B-29 Superfortress touched down on Tinian's runway. Two hundred officers and men were crowded on the macadam. Several thousand more lined the taxiways. A cheer went up as the *Enola Gay*'s crew came down from the hatch behind the nose wheel, and cameramen set off flashbulbs almost as bright as the explosion over Hiroshima. General Spaatz walked up and pinned the Distinguished Service Cross on Tibbets's chest. They saluted. Photographs of the bomb exploding were rushed to Washington for worldwide distribution. The crew was debriefed with shots of bourbon and free cigarettes, and the party got into full swing.

A great day, Joe thought, to be an American.

Vancouver
November 1, Now

Now here was Joe sixty years later, taking a one-way ride between two Japanese thugs with his hands tied behind his back, his past about to catch up with him. Of the almost three million Japanese people who died in the Pacific War, Joe had personally destroyed more than one hundred thousand.

That was a lot of guilt for one old man to carry.

Joe couldn't blame Tokuda for wanting revenge. If the shoe were on the other foot and the yakuza boss had fried Joe's family in the war simply to give Japan a little leverage with the pesky Russians, Joe would've strapped on the six-guns and watch out! No matter how long it took—as the saying went, "Revenge is a dish best served cold"—he'd have hunted Tokuda down.

Wasn't that the American way?

Joe *was* raised on westerns.

When he was young, he'd been a fan of Chester Gould's square-jawed detective. From the early 1930s on, he had followed the celebrated cases of Dick Tracy in the comic strips of his hometown newspaper. There had never been a rogues' gallery like that, with Tracy up against villains like the Mole—not *this* Mole, but one that resembled a rodent—B-B Eyes, Pruneface, the Brow, Flattop, Mumbles, and Sketch Paree. They were, of course, no match for the police, thanks to Tracy's scientific arsenal, which included state-of-the-art devices like the Voice-O-Graf for comparing speech patterns and his best-known marvel, his two-way wrist radio.

Man, did Joe feel old.

It was hard to fathom how an airman who'd once dropped an atom bomb on Japan—ushering in a future of nuclear dread that drove the pre-Hiroshima innocence into the past—had become so out of touch with technologies that were just ordinary to modern young people. No two-way wrist radios for them. Nosiree. They moved about with iPods, BlackBerrys, Palm Pilots, and cellphone cameras that were basically two-way wrist TVs.

Like the gizmo the Navigator had just pulled out of his pocket and was switching on.

"Made in Japan."

Joe winced at his own arrogance. He'd been around in the 1950s, when Japanese technology was a national joke. He remembered laughing along with everyone else at that scene in *The Fly* where the scientist transports a bowl from here to there in his atomizer, and it arrives on the far side with "Made in Japan" inscribed backwards on the bottom.

Joe wasn't laughing now.

He was doomed.

But even in the face of death, his mind went to one of those little nuggets of trivia that later seem so ironic.

The screenplay for *The Fly* was written by James Clavell.

The guy who wrote *Shogun*.

Since they'd tossed his cellphone and hearing aids out of the car, Tattoo, the Mole, the Wheelman, and the Navigator had made no move to communicate with the outside world. That made sense to Joe, despite his unease with technology, for if they'd jettisoned all his electronics to keep the cops from zeroing in on them with tracking devices, it would be foolish to emit signals of their own.

So why now?

Joe figured it had to be so these hoods could survey for traps. Not traps back there, for their wild ride through the fog of the West End had surely left Special O breathing their fumes. First, they had zigzagged down to English Bay, where rolling waves of mist came billowing in from the sea, curling clawed fingers around the windows of his mobile prison. Then they had hugged the shoreline, heading west toward this forest, which Joe assumed was Stanley Park, and where, suddenly, it began to rain.

Now, as the miniature screen in the Navigator's hands shimmered green, they circled around a huge pond—towering trees on the left, rain-pocked lagoon on the right—and that's when the goon riding shotgun wrenched around in the passenger's seat.

Whatever the gizmo in his hand, he passed it back to the Mole.

And as the screen went skirting past, Joe got a look at the digital horror show.

Joe was right. His captors weren't communicating with the counter-surveillance car. No, the Navigator was checking ahead for traps at their destination, and that's why he had linked to a hidden camera aimed across what seemed to be a sushi bar at an executioner's chair that held their other captive: Joe's granddaughter, Jackie.

If the cops were there, they'd have freed her.

Jackie was still tied up, so shouldn't that indicate the hoods were safe?

Well, it didn't.

For while Joe's eyes were damned by the sight of Jackie's naked breasts surrounded by a serving tray of torture knives—What had they done to her? What did they *plan* to do?—the Mole's eyes widened at the sight of what was at Jackie's feet: the severed head of the Sushi Chef.

"The rack is on the track." One of the old guys from Oscar's early years.

"Rack" was their term for a car.

The new guys called a car "wheels."

"Where?" DeClercq asked from the command van, which was already on the move to the West End takedown scene.

"T1 came along the road behind Lost Lagoon and just entered the underpass beneath the causeway."

"They're going into Stanley Park?"

"Affirmative, Chief."

"By which fork? Up through the rose garden or along the seawall shore?"

"The seawall."

"What's traffic like on the causeway?"

"Slow and thin. The fog has kept a lot of cars off the road. There's one lane open going north and one coming south. No cars in the middle lane. It's changing direction."

"Where's your vehicle?"

"Back a bit. I'm on foot."

"Here, Chief," reported the driver. "I'm near the cherry trees at the entrance to the causeway."

"Regroup and take the shortcut up past the aquarium. I want you waiting for them at the intersection with the seawall drive, close to the figurehead of the *Empress of Japan*."

"And tail them?"

"Affirmative."

"Consider it done, Chief."

The command van neared Jervis Street as De-Clercq turned from the bank of TV screens and asked Winter to call the Stanley Park causeway patrol.

"Have them keep the middle lane clear for us, and block all traffic to the Lions Gate Bridge.

Make sure there's a gap at the south end, where the park drive accesses the causeway."

Right away, the sergeant got on the phone.

"The ERT Suburban is coming up on the right," the driver radioed back from the cab of the command van.

"And T2?" asked DeClercq.

"It's parked in front, Chief. Ghost Keeper, the Mad Dog, and their team are at the curb."

Inside the car that was still in play, the hoods were breaking out the hardware.

Outside the windows, the rain and fog were fighting a new Pacific War.

As a recent convert to libertarianism—what was good enough for Clint Eastwood was good enough for him—Joe was an even more ardent advocate for the Second Amendment. All his life, he had known his way around high-powered guns, but it shocked him to see the firepower these goons had onboard. It was bad enough that Tattoo pulled out a Kahr P45, a polymer pistol that smashed the .45 barrier, but then both the Mole and the Navigator fetched Beretta Storm Carbines, black, ugly-looking semi-autos related to swordfish.

These guys meant business.

The Wheelman hunched over the dash, squinting out into the weird weather for signs of anything untoward up ahead, while Tattoo twisted around to make sure that no cop car was hugging their ass. The fog cloaking them degenerated into beggar's rags as the rain tore through the fabric of the mist. Crawling counter-clockwise around Stanley Park, the vehicle ventured deeper into the surreal. Before they could see the Brockton Point Lighthouse, past the Nine O'Clock Gun, they angled north into a creepy quagmire of gigantic monsters. Stacked one on top of another up into the smothering shrouds, a gang of totem carvings crowded in for a final look at Joe before he was executed.

The West End runs up to the south shore of Lost Lagoon, where Stanley Park stretches north to the Lions Gate Bridge. From Jervis Street to Lost Lagoon was no more than seven city blocks, so now the Suburban—with four cops inside—hightailed it along the deserted center lane of the bisecting causeway. The traffic both ways had snarled to a halt, an everyday bottleneck that clenched the teeth of commuters.

"What's the layout in T1?" the Mad Dog asked, pedal to the metal as he overdrove the foglights.

He used the parallel lines of cars to guide him like a luge chute.

"Two bad guys in front and two in back," said DeClercq through the plug in his ear. "The colonel's sandwiched between the two in back. He's American. They're Japanese. He's in his eighties. They're between twenty and forty. He's wearing a light green jacket with a red turtleneck. They're in ninja black."

"Confirmed," said the Mad Dog. "The cutoff from the park drive's coming up. We can't ram T1 with the colonel in it. If these four are quick and armed to the teeth, one of them will shoot Hett before we can bust in."

"The gap's coming up," said Ghost Keeper from the shotgun seat.

"Hang on, Chief. I got some driving to do."

The seaside road around Stanley Park crossed the causeway on an overpass just this end of the bridge. Halfway around the circle, sightseers could abandon the park by way of a short cutoff that gave them access to the causeway before it arched across the narrows to the North Shore. So many accidents clogged the main artery every day that a tow truck stood ready to respond at the junction where the cutoff met the thoroughfare. Currently, that truck deliberately blocked the northbound lane a few yards this side of the exit from the park, creating a gap for the cops.

The Mad Dog spun the wheel and turned in front of the truck. The Suburban drove the wrong way up the tree-lined cutoff to the park road, where it peeled rubber in a clockwise direction toward the seashore. The cops and the yakuza were on a collision course.

Ghost Keeper flicked on the FLIR.

Forward-looking infrared.

"T1's coming to a halt," said the new control, the pair that had spotted the target car driving around Lost Lagoon.

"Where?" asked DeClercq from the command van, which was farther back on the park drive.

"Alongside the figurehead."

"The *Empress of Japan*?"

"Affirmative."

"Where are you?" asked the chief.

"On the T road."

"Did they spot you?"

"I doubt it. If so, would they be stopping?"

"Don't move."

"Roger."

"You've got the eye."

"That's touch and go," the driver said, "depending on the fog. It's in a tug-of-war with the rain."

"Then pitch your foot."

A pause.

"My foot's out, Chief."

"You hear me, Foot?"

"Yes sir."

"What's your name?"

"Singh, sir."

"Okay, Singh. It's up to you. Find somewhere you won't be seen, but keep your eye on T1."

"Roger."

"Mad Dog, where are you?"

"Approaching Lumberman's Arch, near as I can tell. We're using FLIR to pick up heat signatures."

"Chief?"

"Yes, Singh."

"They're vacating T1."

All four yakuza unbuckled their seatbelts. Joe took that to be an ominous sign. If he was about to be butchered, he figured they'd all want to see. Tattoo swung open the rear door on the harbor side, holstering his pistol to free up his hands, then hauled Joe out of the back seat by his biceps and flung him toward the water.

On the other side of the car, the Mole—known

to the yakuza thugs as the Claw—opened his door and climbed out too.

He said something in Japanese.

Tattoo drew his pistol and aimed it at Joe on the ground, then he leaned back over the roof of the car to catch what the Mole was saying.

Joe knew this was it. He was about to die. And his death would seal the fate of Jackie as well. Pearl Harbor had taught him how to stare down the fear of death. *His* death, but not the death of someone put in peril because of him. Staring down the muzzle, Joe felt an overwhelming dread grab hold of him, and he loathed himself for giving in to guilt-driven panic as he exited from life.

Forgive me, Jackie, he prayed.

"They're gonna do him, Chief. They've thrown Hett clear of the car and are about to shoot."

"Clear the air," snapped DeClercq.

Time to earn the big bucks.

"You've got the eye, Singh. Call it," he delegated.

"Hit 'em head-on," said the foot.

A veering jog left, and the Mad Dog had the Suburban zooming along the waterfront curb. The forward-looking infrared caught the heat signatures—and relative positions—of every human body on

its screen. "Hang on," he told the other three commando cops onboard, then the huge Suburban
rammed the stationary vehicle like the *Titanic*
emerging suddenly from the Atlantic mist—
bang!—and plowed it back along the seawall curb.

Smash, smash . . .

Splat, splat . . .

Two red starbursts stained the bulletproof
windshield as the Wheelman's and the Navigator's heads exploded like watermelons hurled
against the glass.

Tattoo and the Claw were both standing behind
the open back doors, so the force of the shove
scooped them off their feet and propelled them
along the road. Tattoo had been near the car, listening to the Claw, so he was thrown straight. The
Claw had been moving away from the car to circle
around to Joe, so the edge of the door clipped him
and spun him off into the park.

One moment, he was there.

The next, he was gone.

Like gangbusters, the strike team stormed out
of the battering ram. On the curbside, the Mad
Dog rushed T1 while the commando from the
back seat knelt down in front of Joe, protecting
him behind his armored vest as the submachine
gun in his hands swept the air for a target.

"Clear!" the Mad Dog shouted after checking inside the car. "Two dead in the front seats. Two unaccounted for."

Ghost Keeper and the commando cop from the passenger's side of the Suburban were somewhere in the rain and fog, playing "now you see them, now you don't" with the hoods who'd been thrown back by the doors.

"Drop it!"

Bam!

Bam!

Bam!

"One down," reported a voice from the haze.

That's when the Mad Dog caught sight of the Claw through the vapor, sprinting toward the aquarium with a 9mm Storm Carbine in his hand.

Like a bucket of water dumped over a drunk, the downpour began. Black clouds let loose a deluge, returning Vancouver to what it called normal weather. The fog was no match for the sudden onslaught, so it liquefied like a waterlogged ghost. Up from the sea and between the scattered trees, the Mad Dog chased the Claw, slopping through a curtain of raindrops. Ironically, the runners splashed toward the Japanese-Canadian War Memorial. The monument loomed at the end of its tree-lined path like a beacon luring warriors to their fate.

The sight of the severed head at Jackie Hett's feet on the Navigator's digital screen had warned the Claw that there was danger lurking up the mountain.

"If something goes wrong," the *kumicho* had told his enforcer, "claw the eyes out of the colonel and put a bullet in his brain. Dump him somewhere fitting."

The figurehead of the *Empress of Japan* had seemed a significant enough killing ground to the Claw.

And it was nearby.

Things had gone from bad to worse, however, and now the Claw was running for his *kumicho*'s life. There was nothing he could do to reverse the situation in the sushi bar, so he had avoided calling Tokuda until the colonel was dead. Those were his orders, and in the yakuza, orders were obeyed.

But different rules applied to the situation he was now in. For botching his assignment, the Claw had to die. If he escaped, he would kill himself with his hara-kiri knife. And if it came to a last stand, he'd go down with honor in a kamikaze run.

After he warned his *kumicho*.

The Claw fished his cellphone out of his black pants. Tokuda's number wasn't programmed in, just in case the phone was seized in a sneak attack, and it was hard to punch in the numbers as he ran full tilt. But a few yards short of the monument's plinth, the phone began to trill.

Then . . .

Bam!

The Mad Dog shot him in the back.

The Claw's arms flew wide as in crucifixion. He dropped the cellphone and the gun, and crumpled to his knees.

With a final spurt, the Mad Dog reached the monument. He was about to grab the fugitive and cuff his arms together when the shot yakuza lunged with his hara-kiri knife. The razor-sharp blade sank to the hilt above the Mountie's groin, where the armor didn't protect his gut.

A grunt escaped the Mad Dog's throat as the Claw spiked him up on his toes and swung him around on the skewer so his back slammed against the column. Blood gushed down his legs and pooled around the gun, which had clattered from his fingers. The Claw used his shoulder to pin the cop against the pillar, then he crooked his other arm up to gouge out the Mad Dog's eyes. Their faces were so close together that they breathed each other's breath, and the blood that spewed from one man's head drowned the features of his foe.

"You're looking at the Rolls-Royce of nine mils, pal. Y'ever seen a Europellet popper like that? Even unmodified out of the box, the P210 will shoot sub-two-inch clusters at twenty-five yards. When accuracy is paramount, it's the closest thing to perfection in a pistol. That's why it's a fixture at European prize shoots. One thing about the Swiss, they know their precision engineering."

Ghost Keeper was too far away to safely take the shot, and the curtain of rain blurred the target at this end, so it was up to the accuracy of the Cree and the SIG.

The slug caught the Claw behind the ear and blew out the front of his temple. Since the day his mother sent him into the woods on his spirit quest, Ghost Keeper had been hunting on the last frontier. What the woods had taught him guided his aim now, and the P210 was as accurate as a Swiss cuckoo clock.

The Claw was dead before his remains hit the ground.

By the time the Cree got to his partner, the Mad Dog was bleeding out.

"A member is down," Ghost Keeper told his open mike. "We need an ambulance, and we need it *now!*"

Hara-Kiri

The TV screen to one side of the executioner's chair jumped to life when a car approached the external camera. How long had it been since Jackie had watched the last car leave? That vehicle had vanished into the tendrils of fog clawing up the mountainside. But this car materialized from a sheet of rain.

Here we go, she thought.

And she didn't know which would be worse.

The return of whoever had hacked off the Sushi Chef's head with what Jackie—judging by the clean cut across the neck and all the samurai films she'd seen—concluded was a sword?

Or the return of Tokuda's yakuza gang, unaware that someone had taken out her would-be torturer at the top of the stairs?

Knock, knock . . .

Who's there? she thought.

Whoever sat behind the tinted windshield of the car had a remote control that opened the garage, and after the vehicle was inside, the TV went black again.

Moments later, the Third World War erupted overhead. Deafening explosions reverberated down the stairs, quickly followed by storm troopers armed with laser-guided weapons.

Sweep . . .

Sweep . . .

Sweep . . .

"She's alive!" someone shouted.

And the next thing she knew, Dane Winter was releasing her from the chair and using his jacket like Sir Walter Raleigh to hide her naked breasts from macho cop eyes.

"Say something," her partner said.

"Man, do I have to pee."

"How'd you find me?" Jackie asked, rubbing circulation back into her numb wrists.

"If you and I were sent to Tokyo to kill Tokuda, how do you think we'd find our way around?"

"A navigation program. A GPS map."

"One thing about the Japanese, they love their digital magic. What the yakuza used to navigate through Vancouver was a global positioning system with pinpoint accuracy. They punched in their destination—this house atop the mountain—and the software offered up every possible route to evade us. At any given map point, they knew where they were, so all the wheelman had to do was follow his navigator's directions: 'Turn left here. Turn right there. And gun it three blocks straight ahead.' "

"Reverse engineering?" said Jackie.

Dane nodded. "DeClercq had several problems. A clock was ticking. He didn't know where you were. And if he did, he couldn't have your kidnapping turn into a hostage situation. So as soon as he got intel that the yakuza were using a navigation system, his priority was to seize one of their cars before they could erase this destination and destroy the equipment."

"Which you accomplished?"

"Uh-huh. In the West End. Before they knew what hit them, they were dead. We had not only their destination—the *address* here—but the remote control to this garage as well. Since the windows are tinted, we had a Trojan horse."

"Slam, bam, thank you, man," Jackie said.
"That's what partners are for."

The headless corpse of the Sushi Chef lay
sprawled in a pool of blood at the top of the staircase from the sushi bar. Near him was a *katana*,
the big samurai sword, which appeared to have
come from a *daisho* rack on the far side of the
room. Whoever had done the beheading had
waited at the mouth of the stairs, and as the yakuza finished ascending from below, that person
swung the sword in a sweeping arc—Jackie could
almost hear the swish—lopping off his head and
sending it bumping down the stairs to her feet.

Ouch!

What jumped into her mind was a Second
World War photo from *Life* magazine. In it, a
blindfolded Australian captive in tropical khaki
wear kneeled on the ground, oblivious to the fact
that a Japanese soldier with a samurai sword was
about to whack off his head.

Then she remembered an even more visceral
photo she'd seen reproduced on the cover of an
Italian magazine. It showed a kneeling Chinese
peasant, his face scrunched up in fear, an instant
after a samurai sword had swept through his
neck. The head was still in position above a neck-

lace of spraying blood, and the Japanese swordsman stood frozen in the follow-through of his blow.

Those images, of course, were history to her. But then she thought of Nicholas Berg, the Jewish-American businessman whose decapitation in Iraq had sparked a modern uproar when it was broadcast on the Internet.

Jackie shuddered.

What a dreadful way to go.

"This guy was lucky," Dane said, "compared with what happened to the old man over there."

He ushered Jackie across the floor to a *shoji* screen that hid the other cadaver from view. The room felt very Japanese, all *tatami* matting and Oriental antiques. Watercolors and decorated fans hung on the walls. A delicate sake set adorned a short *kotatsu* table. A sheet covering a section of the floor was all but red from too much blood and piled high with spilled guts.

"Ugh!" Jackie exclaimed.

"A true samurai," Dane said, "was always armed with a pair of swords stuck through his kimono belt. One to kill his enemies. The other to kill himself."

"Both got used," said Jackie.

"So what do you think happened?"

"Tokuda and his henchman were downstairs with me. Tokuda was eating sushi. A closed-circuit camera showed the arrival of a car, and I thought Tokuda said the Japanese word for 'son.' He left the sushi bar and climbed the stairs, leaving me with the Sushi Chef. Tokuda must have been ambushed up here. He was knocked out, stunned, gagged, or something. His henchman heard a noise—I saw him cock his head—and went to investigate. When he reached the top of the staircase, the swordsman struck, and his head came bouncing down to land at my feet. Then I heard grunting and a voice upstairs. I couldn't tell if it was male or female. After that, the camera showed the same car leaving the scene."

"There must have been a falling-out among the hoods," Dane concluded. "Some disgruntled yakuza whacked both his boss and his boss' faithful bodyguard."

"I suppose," Jackie said. "That would explain this."

"How so?"

"It looks to me like someone thought the yakuza boss should have committed hara-kiri to atone for some dishonor. And because he didn't, the killer performed it on him."

Genjo Tokuda was kneeling on the bloody

sheet. Each wrist was lashed to an ankle, and then the cinched limbs were tied to a heavy wooden chair. The weight of the furniture kept Tokuda upright, even in death. The old man's gray kimono had been parted to expose his naked belly. Following the time-honored ritual of seppuku, the shorter *wakizashi* sword from the *daisho* rack had been plunged into the left side of his abdomen. The hara-kiri blade still protruded from Tokuda's stomach. The pinkish-brown coils of the *kumicho*'s intestines had spilled out onto the floor. His vacant eyes stared down at the mess he'd made.

"I wonder how long it took him to die?" said Dane. "There was no swordsman to lop off his head."

"Oh, there was a swordsman, all right," Jackie speculated. "But he stood by, taunting Tokuda as he died in excruciating pain. It had to be a he, if the killer was yakuza. The gangs don't trust women and won't let them in."

"He isn't gagged. And there's no chafing around the mouth, like I'd expect to see."

"All I heard was grunts."

"You'd think he'd have screamed blue murder."

"Tough old guy," Jackie said. "Where'd he find the courage to go through death like that?"

"*Bushido*," said her partner.

Flamethrower

November 2, Now

Lyn Barrow felt liberated. She was almost free of the past. If not for the Japanese soldiers who had overrun St. Stephen's during the fall of Hong Kong, what might her life have been? She would have been the only child born to Viv and her mother's lover, Captain Richard Walker. Would they have married, settled in England after the war, and raised her as the daughter of a loving two-parent family? Would she, too, have met a dashing beau, and would they have enjoyed a storybook romance in exotic locales?

Probably not. That's why romance fiction racked up the sales. If readers were actually living such exciting lives, there'd be no market for heart-throb fantasies.

But maybe.

If only she'd stood a chance.

Instead, Genjo Tokuda had ruined Lyn's life. A man she had never met had destroyed her mother, by raping her amid a pile of hacked-up bodies and then imprisoning her for close to four years in a brutal concentration camp that stank of never-ending fear. That had shackled Lyn with a chain of monstrous burdens she'd never been able to shrug off.

But now she was *almost* free.

Viv's death had emancipated Lyn from her role as caregiver to a broken-down wreck.

And Tokuda's death had satisfied her craving for revenge.

If only he had screamed!

You'd think any man whose intestines had been spilled out in front of him would scream and scream and scream with horror, if not from pain.

But Tokuda hadn't.

All he had done was grunt.

And then he had died from loss of blood.

And that was it.

Oh, well, Lyn thought. At least he's dead. And I have the comfort of knowing he died by *my* hand.

So the only loose end was Tokuda's son.

And now he too had to die.

For until her half-brother was gone from her life, Lyn knew she'd never *really* be free.

It was supposed to happen like this.

First, they would ambush Joe Hett's son, Chuck, and hurl him from the kamikaze plane, which would then dive-bomb the war vets' convention. But that was only meant to tear the heart out of that Yankee airman, to soften him up for the payback yet to come and to mask the motive for the attack until Tokuda and his Pacific War enemy were face to face. Abducting Hett's granddaughter would be torture enough. Imagine the horrors that would eat at his mind after what had been done to his son. But that would be nothing compared with what the colonel would witness once he, too, was in the yakuza's clutches. Having slit Hett's eyelids off to make sure he couldn't blink, the Sushi Chef would strip Jackie down to her bones. And finally—in an imitation of the Hiroshima bombing—the *kumicho* would use a blowtorch to fry the colonel alive.

Smoked meat.

But now the *kumicho* was dead, so it was left to Kamikaze, his new-found son, to find a suitable killing ground and char Hett's aging flesh from his skeleton.

The police car dropped Joe off at the front doors of the hotel. The excitement of yesterday had spiked his blood pressure into the danger zone, so St. Paul's Hospital had checked in an unwilling patient for overnight observation. Here in the hotel lobby, Joe veered toward the conference area, which was cordoned off by yellow crime-scene tape.

The huge convention hall was all but deserted. The forensic techs didn't want their evidence contaminated by a thundering herd, and those responsible for the structural integrity of the building didn't want to risk a thousand-plaintiff lawsuit should the roof collapse.

Ducking under the tape, Joe entered the hall.

Like the pier on which it was built, the rectangular vault extended into the harbor from the south shore. The kamikaze plane had slammed into the west side, so that's where a dozen clue hunters in white coveralls, hoods, and foot bags were looking for evidence.

Strung about Joe's neck was a police pass, which gave him the authorization to breach the tape.

No one stopped him.

The central and eastern two-thirds of the hall had been cleared as a path of contamination. That meant the techs had all they wanted from it. Joe paused inside the door to gaze at the kamikaze wreck before slowly making his way along the exhibit stalls lining the opposite side of the hall. The memories of an old man are the deeds of a man in his prime. So sayeth Pink Floyd, according to Jackie. Joe passed an eclectic mix of artifacts and recreations from the Second World War, the Korean War, and the Vietnam War. Mannequins wore uniforms from various combatants. Regimental and division flags flapped in an artificial breeze, thanks to the pins holding them up. Medals and patches and plaques and emblems from every unit were on display, as were weapons and anti-aircraft shells. A statuette of Douglas MacArthur, corncob pipe clenched in his teeth, dominated a booth headlined "I Shall Return." Etched beneath his feet were the words *"Gaijin Shogun"*—meaning "foreign military ruler"—the nickname he earned while occupying Japan.

Kamikaze looked like a man who'd just come in from the rain. Actually, his loose raincoat was stuffed with four Molotov cocktails in separate inside pockets. Each bottle was topped with a flammable wick. A flick of one of several lighters in the external pockets of the recently initiated yakuza's coat and—*foom!*—fiery death would be at hand.

The trench coat came with a pull-up hood. Staring out through the face hole, he watched Joe Hett duck under the crime-scene tape.

The Pacific War convention hall.

What better killing ground?

At the far end of the hall—the far end of the pier—Joe stood in front of the podium where he was supposed to deliver that keynote speech. The lectern was backed by two photographs that encapsulated his and America's involvement in the war.

The photo on the left was the one from *Life* magazine. Staring up at himself, Joe recalled that defiant young man. With his dog tags flung out from his naked chest and his eyes flashing above the bloody streak in his shaving cream, the warrior blasted away at the Japanese Zero over his head.

Now, a lifetime later, Joe thought back to what the world was like before Pearl Harbor—back to the reality he had known just an hour before this photo was taken. His country was minding its own business, and even the Nazis' conquest of Europe couldn't suck America into Hitler's war.

"Dad, I want to fight."

"Where?"

"In Europe."

"Why?"

"Because it's the right thing to do."

"Red," his old man had said, shaking his head, "never provoke an enemy who's willing to die for his beliefs unless you're also willing to give up your life—*yours*, and not someone else's—for what you believe. War *is* hell, son. I saw it in the trenches. If your enemy is willing to fight to the last man, you gotta be fucking sure that *you* are too."

"I am."

"Ichioku Sotokko," Genjo Tokuda said when he and Kamikaze had talked of life and death the other night. "All one hundred million for *Tokko.*" That slogan was broadcast to the Japanese people in speech after speech during the Pacific War. Its underlying meaning was, "Every Japanese has the spirit to become a member of the Kamikaze Special Attack (*Tokko*) Corps."

"I knew a lieutenant in the army named Hajime

Fujii. After he became an officer, he switched to the air force and volunteered to join the kamikaze. Three times, he was rejected because he was a father with two young children. One day, he returned to his home near Tokyo and found a letter from his wife on the table. 'I know that because of us,' she had written, 'you cannot exert your utmost for the country. Therefore, allow us to take leave of the world before you join us. Please fight with nothing weighing on your mind.'

"The next day, his wife and two children were recovered from the Arakawa River. She carried their one-year-old daughter on her back and had tied their four-year-old daughter to her wrist. All three wore their best dresses.

"Freed of all impediments by the sacrifice of his wife, Lieutenant Fujii took off from an air base near Hiroshima and led nine attack planes in a kamikaze dive against the American warships off the coast of Okinawa.

"I was there. I saw them die honorably. We called their squadron *Kaishintai*. 'A spiritually satisfied unit.' That was not long before the Americans"—he touched his scarred face—"did *this* to me."

So now Kamikaze stood behind the crime-scene tape and watched as the atomic bomber who had wiped out his ancestral line in Hiroshima faced his fate.

The photo on the other side of the lectern was a shot of the mushroom cloud boiling over Japan as the *Enola Gay* made its sharp bank out of harm's way. But the black-and-white shot didn't capture the colors of hell.

What Joe had told his father was the truth: he *was* willing to die for his beliefs. What he wasn't willing to do, and had done unknowingly, was kill non-combatants for power politics.

Now, confronting that accursed blast, he recalled what Chuck had once said about the Vietnam War.

"Red?"

"Yeah, son?"

"I wonder why it took three decades for America to acknowledge the heroes of the My Lai Massacre? Back in '68, when I was fighting in 'Nam, we heard about Lieutenant Calley going berserk at that village, and about how GIs had indiscriminately shot Vietnamese civilians. That was a pivotal point in ending the war. Calley got life in prison—until Nixon made sure he went free."

"War crimes happen."

"Sure, but why did we hide the flipside of the

coin? What stopped the massacre was a single chopper crew. They flew over the bloodletting as it was under way, landing between those rogue GIs and the terrified villagers. They had to point their chopper guns at their own comrades to stop them killing. Two of them covered the pilot while he confronted the leader of the marauding forces, and that led to the ceasefire order. The crew coaxed some villagers out of a bunker for evacuation, then flew a wounded child to a hospital."

"They did the right thing, Chuck, and they got medals."

"In 1998! And only after a letter-writing campaign. It makes you wonder."

"What brought that on?"

"Retirement," Chuck said. "That's the kind of American hero I wish I'd been."

Now Chuck was dead, and Joe faced the mushroom cloud that was really aimed at Russia.

All those civilians slaughtered or slowly tortured to death through radiation sickness.

How he wished he could take back the bomb.

Joe would give his life to put that genie back in the bottle.

"'I'll meet you at Yasukuni Shrine,'" Genjo Tokuda had said during that talk with his son.

"That's the farewell that the kamikaze—and the rest of us too—exchanged before going into battle. 'A man must live in such a way that he is always prepared to die.' Confucius teaches us that. 'Only by reason of having died does one enter into life. The future life is the all-important thing.' We learn that from Buddhism. Honor means fighting to the bitter end. Surrender equals dishonor. It is only at the moment that he determines to die that a man attains purity. The discipline required of all samurai comes down to a readiness for death. Followers of *bushido* must fight on until every sword is broken and the last arrow is spent. There, my son, is the difference between cowardly Western and honorable Japanese philosophies. The West tells its soldiers how to live. We tell ours how to die."

For the first time in his wretched life, Kamikaze actually *felt* like a man. What had Dickens written at the end of *A Tale of Two Cities*? "It is a far, far better thing that I do, than I have ever done. It is a far, far better rest that I go to than I have ever known."

His life was a tale of two cities, and he had lived it miserably in the wrong one.

Tokyo.

That's where he belonged.

Now, as he ducked under the crime-scene tape,

Kamikaze focused on his father, who was waiting for him at the Yasukuni Shrine. In his mind, he saw the great bronze *torii* gateway and the broad approach lined with cherry trees, rows of stone lanterns, and statues of national heroes. Almost all of Japan's fallen soldiers, sailors, and airmen were registered as *kami*—as gods—at the shrine, an apotheosis that Kamikaze yearned to experience. There, among the guardian spirits of their nation, Genjo Tokuda bowed toward his son.

"I'll meet you at Yasukuni Shrine," Kamikaze said to himself as he lit the wick of the Molotov cocktail and began his run at the atomic bomber.

They called them "Judy bombers," back in the war.

Yokosuka D4Y3 Suisei planes.

Those diving devils that so plagued American warships.

Kamikaze attacks were unlike anything ever experienced in the wars of the Western world. Shintoism had no taboo against suicide. Instead, it was the ethical duty of the kamikaze to "bleed the enemy white" in any way possible.

Of the many Pacific War exhibits in the convention hall, none had the psychological lure of this kamikaze plane. Steps led up to the cockpit of a recreated Judy bomber, where vets could strap themselves in—as Joe was doing now—to relive what it would have been like to embark on a crash dive. The windshield in front was actually a video screen, and the headphones he clamped over both ears provided the sound effects. Joe punched a button and found himself gripped by the white-knuckle dread of a suicide run.

So engrossed was he in this digital fantasy that he missed the real-life attack closing in on him.

"Something's not right," DeClercq had said at Special X last night. He was debriefing Jackie on the deaths of Genjo Tokuda and his henchman, the Sushi Chef.

"What, Chief?" she'd asked.

"Every yakuza who flew in from Tokyo is dead, and each played a part in Tokuda's revenge against your family. The thugs he brought with him were hand-picked to carry out a personal vendetta. Tokuda was retired. Gang power had already passed to the next generation. So what's to be gained by killing him?"

"You think it was an outsider?"

"Could be the local yakuza. The goons who supplied the guns and the mountain house. Are they sending a message to Tokyo that they want independence?"

"If so, what's our move?"

"First, I want to be sure we're not missing something. Could it be that your grandfather is still in danger?"

"The killer didn't kill me."

"You're not the target, Jackie."

"What would be the motive for killing both the yakuza godfather *and* his wartime enemy?"

"I don't know. But I want to be sure that the colonel is off the hit list. There's only one way to determine that. After your granddad gets out of the hospital tomorrow, we offer the killer a chance to strike somewhere that fits Tokuda's vendetta."

"Where?"

"A shooting gallery we control."

So that's why Red had walked to the far end of the convention hall pier, and why the forensic techs combing the kamikaze crash scene were really ERT cops, and why Jackie—the moment the hooded intruder exposed his criminal intent by lighting the wick on the gasoline bomb—had reached inside the pocket of her white coveralls and yelled, "Stop! Police!"

Kamikaze heard the shout and knew that this was it. Chances were those forensic techs weren't armed, but police who were would respond within minutes. By then, he'd have hurled his gasoline bombs at the American colonel. Frying him alive in the cockpit of the mock kamikaze plane was a fitting revenge for the war crime he'd committed against Hiroshima. Then Genjo Tokuda's son would be worthy to meet his father and the samurai deities at Yasukuni Shrine.

"Banzai!" the attacker bellowed, breaking into a run, his crooked arm ready to throw the flaming bomb.

He never reached his target. There was only one defense to a kamikaze dive, and that was to fill the air with as much flak and shrapnel as you could, in the hope that something would hit the plane before it hit you. Because DeClercq was a tactician, that was his strategy, and every marksman lining the wall to Kamikaze's side had earned the sharpshooter badge worn above the cuff of the red serge uniform.

Several shots hit the bottles tucked inside the open coat, spewing a mist of gasoline about the charging figure, and the flaming wick on the Molotov cocktail in his hand ignited that halo in a whoosh of hellfire. Unlike his Pacific War counterparts, Kamikaze was dead before he hit the deck.

Who?

The morgue stank of burnt flesh, but unlike those wimpy TV cops who wore face masks, dabbed the skin under their noses with Vicks VapoRub, or dashed out to the john to hurl their Cheerios, the two Mounties toughed it out. If Gill Macbeth, the forensic pathologist, could stomach the smell, then Jackie and Dane wouldn't shrink from their job either.

"I've always wondered," Gill said, probing the body she'd opened up with a Y incision, "if I'd get one of these."

"A cross-dresser?" Jackie asked, holding up an evidence bag containing a pair of women's red panties that had been removed from the man stretched out on the autopsy table.

"I heard a story once," said Dane, "about a cross-dressing hit man in Japan. A gang war was raging between two yakuza factions. A pair of hoods schemed to go after the rival leader, a gangster named Akasaka or something like that. They hatched a plan to dress one of the hit men up as a woman and have him case the bar the gangster was known to frequent. Before long, the transvestite was popular in the bar, and he began entertaining Akasaka with his impersonation. One day, the boss walked in with just two bodyguards, so that's when the assassins struck. The second hit man entered and shot the yakuza boss five times, then took out one of the bodyguards with his last bullet. The cross-dresser knifed the other bodyguard. When I heard the tale, neither had been caught."

"This is much more than that," said Gill, pointing one of the tools of her trade at the open abdomen.

The cops peered at the organs she indicated with the blade.

"They don't match," said Dane.

The face and hands of the remains were charred black from the flames. The eyebrows were gone, but hair in the hood had been singed or saved in patches. Some of the fabric was burned right into the skin. The unexposed flesh beneath the killer's clothes had been mostly spared, and Gill had recovered fingerprints from the hand that had gripped the Molotov cocktail.

"I knew something was wrong when I palpated the scrotum," said Gill. "One of the testicles was missing. When I opened him up, I thought I'd find an undescended testicle in the abdomen. Instead, I found a mass on that side of the body."

"What sort of mass?" asked Dane.

"The mass you see. That's an ovary, a fallopian tube, and part of a uterus."

"The guy's a hermaphrodite?"

"A chimera, to be exact. In the past, as you know, I've had a case of chimeric blood. That's not uncommon. Twin embryos will often share a blood supply in the placenta, resulting in stem cells passing from one twin and settling in the bone marrow of the other. About 8 percent of non-identical twins have chimeric blood."

"But this guy's the real thing?" Jackie said.

"Yes. But genetically he's not a guy at all. He-and-she amount to a guy and a gal in one body. What you see before you is literally Dr. Jekyll and *Sister* Hyde."

*   *   *

Normally, Gill said, a single egg from Mom will join with a single sperm from Dad to produce an embryo that gets half its DNA from each parent. If that embryo splits in the womb, the result will be identical twins with the same DNA. An incomplete split produces Siamese twins. Both identical twins and Siamese twins are always of the same sex.

Non-identical twins result when two different eggs from Mom and two different sperms from Dad join up in the womb. Again, each embryo gets half its DNA from each parent, but the twins look different because each has a unique set of genes. Mom, of course, must be the mother of both twins. But if she had sexual relations with *two* men, each twin could come from an egg fertilized by a different father. In fact, there have been cases where the father of each twin was of a different race.

What we have here, Gill concluded, is the equivalent of Siamese twins from non-identical embryos. Instead of one embryo imperfectly splitting in two, two distinct embryos fused together as one. A single child was born, but it was made up of two *complete* genetic cell lines—not a half-and-half DNA composition, like the rest of us

374

have. In Greek mythology, a chimera was a monster created from hybrid parts: the head of a lion, the body of a goat, the tail of a serpent. This hermaphrodite is genetically *two* people—a he-and-she composed from the fusion of a boy and a girl.

It looks like a man on the outside.

But a woman hides within.

"Thus the red panties," deduced Dane.

"Imagine having dual identities," Jackie said. "One male and one female. What would that do to your mind?"

"Norman Bates in *Psycho*," said Dane. "But with a physiological abnormality."

"I'm no psychiatrist," Gill added. "But I grasp most of the terms. Intersex condition. Transsexualism. Androgyny. Klinefelter's syndrome. Gender dysphoria. Sexual-identity crisis. Gender blurs. Gender bends. Gender switches. There's nothing more complex or unfathomable than sex."

"If only we knew their background," said Dane. "I wonder where they were born and raised, and if there were any childhood traumas? Do you think the mother passed them off as a boy or a girl? Could it be that one saw the other as its imaginary twin? Or suffered from a dissociative identity disorder, like Jekyll and Hyde?"

"Why no corrective surgery?" Jackie asked.

"Perhaps it wasn't available," said Gill. "And by the time it was, there was no way he-and-she could choose which should live and should die."

"So both chose life and took turns living it?"

The forensic pathologist shrugged and picked up Roger Yamada's brain. Gill held out the Japanese diplomat's mind as if she were Hamlet addressing Yorick's skull.

"Biology affects psychology in weird ways. We'll never solve the mystery of who did what in there."

Dane nodded. "It's a genetic whodunit."

Samurai Sword

November 3, Now

Knock, knock . . .

"Enter," said DeClercq, turning from the Strategy Wall, where he was taking down the photos and reports that had given him an overview of the yakuza case.

Wearing the full dress uniform of the U.S. Air Force, Colonel Joe "Red" Hett stood framed in the doorway. A "full bird colonel"—which is how the military distinguished him from lesser ranks—he wore a large silver eagle affixed to his chest. A military historian and strategist at heart, the chief superintendent grasped the symbolism of the American insignia. Gold is the deepest in the earth. Silver is higher. Railroad tracks run across the land. Oak trees soar skyward. Birds fly above them, but not above the stars. So stars are saved for the highest ranks: generals and admirals.

Hett saluted.

DeClercq saluted back.

"The full Monty? What's up, Colonel?"

"I came to thank you."

"The dress blues are for me?"

"The girl you saved is the most important person in my life."

"*You* saved her, Colonel. Offering yourself up as bait took a lot of guts."

"That decision was easy. You called the hard ones."

"In your case, it was actually a constable named Singh."

"Thank Singh for me."

"I will."

The Mountie motioned the colonel to one of the chairs facing his U-shaped desk and then sat down in its partner. Beyond the windows, it rained, rained, rained.

"When do you leave for sunny New Mexico?"

"I thought I'd stick around a while and enjoy your weather. Truth is, I'm living in overtime, and I'm going to spend a few weeks of it with Jackie."

"I'm told your son was cremated. I'll give her time off so you two can take his ashes home."

"We're going to spread them here. I like the tradition of laying a warrior to rest where he fell in battle. There's a rock with a strange name off Stanley Park—"

"Siwash Rock?"

"Right. Siwash Rock. The legend that goes with it is about clean fatherhood. What better epitaph could there be for my son? We plan to scatter Chuck's ashes there on Veterans Day. Remembrance Day, to you. A name I think fitting, by the way. Jackie will remember her dad every time she jogs by."

Knock, knock . . .

"Enter," said DeClercq.

Both men turned toward the door, where Sgt. Dane Winter stood with a sword in his hand.

Again, Hett wondered if Winter was bedding Jackie. He hoped so. A good-looking couple. And he might greet a great-grandchild before he passed on.

"I saw you downstairs," the sergeant said, "and thought you might want this. It's the hara-kiri sword that took Tokuda's life. Prints on the handle matched Yamada's. There'll be no trial. So the sword is yours as a war trophy."

The colonel stood up and received the weapon as he might have a flag from his son's coffin. With one hand gripping the handle and the other holding the sheath, he yanked them an inch or two apart like samurai do in the movies.

"Have you read *From Here to Eternity*, Sergeant?"

"No," said Winter.

"I knew James Jones. He was at Pearl Harbor."

"Sir?"

"And I know the ending of his book by heart:

" '*Mother, do you think the war will last long enough so I can graduate from the Point and be in it? Jerry Wilcox said it wouldn't.'*

" '*No,' she said. 'I don't think it'll last that long.'*

" '*Well, gee whiz, mother,' her son said, 'I want to be in it.'*

" '*Well, cheer up,' Karen said, 'and don't let it worry you. You may miss this one, but you'll be just the right age for the next one.'*

" '*You really think so, mother?' her son said anxiously.'* "

"Written when, Colonel?"

"1951."

"So Jones got it right?"

"Yes," replied Hett. "Vietnam came along in time for my son, and but for a twist of fate in where she was born, my granddaughter would likely have been in Iraq. Hetts have served in every conflict since the American Revolution."

"Your loss is our gain."

"We're a warrior nation. You might have noticed that. Oh, but we do love our wars. We love to thump our chests and wave Old Glory. But ever since I dropped that bomb, we've been cursed. The Korean War left us with that threat. The Vietnam War was bogus and an utter defeat. And now the oil hawks have taken on *millions* of vengeful suicide bombers, and the new kamikazes will be coming for us from here to eternity. Our enemies have our number. They see our Achilles heel. We're unable to win a guerrilla war. We fear body bags, which is why we hide them from sight. We want to do our shock-and-awe killing from the height of the *Enola Gay*. Our enemies, on the other hand, parade their dead through the streets and swear in blood to follow them to the grave."

The colonel slammed the sword back into its sheath.

"Do me a favor, Sergeant?"

He handed Winter the hara-kiri sword.

"Take this to the Lions Gate Bridge and hurl it into the sea. I'm an old man, and the Pacific War was a *long* time ago. I really don't have the stomach for this sword."

Author's Note

This is a work of fiction. The plot and the characters are a product of the author's imagination. Where real persons, places, incidents, institutions, and such are incorporated to create the illusion of authenticity, they are used fictitiously. Inspiration was drawn from the following non-fiction sources:

Allen, Thomas B., and Norman Polmar. *Code-name Downfall: The Secret Plan to Invade Japan—and Why Truman Dropped the Bomb*. New York: Simon & Schuster, 1995.

Alperovitz, Gar. *The Decision to Use the Atomic Bomb: And the Architecture of an American Myth*. New York: Knopf, 1995.

Archer, Bernice, and Kent Fedorowich. ''The

Women of Stanley: Internment in Hong Kong, 1942–45." *Women's History Review* 5, no. 3 (1996).

Arroyo, Ernest. *Pearl Harbor*. New York: Metrobooks, 2001.

Axell, Albert, and Hideaki Kase. *Kamikaze: Japan's Suicide Gods*. London: Pearson, 2002.

Banham, Tony. *Not the Slightest Chance: The Defence of Hong Kong, 1941*. Vancouver: University of British Columbia Press, 2004.

Bruno, Anthony. "The Yakuza: The Japanese Mafia." Court TV's Crime Library. Accessed at www.crimelibrary.com/gangsters_outlaws/ gang/yakuza/1.html.

"The *Enola Gay* and the Atomic Bombing of Japan." The History Channel, 1995.

Ferguson, Ted. *Desperate Siege: The Battle of Hong Kong*. New York: Doubleday, 1980.

Feifer, George. *Tennozan: The Battle of Okinawa and the Atomic Bomb*. New York: Ticknor & Fields, 1992.

Ferrell, Robert (ed.). *Dear Bess: The Letters From Harry to Bess Truman, 1910–1959*. New York: W.W. Norton, 1983.

Frank, Richard B. *Downfall: The End of the Imperial Japanese Empire*. New York: Random House, 1999.

Giovannitti, Len, and Fred Freed. *The Decision to*

Drop the Bomb. New York: Coward-McCann, 1965.

Gow, Ian. *Okinawa 1945: Gateway to Japan*. London: Grub Street, 1986.

Great Battles of World War II. London: Marshall Cavendish, 1995.

Hersey, John. *Hiroshima*. New York: Knopf, 1996.

Hill, Peter B. E. *The Japanese Mafia: Yakuza, Law, and the State*. Oxford: Oxford University Press, 2003.

"Hiroshima: The Decision to Drop the Bomb." The History Channel, 1995.

"Hiroshima: Why the Bomb Was Dropped." ABC Nightly News, 1996.

Johnson, E. Pauline [Tekahionwake]. "The Siwash Rock." *Legends of Vancouver*. Vancouver: David Spencer Ltd., 1911.

Kaplan, David E., and Alex Dubro. *Yakuza: Japan's Criminal Underworld*. Berkeley: University of California Press, 2003.

Life Magazine. *Pearl Harbor: America's Call to Arms*. New York: Time-Life Books, 2001.

Lindsay, Oliver. *The Battle for Hong Kong, 1941–1945: Hostage to Fortune*. Staplehurst, UK: Spellmount, 2005.

———. *The Lasting Honour: The Fall of Hong Kong, 1941*. London: Hamish Hamilton, 1978.

Lord, Walter. *Day of Infamy*. New York: Henry Holt, 1957.

McKenna, Brian. "Savage Christmas: Hong Kong 1941." *The Valor and the Horror*. Toronto: National Film Board of Canada, 1992.

"Okinawa: The Last Battle." The History Channel, 1983.

Pearson, Helen. "Human Genetics: Dual Identities." *Nature* 417 (May 2, 2002).

Prange, Gordon W., with Donald M. Goldstein and Katherine V. Dillon. *At Dawn We Slept*. New York: McGraw Hill, 1981.

———. *Dec. 7, 1941: The Day the Japanese Attacked Pearl Harbor*. New York: McGraw Hill, 1988.

Robertson, David. *Sly and Able: A Political Biography of James F. Byrnes*. New York: Norton, 1994.

Saga, Junichi. *The Gambler's Tale: A Life in Japan's Underworld*. New York: Kodansha International, 1991.

Seymour, Christopher. *Yakuza Diary: Doing Time in the Japanese Underworld*. New York: Atlantic Monthly Press, 1996.

Takaki, Ronald. *Hiroshima: Why America Dropped the Atomic Bomb*. Boston: Little, Brown, 1995.

Thomas, Gordon, and Max Morgan-Witts. *Enola Gay*. New York: Stein and Day, 1977.

Time-Life Books/BBC. *Secrets of WWII: Target Oki-*

nawa: The Greatest Sea/Air Battle in History. London: Nugus/Martin Productions, 1998.

Truman, Harry S. *Memoirs*. Garden City, New York: Doubleday, 1955, 1956.

Wheeler, Keith. *The Road to Tokyo*. New York: Time-Life Books, 1979.

Whiting, Robert. *Tokyo Underworld: The Fast Times and Hard Life of an American Gangster in Japan*. New York: Vintage, 2000.

Willmott, H. P. *The Second World War in the Far East*. London: Cassell, 1999.

Yahara, Colonel Hiromichi. *The Battle for Okinawa*. Translated by Roger Pineau and Masatoshi Uehara. New York: Wiley, 1995.

The fictional portrayal of Harry Truman is based largely on the above primary and secondary sources, including Truman's memoirs and his letters to Bess Truman (edited by Robert Ferrell).

General Curtis E. LeMay—known as "Iron Ass" and "Bombs Away LeMay" by one side, and as "Brutal LeMay" by the other—directed both the firebombing and the atomic bombing of Japan. The LeMay quote "We're going to bomb them back into the Stone Age" actually refers to Vietnam and appears in his autobiography, *Mission with LeMay: My Story* (New York: Doubleday,

1965), which was co-authored by MacKinlay Kantor. In the Stanley Kubrick film *Dr. Strangelove or: How I Learned to Stop Worrying and Love the Bomb*, the gung-ho, cigar-chomping, "acceptable casualties" character of General Buck Turgidson, portrayed by George C. Scott, was inspired by LeMay.